"What are you thinking about?"

"Was I thinking?" asked Harlow.

"Yeah." Vander pointed to her brow. "You've got your thinking face. You're thinking about something."

"Aren't humans normally thinking about something?" she asked.

"Fine, it's your pondering face."

Harlow laughed. "I was just letting my mind wander."

"You don't have to tell me what you're thinking about. But you have this kinda frown. Not a bad frown. It's—it's cute. And the line in your brow. That's how I know you're hatching a plan, and I wanna be prepared."

What could she tell him? *I've been thinking about Trey Tucker, a perfectly nice, completely practical man I was ready to settle for, until I met you. And you are the least practical partner I can imagine. But when you look at me, I feel like I've been dipped in starlight. I feel like I shine so brightly anything is possible.*

Yeah, it probably wasn't appropriate cattle-herding conversation.

Dear Reader,

Welcome back to Pronghorn, Oregon, the contentious, quirky little town bouncing back after a few rough decades. As five young teachers breathe new life into the high school, the citizens of Pronghorn have to contend with their own growth as well.

"Don't draw undue attention to yourself" is one of the many unspoken rules of Pronghorn. It's a rule Harlow Jameson was never able to accept as a precocious child and has no interest in following as a high-achieving adult. When she's sentenced to community service helping the handsome, enigmatic new science teacher stage a holiday pageant, she wants to pull out all the stops and blow the lid off the tiny town. Vander Tourn moved to Pronghorn after a rough patch in his own life, finding refuge in the small community. He never expected that his inclination to retreat behind his old guitar would land him center stage with a beautiful, ambitious woman.

As Harlow and Vander inspire growth in one another, the town begins to change, too. From coming to terms with an espresso machine to taking credit for their unique talents, the citizens of Pronghorn abandon the old rule of keeping their heads down and staying in one lane. Success by its nature includes change, and change isn't always comfortable. In this book, characters explore the challenge of stepping up and into the limelight.

I'd love to hear what you think of Harlow and Vander's story! You can find me on social media and at my website, anna-grace-author.com.

Happy reading!

Anna

MISTLETOE AT JAMESON RANCH

ANNA GRACE

HEARTWARMING

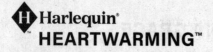

Harlequin®
HEARTWARMING™

Recycling programs for this product may not exist in your area.

ISBN-13: 978-1-335-05131-8

Mistletoe at Jameson Ranch

Copyright © 2024 by Anna Grace

Harlequin Enterprises ULC
22 Adelaide St. West, 41st Floor
Toronto, Ontario M5H 4E3, Canada
www.Harlequin.com

Printed in Lithuania

MIX
Paper | Supporting responsible forestry
FSC® C021394

Award-winning author **Anna Grace** writes fun, heartfelt romance novels about complex characters finding their way with humor and heart. Anna's Oregon roots and love of family and community shine through in her Harlequin Heartwarming series, Love, Oregon and The Teacher Project.

Whether exploring the West in a remodeled Sprinter van or wandering new city streets in search of an art museum, Anna loves to travel and spend time with friends and family. You can find her on social media, where she's busy stamping likes on images of cappuccino, books and other people's dogs.

X: @AnnaEmilyGrace
Instagram: @AnnaGraceAuthor
Facebook: Anna Grace Author
Website: Anna-Grace-Author.com

Books by Anna Grace

Harlequin Heartwarming

The Teacher Project

Lessons from the Rancher
Winning the Sheriff's Heart

Love, Oregon

A Rancher Worth Remembering
The Firefighter's Rescue
The Cowboy and the Coach
Her Hometown Christmas
Reunited with the Rancher

Visit the Author Profile page
at Harlequin.com for more titles.

To my fabulous writing partner, Kristine Lynn.
May we always be a little too big for our britches.

CHAPTER ONE

THE CAT SAT UP, alert in the middle of the empty two-lane highway running through Pronghorn. She turned her head briefly at the sound of the car door slamming, then twitched her crooked tail.

"How are you still here?" Harlow asked the cat.

Connie narrowed her eyes.

Par for the course. Harlow Jameson was used to being watched with suspicion in Pronghorn.

Harlow checked her makeup in the reflection of the driver-side window. Less polish, more residual dust than her normal look, but it would do for Pronghorn. Clothing and makeup served as her armor in Nashville: shiny, expensive and denoting status. People didn't mess with a woman who could afford bespoke Miron Crosby boots.

But around here, they'd take potshots at her no matter what she was wearing.

Harlow glanced down the street. Nothing had changed. The weathered wood of Mac's store looked like a parody of a ghost-town building. The Restaurant was bizarrely still in business, still had the same sandwich board out front informing prospective patrons of the two choices offered that day. Or warning them. Connie the cat still lounged in the road in front of the school, glaring at strangers.

Of course, Harlow wasn't a stranger. She'd grown

up in Pronghorn, still owned the family ranch out-side of town. But if she hadn't fit in around here as a young person, relocating to Nashville had sealed her fate.

Moving away was a mortal sin in these parts. It suggested there was a better life elsewhere. The cat didn't like her any more than anyone else in town.

"You know you're going to get smushed one of these days," Harlow said.

Connie stretched out, impossibly long, in the mid-dle of the highway.

"Suit yourself."

Harlow readjusted her wool and cashmere coat and turned in the direction of the store. She took two decisive steps, then stopped cold.

Are those Christmas lights hanging outside of the sheriff's office?

Harlow stepped into the road to investigate. Christ-mas lights and a handmade garland of pine and juni-per hung under the eaves of the brick building that housed the sheriff's office and the post office.

Weird.

Harlow took another step toward the store when something else funny caught her eye. Over the door of the old school someone had painted:

Pronghorn Public Day School, Proud Home of the Pronghorn "Pronghorns"

Harlow leaned back so she could see the parking lot. Sure enough, a few old trucks were lined up in the faded parking spots, and a collection of bicycles had been haphazardly attached to a brand-new bike rack.

"I thought the school closed down," she said to the cat.

Connie rolled onto her back, exposing her belly to the weak December sunlight.

Something was off. Harlow was standing in Pronghorn, but also *not* Pronghorn.

She pulled off her sunglasses and turned slowly, examining the town. She let the details come to her, as she would when studying the evidence in a legal case.

Holiday lights and fresh, elegant garlands adorned every one of the old brick buildings on Main Street, not just the sheriff's office.

Mac's store had a sign affixed to the side advertising ice cream. Underneath was another sign:

Coming soon! Espresso!

And pinned to the second sign was a sheet of paper that read Maybe.

The restaurant still bore its title—"The Restaurant"—in yellow paint on the side of the building. But it, too, was decorated for Christmas. It also included a snug outdoor seating area with heaters. Harlow squinted as she read the sandwich board out front. There were *three* choices of entrée. Half again as many choices as had ever been offered there before.

Harlow's heart sank a little. She didn't like the proprietress, Angie. And Angie didn't like her, but three choices on the menu? Something must have happened to the surly woman who ran the one restaurant in a fifty-mile radius. She might be hurt or sick or no longer with them. Harlow didn't wish ill on anyone, not even Angie, and certainly not on the three boys the cantankerous chef was raising on her own. But if dining at The Restaurant now included choices and ambiance, Angie was no longer in charge.

Harlow shook her head.

Or maybe she was dreaming, because this couldn't be Pronghorn. Pronghorn was sad and beleaguered, on the verge of vanishing completely. Pronghorn was *not* cheerful. It was not cute and Christmassy. Pronghornians weren't the type of people to put up Christmas decorations only to have to take them down a month later. If one needed evidence of what Pronghorn had become, the old City Hotel was the perfect symbol. Once bustling and glamourous, the building was now an empty shell, falling apart at the seams.

For confirmation, Harlow spun around to face the City Hotel.

It did not comply with her memories.

Sparkle lights hung from the eaves. A colorful garland of pine, juniper and dried flowers framed the entrance to the courtyard. Fresh wreaths hung outside the upstairs windows facing the street.

What in the sagebrush was going on here?

"Can I help you, ma'am?"

Harlow lifted her head, ready to demand an explanation as to why her hometown, which was supposed to be dying, was all gussied up like a California spa. Then she locked eyes with the speaker.

It was a cowboy sauntering out of the hotel, wearing jeans, boots and a canvas jacket. The dark eyes she was staring into shone from under his Stetson. He stopped in front of her, a charming and almost shy smile spread across his face.

Was that a Gibson guitar slung across his back?

"You look lost," he continued.

Emotionally lost? Or metaphorically?

Lost in the multiverse, maybe.

Also, why was the world's most gorgeous cowboy asking her if *she* was lost? He should know better; Pronghorn was no place for interesting people.

She slapped around in her befuddled brain for her manners and managed to come up with what she hoped was a self-assured smile. "I was heading to the store." She pointed to Mac's.

His grin grew conspiratorial. "I'll warn you, the espresso machine has arrived, but Mac hasn't quite figured out how to use it yet. He's been serving real strong instant coffee until he's got it all under control."

Harlow laughed. "Now *that* sounds like Pronghorn."

"It's not bad if you put a scoop of ice cream in it." He held her gaze, his smile growing hopeful. "My treat if you're brave enough to try."

Who was this handsome, funny, guitar-wielding guy with espresso advice? The cowboys around these parts were supposed to be like Pete Sorel or Ed Gonzales, old and grumpy.

Harlow allowed her gaze to connect with the decidedly *not* old nor grumpy cowboy. A spark lit, and color rose to his face. He kicked the toe of his boot against the sidewalk.

But as much fun as flirting with this man was, she still needed answers.

"Mac *actually* has ice cream?"

"Oh, yeah." He nodded toward the school. "When school lets out, the kids swarm the place."

She glanced over her shoulder at the cat, as though Connie could corroborate his story. The feline stood and stretched, then walked over to the cowboy and rubbed against his legs. He bent and scooped up the cat.

"Have you met Connie?" he asked, scratching around her ears, then rubbing her chin. Connie gave Harlow a smug look, then rubbed her furry nose against the man's chin and purred loudly.

"We're acquainted."

"Connie's our welcome committee here in Pronghorn."

She gazed at the man, snuggling a cat in front of the holiday-decorated hotel. Part of her wanted to play along and let the handsome stranger show her around. But in twenty seconds, some Pronghorn native was going to wander into the street and recognize her, and it would all be over. Or worse yet,

Sheriff Weston would start yammering about her cattle again.

The cat shot her a look, reminding Harlow she'd already been recognized. Then she jumped from the man's arms and returned to her post in the middle of the highway.

It was probably time for Harlow to rip off the Band-Aid.

"Look, I'm not lost. There's only like ten buildings in the whole town, so even if I was, I could probably find my bearings pretty quickly."

He laughed and kicked the toe of his boot against the sidewalk again. "Yeah, I know. I was just excited to help a stranger." He looked into her eyes and smiled as he added, "Get my local cred by helping out a pretty newcomer."

Pretty newcomer? That was probably the nicest thing anyone had ever said to her in Pronghorn. As a child, she'd been awkward and self-conscious to an extreme. Over the years she'd learned to embrace her larger frame and curves, cultivating a style a former boyfriend had described as Nashville Goddess. But as a kid she'd felt like a giant among pixies. Her parents didn't believe in spending money on frivolous things like stylish clothes, or even new clothing. No one thought to help her manage her tempestuous teenage complexion, or work with her thick mane of hair.

In college, she figured out how to present herself, as quickly as she'd figured out how to ace her classes. But as she'd changed and grown more confident in herself, Pronghorn seemed to resent her more and more. By reaching for more for herself, she'd betrayed those who didn't do the same.

So how was it she now stood in the middle of a festive Pronghorn street with an adorable cowboy calling her pretty and asking to buy her instant coffee with a scoop of ice cream in it?

Harlow's heart reached out to tug on her frontal lobe, asking if it could run outside to play.

No.

Harlow was no stranger to charming men. In Nashville, the streets were swarming with well-mannered, good-looking people who used every skill at their disposal to scale the cliffs of the country music industry. To those in the know, Harlow was an up-and-coming intellectual property lawyer. She'd earned a reputation for fiercely protecting the work of big-name stars, as well as working overtime to care for fledgling singer/songwriters in a system rife with wolves. She knew how to wear her Wranglers and didn't have any dreams of fame herself. Harlow was an artist's dream date.

So yes, she'd been flirted with a time or two. But not like this. Not with a chivalrous cowboy on the spruced-up streets of her hometown.

Not with someone who had her heart spinning ahead of her good sense like a tumbleweed.

"You're new to town?" she asked.

"Yep." He grinned, like living in Pronghorn could possibly be considered a good thing.

"And you want to gain your local status?"

"Of course."

"Then explain this to me." She waved a hand, indicating the holiday cheer.

He looked around, confused. *Right.* He was new to town. He didn't understand that tasteful, handmade garlands, glittering twinkle lights and even the possibility of espresso didn't fit the town's MO.

She tried again. "I thought the school had closed down." *And put all future Pronghorn teens out of their misery.*

"Oh, no. Well, yeah. It did. But we got it up and running at the end of August."

"We?"

He gave her the biggest grin yet. "I'm one of the new teachers."

A teacher? This guy was wasting his charisma teaching? She stared at him expectantly, waiting for him to explain that education was a stopover career, like how Harrison Ford was once a carpenter before he became *Harrison Ford.*

His smile was slow and easy as he gazed into her eyes. "I teach science."

It was not a sentence anyone should have found attractive, but somehow it transported her to a dreamy place of Bunsen burners and plastic safety goggles.

Yeah, she could certainly believe the guy knew a thing or two about chemistry.

Harlow broke eye contact and fixated on Mac's *maybe* espresso sign. "You're a teacher?" she clarified, then gestured to his guitar. "Not a musician."

"No, I'm on my prep period. I came to grab my guitar because my physics students are struggling with linear momentum, so I wrote a song about it."

She shook her head, laughing. It was all so absurd.

"Music can be really helpful in the classroom," he defended himself.

"Sorry. No. That's amazing. You're writing songs to help your students learn. I love it. I'm just a little thrown off by—everything. I need to put all the facts in order here."

"I'm happy to help."

"The school is open again?"

"Yeah, it's doing great. Kids are back in class, and we even have a few exchange students."

Kids from other countries came here on purpose?

"And how did they find *you*?" *Or rather how did they manage to get someone like you to come to the middle of nowhere for what has to be abysmal pay?*

"I'm one of five new teachers recruited to work here. We live at the hotel." He gestured over his shoulder.

"The hotel is gross and dilapidated," she reminded him.

He shook his head. "No, it's all fixed up. It's great. We love it."

How long had it been since she was home last? She'd spent some time at her ranch in the spring but managed to avoid coming into town. Come to think of it, she hadn't set foot in Pronghorn for well over a year. Things had changed, but why? And how?

"Whose idea was it to revive the school?" she asked.

"I think a lot of people were invested in the idea. Colter Wayne put up seed money, and most folks in the area donated. Then, well, do you know who Loretta Lazarus is?"

"Yeah, I know Loretta."

Everyone knew Loretta.

"She kinda Frankensteined a school together."

"I bet she did."

And this guy was the lightning bolt that brought it to life.

A LOT OF good things had happened to Vander when standing in this very spot. It was where he got off the bus and saw the town for the first time. His co-workers, the people he now considered his closest friends, had vowed to face the challenge of reviving the small school here.

He had his first herding experience in this spot, wrangling a group of curious pronghorn out of the hotel courtyard and back into the fields surrounding the town.

It was where he'd been offered his second job, assistant to the foreman at Jameson Ranch.

But standing here, talking to a smart, beautiful woman? The best. He needed to get back to his classroom, but he had about twenty minutes before fourth period started. And since there were only six students in physics, getting the class settled down and taking roll wasn't a big ordeal.

"What brings you into town?" he asked.

"Not espresso."

Vander laughed. He hadn't asked out a lot of women in his life. As an introvert, he was possessive about his free time. His last relationship had taught him he didn't have the best instincts when it came to women. But he intended to see what this woman thought about very strong instant coffee with a scoop of chocolate caramel ice cream in it. "Sure you don't want to give Mac's substitute creation a try?"

"Tempting. But honestly, I'm feeling like my understanding of linear momentum is a little shaky." She flipped her shiny dark waves over one shoulder. "If I could just hear a song about it, that would probably clear it right up."

He laughed again. "You're welcome to join my class. Anytime." Every day, as far as he was concerned. Unless...wait. He might not be correct. "I mean, you might need a background check or something. I don't really know much about it, but I'm sure Aida can run it for you."

"You're on a first-name basis with the sheriff?" she asked, implying that she, too, was on a first-name basis with the sheriff.

"Yeah, she's great. She's actually engaged to my friend Tate."

"Aida Weston is getting married?!" She looked around, as though this were proof that the universe was unraveling. "Like, to an actual person? Tate's not a soccer ball."

Vander threw his head back as he laughed. This woman, for all she'd been standing bewildered in the street, clearly knew the area. Aida Weston was a local soccer legend.

Which meant maybe she lived nearby. Maybe they could get together and talk about linear momentum *outside* of class.

"Tate's a real person. He's a PE teacher, a great guy. He's crazy about Aida."

"Wait, there's more than one attractive male teacher in town?"

Vander coughed. Did she just call him attractive?

Maybe he needed to reel this back in? His last relationship had broken down over a lack of shared values, and his student-teaching experience made him wary of trusting anyone he didn't know well. But there was something about this woman's absolute confidence that drew him to her. Besides, he was only thinking about ice cream and coffee, it wasn't like he was considering opening up a joint checking account.

He glanced at her again, but she was looking across the street at the sheriff's office, eyes narrowed.

"Weeelll, I'll tell you, Aida Weston knows all about my past."

Okay, so maybe she grew up around here. Was she visiting family?

"What brings you to town?" he asked.

"I'm hosting some friends at my ranch in a few weeks. I want to make sure the place is in order, and I like to take a few weeks every year for some solitude and reflection."

Solitude and reflection? This was clearly the woman he was meant to spend his life with. Vander kicked the toe of his boot against the sidewalk, trying to think of some kind of date he could ask her on besides the coffee. Maybe she liked horses?

"And I'm here, specifically in Pronghorn, to get some groceries."

Vander winced on her behalf. She laughed.

"Your reaction suggests that a cute little deli with an olive bar has not yet opened up in Pronghorn, despite the alarming changes elsewhere."

"It's still just canned soup and crackers," he said. "Two new items a year is probably max growth for the store."

She nodded, as though expecting this.

Should he invite her over for dinner? Willa Marshall, the school's English teacher and the first person Vander turned to with any kind of a problem, had put stew ingredients in the slow cooker before they left for work. The teachers planned to warm up some rolls to go with it that evening. His friends wouldn't mind one more person at the table, and certainly not someone as interesting as this woman.

Vander opened his mouth, contemplating the best way to phrase the invitation. By this point in their brief meeting, he wanted to take her out for instant coffee, sing to her about linear momentum and serve her a bowl of his friend's stew. Vander had never been real smooth with women, but even he could tell this wasn't anyone's dream date. If Tate were here, he could help him plan something, but this seemed like a moment he was supposed to seize.

She sighed before he could get started. "My housekeeper got sick, so she wasn't able to fly ahead and stock the house like she normally does. I'll roll into Lakeview tomorrow, but right now there is literally no food in the fridge."

Vander had managed to put together seven words of a dinner invitation, but something stopped him. *Housekeeper.*

"I mean, it's not *her* fault she's sick," Harlow continued. "But I'm seriously *not* happy with whoever sneezed around her."

"You travel with a housekeeper?"

"When I come back to the ranch." She readjusted the black leather bag on her shoulder. A gold clasp and detailed stitchwork caught his eye.

Vander studied the woman more carefully. She probably didn't wake up with perfect glossy brown hair and careful eye makeup. Her clothes were understated, but the long wool coat and soft-looking sweater underneath coordinated expertly.

Vander knew he had a tendency to be judgmental. He used up a lot of his grace and goodwill for people under the age of eighteen and tended to be critical of the choices adults made. It wasn't his best trait.

He tried to look at the situation from her perspective. So she had some money. Not a big deal. She could afford to have someone grocery shop for her. That was fine.

It was just kind of disappointing since it meant they weren't going to fall in love over rapidly melting chocolate caramel ice cream in Folgers coffee.

"I try not to come into Pronghorn when I visit, but I tried fasting once, and it did not go well." She glanced over her shoulder at the store, then sighed. "Crackers and soup it is."

Now Vander was confused. "Why wouldn't you come into town?"

"Why would I?" She gestured to the adorable, quirky place Vander had come to call home. "This place is dead."

"It's not dead. The Warner Valley is home to forty-two species of mammal wildlife and is part-time home to the largest population of pronghorn in the US."

She raised her hands in emphasis, like they were sharing a joke. Which they weren't. "Exactly. There are more antelope than people."

How did she not see that as a positive?

Vander had never fit in anywhere until he came to Pronghorn. From the moment he stepped off the bus in this tiny town in the middle of nowhere Oregon, he knew he was home. The lack of reliable internet, and thus lack of a relentless dependence on social media by the inhabitants, cemented the feeling. That didn't mean the last few months had been easy. Within the first two weeks of classes, a community group had tried to shut down the school.

The students had to readjust to in-person education. Negotiating the realities of a small town was no joke. But never in his life had anything felt more important than the work he was doing. In Pronghorn, he'd met his closest friends, was respected as a teacher and was learning to handle horses.

It was a blessed shelter after the emotional hurricane that had blasted everything he thought was sacred and solid in his life.

"Pronghorn is thriving," he said. If she didn't live here, she couldn't know. He led with what seemed to be the most important recent event to native Pronghornians. "We tied the league championships in soccer."

She gave him a deadpan look.

"We tied with Westlake Charter," he clarified. "Those kids were good."

She laughed. Not the beautiful, sparkling fun laugh he'd heard moments before but something hard and intentional. It was a laugh meant to dismiss. It was the laugh of a mean kid playing keep-away in grade school, seeking differences to point out in junior high, taming sycophants in high school.

As an adult, Vander had been disappointed but not surprised to find that the cliques still existed. There were still people who believed in social rank and did their best to sort everyone into it as they kissed up and kicked down. He'd been pretty uninterested in these folks for most of his life, until one of them came after him.

A frisson of discomfort ran down his spin. Vander

twitched off the uncomfortable feeling. He was in Pronghorn to get away from people who laughed like that.

It wasn't that everyone around these parts got along all the time, not by a long shot. But they understood they were in this together. At any given time, one person's skill set might be what another needed to survive. The school had given them ample evidence of the difficulty but ultimate value of coming together.

"Pronghorn is fantastic," he said. "I wouldn't want to live anywhere else."

"The town goes dark at 6:00 p.m.—"

"Because we're part of the world's largest Dark Sky sanctuary."

She tilted her head to one side, baffled.

Vander tried to explain, but how did she not know this already? "Two and a half million acres of the Oregon outback is free from light pollution. You can see the Milky Way from here."

"Sounds like a party," she said dryly.

"It can be."

It actually had been a party in the hotel courtyard when he and his friends first discovered how much they could see in the night sky. Tate had nearly gotten a ticket for disturbing the peace from his own fiancée that night, he was so excited about seeing their galaxy stretch through the sky like something out of Star Wars.

Her brow furrowed. "Pronghorn is tiny. It could

get absorbed by the sagebrush and prairie grass at any minute."

"Not if people work together to save the town."

"Why does it need to be saved? Towns die. It happens. That's the natural cycle of things."

"Towns go through good times and bad," Vander corrected, really wishing Luci, the social studies teacher, was here to back him up. "And this town is perfectly healthy."

"And the evidence of that would be?"

It really was too bad she hadn't been here for the Westlake Charter game. Instead he gestured toward the store, but even he understood the possibility of espresso wasn't the most compelling argument.

She shook her head. "Even on its best days, you have to admit Pronghorn is weird."

"*Interesting* is a better word."

"This town literally has a commune—"

"It's an intentional community," Vander reminded her.

"Intentional community," she repeated. "Where everyone wears orange and walks around talking about the sun like it's taking care of them."

Vander'd had a few run-ins with the Open Hearts Intentional Community early on, as their beliefs didn't always mesh perfectly with modern scientific thought, but they'd worked it out.

"Technically, the sun is taking care of us. There'd be no life without it."

She sniffed and twitched one eyebrow, as though the argument were beneath her.

"I'm not saying Pronghorn is perfect." Vander glanced around. "But it's full of good people—"

"It's full of stubbornly bizarre people who seem to think their way of life is somehow special."

As though to prove her point, Pete Sorel's big, white, double-wheeled truck rumbled by, waving both an American and a Senegalese flag, a multitude of international flag bumper stickers on the back.

The woman watched the truck, brows furrowed. Then she gave her head a sharp shake.

"I think this town is great," Vander said. "I'm sorry you don't agree. I really am. But if you don't like it, that's your problem."

Her face fell, as though he'd hit the one sensitive nerve she had. Like it was fine for her to insult his home, but by suggesting that was her problem he'd somehow crossed a line.

He'd said the wrong thing, again. But so had she, and he wasn't going to apologize to someone who'd started the argument in the first place.

"Sorry." She brushed her pretty hair off her shoulder. "I shouldn't have said anything. Enjoy this weird, small town and its weird, small inhabitants."

"You got it." Vander backed away across the street, making sure to step carefully over Connie. "Have fun judging everything you don't understand."

She waved. "I intend to."

"Mr. V?"

They both turned to look at the steps leading up to the school.

Mav, a student wearing the orange of Open Hearts, leaned out the front door. "Ms. Marshall wants to know if you're available to help her. A couple of pronghorn got into the library, and they're scaring the hedgehogs."

"I'll be right there," he said. Vander took one last look at the beautiful woman.

She crossed her arms, as though Mav had proved her point.

Vander kept his gaze steady, like he'd learned to do with the horses he worked with. "Enjoy your stay." He tipped his hat and stalked up to the school.

It would have been perfect if he could have kept it at that. But something in him rebelled against the high road. He wanted to know if his words had affected her. There was no reason for him to care. Elegant women who didn't like Pronghorn weren't his concern. She had zero positive qualities, and if she did her best to never set foot in Pronghorn, he'd likely go his whole life without seeing her again.

And yet.

Vander's excuse was he wanted to take a moment to compose himself before entering the school, which he did. But he didn't need to take one more look at the pretty woman to do that.

He glanced back in time to see her take three decisive steps toward the store. Then she stopped. After a second of hesitation, she spun around and tried to shoo Connie out of the middle of the street. When the cat refused to move, she picked her up and set her on the sidewalk.

"Lounge on the sidewalk," she commanded.

Connie twitched her crooked tail in annoyance.

The woman readjusted her handbag and sunglasses, then resumed her journey toward the store.

Connie watched her walk away, then sauntered back to her spot on the warm pavement and stretched out again.

Good cat.

CHAPTER TWO

HARLOW FORGOT TO square her shoulders and brush her hair back before entering Mac's store. A rookie mistake, but she was still shaken by the argument with the handsome cowboy teacher.

Also shaken by the fact that there *was* a handsome cowboy teacher in Pronghorn to argue with in the first place. A cat-snuggling Pronghorn enthusiast who wrote songs for his students to explain important concepts. How was that fair? Back in her day, school was all lectures and worksheets, occasionally broken up by a dull documentary. Heaven help you if you already knew the information being taught and tried to relieve your boredom by pulling out a book.

Given her morning, it wasn't a huge surprise she forgot to center herself before heading into a public space in Pronghorn. By the time the sleigh bells attached to the door jingled in response to her entrance, everyone was already staring.

Harlow suppressed a sigh.

"Howdy," she addressed all three people as though they were a jury she needed to win over.

Mac nodded to her, then glanced self-consciously to the right. As described, there was an ice cream counter, with four different kinds of ice cream. Behind it was a midlevel Breville espresso machine with a red-lettered sign taped on the front reading Caution!

"Harlow." Pete Sorel, the grizzled old rancher, touched the tip of his hat. It could almost be considered a kind greeting. Like, he wasn't actively scowling, *and* he made eye contact. The effect was lost when he followed with, "You know the sheriff's been looking for you."

Harlow was about to respond when a woman moved to stand in front of some type of display table, speaking quickly. "Harlow Jameson? Well. I didn't expect to see you in town. Aren't you staying out at that fancy new ranch of yours?"

"Hi, Raquel," Harlow said flatly.

"We probably don't have the same fancy groceries you'll find in Nashville, but Mac's store is good enough for the people around here."

"I just came in to grab some soup." Harlow raised both hands in innocence but kept eye contact with Raquel and lied, "Nice to see you."

Raquel glanced at Mac, then Pete, then finally crossed her arms and returned her focus to Harlow. "I guess I'll be the one to remind you that this is a small town."

"Thanks for the tip?"

"Mac has limited shelf space." Raquel took another stab at the obvious. "So keep that in mind before you stock up."

This was *so* Pronghorn. Harlow hadn't seen Raquel in over two years. Her daughters were probably in high school by now. Anywhere else in the world, there'd be a give-and-take of *hello, how are you, how's the family*, but here? Just a sharp, quick reminder; she didn't fit in.

Harlow remembered the unspoken rules of this little town all too well, even if she'd never been big on following them. Don't stock up at the store or you're being antisocial by not stopping in once a day. Eat at least one meal a week at The Restaurant, or you're unsupportive of local business. Don't draw undue attention to yourself. Don't question the status quo.

Leaving town, making it through undergraduate and law school in five years, developing a successful career and achieving financial independence all fell firmly within the category of drawing undue attention to oneself.

"I'll try to hold myself back." Harlow had done her due diligence and chatted. She could now grab her soup and get going. She gave the biggest, fakest smile she could muster. "Nice to see you all."

Raquel narrowed her eyes at Harlow, her lips pressed into a flat line to match. Pete grumbled something about it being good to see her back in town, then returned to his conversation with Mac about a postseason soccer game. Raquel spoke over him, relaying information about an upcoming Christmas pageant. The three Pronghornians had done their due diligence, too, putting her back in her place, and would be happy to ignore her for the duration.

Harlow took a few steps backward, aware of another element once foreign to Mac's store: background music. It took a moment to place the soft Christmas tune as Willie Nelson's "Pretty Paper." Her eyes darted to the counter behind the cash register. An actual record player was spinning what had to be the original vinyl from the late seventies.

Mac noticed her noticing the record player. He seemed slightly uncomfortable, as though by having good taste in music and sharing it, he might be breaking rule three as well. The tiniest flicker of connection wavered between them.

Harlow turned to the aisles, categorizing more subtle changes as she selected her items.

Mac's store was clean, for one. Someone had gotten after it with a scrub brush and some Windex. She drifted down an aisle with fishing gear on one side, first-aid supplies and packaged cookies on the other. Winter sunlight beamed through the windows. The limited selection looked a lot better on tidy shelves. Harlow grabbed a sleeve of Nutter Butter cookies. It wasn't the sort of thing she'd ever buy herself back in Nashville, but when in Pronghorn...

Harlow rounded the end of the aisle, noticing little notes posted at the edges of the shelves. They were item recommendations, like this was a boutique wine shop. When she finally came to the soup, Harlow found a small note proclaiming Campbell's tomato to be Mateo's Favorite!

No clue as to who Mateo was or why he liked Campbell's tomato soup so much, Harlow grabbed a can and its twin product, chicken noodle.

As she turned the corner, another oddity struck her. Possibly the oddest thing yet—a new selection of postcards. It was weird Mac was still shelving postcards at all. Who even bought postcards anymore or sent them? Who supplied them? But not only did Mac maintain the tall, slim rounder of images of Hart Mountain, Warner Valley, Albert Rim and Crump Lake, he appeared to have a fresh set of cards. Like the others had sold out, and he'd had to restock.

Mac looked up from where he was speaking with Raquel, or rather listening to Raquel who was still yammering on about the rumors she'd heard about a Christmas pageant.

"I moved the crackers," he said, anticipating Harlow's next move.

Mac moved the location of an item? End times must be upon them.

Harlow located a box of saltines. She was tempted to grab a second box to annoy Raquel, but she managed to refrain. Who knew how long the transaction would take if she gave in to the urge to stir up trouble.

On her way to the cash register, she passed a small table holding an intriguing display. Harlow risked a brief glance. She didn't want to spend one extra minute in the store, and she certainly didn't want to look interested. Because she was observant, her brief glance generally registered more than most people's long gander.

The table held a collection of high-end, handmade jewelry. Smooth, modern silver designs, turquoise and sunstone: these were actually pieces she would wear.

Harlow took a step closer to the table.

"Are you ready to check out?" Raquel asked quickly and somewhat nervously. She moved away from the counter and stood in between Harlow and the table of jewelry.

Odd.

Harlow laid her selection on the counter. She was tempted to order Mac's "espresso" with ice cream, like the science teacher had suggested. She was legitimately curious, and she had to give Mac props for even trying with the coffee drinks.

Before she could ask, the bells on the door jingled, and a gust of cold air blew in, then continued to blow as someone stood in the doorway without entering.

"I have been all over this town, looking for Vander Tourn," someone said.

Harlow turned to see who was complaining about what couldn't be more than a fifteen-minute search.

Oh, no.

Loretta Lazarus, the woman who ran this town with the focus and precision of an attention-deficit chicken. She was everywhere, in everyone's business, clucking and preening. Whoever this Vander was, Harlow did not envy him.

Fortunately, Loretta was so self-absorbed she hadn't noticed Harlow yet but was craning her neck to look throughout the store, as though this Vander guy were crouching behind the Frito-Lay stand. Which he might be, given Loretta's determination to find him.

Mac made silent eye contact with Harlow as she slid a ten-dollar bill across the counter. She widened her eyes ever-so slightly. It felt good, sharing a brief moment of mutual irritation with another citizen of Pronghorn.

Then Loretta stepped fully into the store.

"Oh." Her voice was loud and fully disappointed as she looked Harlow up and down. "It's you."

"It is."

Loretta crossed her arms, the yellow polyester of her suit jacket straining at the elbows. "So, the prodigal apple has come back to the tree. Well, I, for one, am glad you finally came to your senses."

"I'm just here for a visit."

"That's what the salmon always say."

"I don't think salmon say anything." Harlow accepted her change from Mac, remembering to put both nickels and pennies in the Share a Penny cup.

"Mark my words, a few days back in Pronghorn, and you'll never want to leave."

A few minutes in the store, and she couldn't wait to get out.

"My life is in Nashville," Harlow reminded Loretta, and everyone else. Then she muttered, "You won't have to put up with me for long."

Loretta spread her arms wide and said, "What could they possibly have in Nashville that they don't have here?"

Everyone stared at Loretta. Even Pete had the grace to clear his throat. Then Raquel rushed in, with an artificial sweetness to her voice that made substituting instant coffee for espresso seem authentic.

"Loretta, this town has always been far too small for Harlow." Raquel levied a fake smile at Harlow. "Her tastes are too elevated for us."

"Be that as it may," Pete interjected. "I hope you get your fences mended while you're here. Good fences make good neighbors."

Harlow opened her mouth to tell him she was planning on getting a crew to fix her fences as soon as she could assess the damage—a job her foreman should have been on weeks ago.

But Raquel spoke before Harlow could get a sound out. "Oh, her neighbors are all in *Nashville*," Raquel said. "Or didn't you hear that part?"

"I don't see why you're so stubborn." Loretta batted long, tangly eyelashes at Harlow. "This town is good enough for the rest of us, what makes you so special?"

Wow. They did not waste time getting under her skin in Pronghorn.

Even though it had all been said before, their words peppered her like mosquito bites. One person's derision isn't so terrible, but an entire town vocalizing their dislike of you? It hurt. Even in a town so tiny a mapmaker would have trouble finding a pen small enough to make the dot representing it.

Yet here she was again, the center of disapproval

in Pronghorn. Less than five minutes in Mac's store, and she felt as small and worthless as she had as a child. Why did she even try with these people?

Harlow picked up her small sack of groceries.

"You need anything else?" Mac asked, glancing at the ice cream.

"I'm good." Harlow headed for the door and didn't even bother saying goodbye. She was done with this town.

IT HAD BEEN well over a minute of composing himself before Vander finally ducked inside the school and trotted through the entrance hall. Assaultingly yellow lockers lined the walls. Above them hung a barrage of painted wooden signs the school's volunteer "principal" Loretta Lazarus had found at a Goodwill hundreds of miles away in Pendleton. He didn't love the idea of people learning core values from distressed pieces of plywood, but Vander could admit there were some good messages for students up there.

Believe You Can and You're Halfway There
Everything is Figureoutable
These Are Your Good Old Days

Others made less sense in a school setting.

Laundry is Loads of Fun!

Over time, the signage had gone from baffling to just another colorful piece of the mosaic. If somewhere in the mix was a sign informing students of other people's Lake Cabin Rules, it wasn't like taking time out to play a board game was bad advice.

Vander turned down the main hall of the school, where the teachers had their classrooms, and the gym and the library stood on opposite sides at the end. Noise spilled from the library, scene of today's antelope invasion.

Vander looked up in time to see a couple of pronghorn run out, followed by Luci.

"I'm herding!" she called over her shoulder to him.

"Great job!"

Luci, in her argyle sweater, loafers and tortoiseshell glasses was an unlikely wrangler, but she'd helped Vander deal with the antelope a time or two and was doing great.

Ilsa, an exchange student from the Netherlands, ran ahead and opened the big double doors at the end of the hall. Vander joined Luci in ushering the final pronghorn out of the building.

"And stay out!" Luci called as the nimble creatures trotted out of the school and onto the prairie.

One of the pronghorn looked back at Luci with a glance, suggesting she had no interest in following her directive.

Luci brushed her hands together and picked a miniscule piece of lint off her sweater. "Where were you?" she asked as they headed back inside.

"I needed to grab my guitar." He kept it at that. No need to rehash his uncomfortable conversation. Definitely no need to review the part of the conversation that had been pleasant.

Vander poked his head into the library and waved at Willa. Her intermediate English class sat at the large library tables, cutting up old copies of *Field & Stream* magazine for collages. "Whatcha working on?" he asked Mav.

"We all got to pick a book to read," he said, holding up a copy of *Dog Songs* by Mary Oliver. "And now we're making a collage to explain the major themes in the book."

"Cool." Vander nodded, scanning the table to see students cutting out pictures of fish, elk and people in Realtree camo. Inasmuch as the library held a tiny collection of literary fiction, half a Funk & Wagnalls encyclopedia collection, the complete works of Barbara Cartland and every *Field & Stream* magazine going back for forty-seven years, it was an ambitious project. But if the kids of local ranchers, those from the commune and the nine international exchange students at the school had learned one thing in the last few months, it was to creatively use the resources they had at hand.

Bloom Where You're Planted, as a piece of plywood in the entrance hall might suggest.

Vander scanned the students again. A conspicuous absence stood out.

"Is Nevaeh here?" he asked.

Willa pressed her lips together and shook her head.

Vander spoke quietly so the other students couldn't hear his concern. "She's gone again?"

"I tried calling, but no one answered," she said. "I

was hoping her attendance in December would be better. We only have three weeks before vacation."

"Missing the first school day of December isn't a strong start."

"Did you talk to her?" Willa asked. "She trusts you more than any of us."

"I did. We had a real good conversation on Friday." Nevaeh had drifted into his room after lunch and asked to help clean up from the osmosis and diffusion lab they'd done earlier. As the two of them organized lab reports and wiped down tables, Vander had brought up his concerns around her attendance. "She really seemed to get it."

Willa placed a sympathetic hand on his back. "You did your best, which is all we can do."

Vander needed his best to get better where Nevaeh Danes was concerned. She was so quiet, rarely speaking with the other kids and only really comfortable when talking with Vander. Her attendance was erratic, and when she was in class, she seemed to constantly be apologizing for her existence. There wasn't a lot of support for school at her home. The system had failed the family in the past, and no one was ready to concede that the new teachers might be running things a little differently.

"It's every ten days," he said quietly, finally understanding what Nevaeh was doing.

"What do you mean?" Willa kept her eyes on her students as they worked, but Vander could feel her full attention on his words.

"Nevaeh comes to school once every ten days.

Legally, that's what you have to do to keep from being considered truant."

Willa closed her eyes slowly and nodded. "Her family won't get fined if she makes an appearance for at least one class, every ten days."

"They won't get fined or hassled."

Frustration compounded in his chest. It seemed like Nevaeh wanted to be in school. She hadn't made friends given her infrequent attendance and habit of hanging out in his classroom during breaks. Vander often asked her to help him organize his shelves or set up for labs so she could feel like she was a part of things. He'd discovered a closet full of old microscopes he was planning on cleaning up and trying to get working for class. He'd thought Nevaeh might like to help with the project, then every time they used the microscopes in class, she could take ownership for the working equipment.

The realization that Nevaeh was intentionally skipping school lodged in his chest. And while meeting a gorgeous woman and then arguing with her was on nowhere near the same scale of importance as Nevaeh, he still felt all tangled up about it.

"I'm having a bad day," he told Willa.

She patted his back. "I'm sorry. Would you like to hold one of Luci's hedgehogs?"

He shook his head. "They're nocturnal. I don't wanna bug 'em."

"You are a good egg, Vander Tourn," Willa said, wrapping her arm more fully around his shoulder.

"I feel like a scrambled egg."

She laughed.

Vander glanced at the clock. "I gotta get to class."

"And we need to clean up," she said. "Students, let's start picking up. We'll have time to finish this project in class tomorrow, so make sure to save the pictures you've cut out and then stack the magazines neatly."

"Look at mine!" Sulieman, an exchange student from Senegal, held up his collage. Vander had no idea what book the kid had read, but he'd managed to arrange men and women modeling hunter gear to look like they were playing soccer with balls created out of vegetation.

"Creative," Vander said.

"I know," Sulieman replied, then glanced at Taylor Holms to see if she'd noticed.

She had. Taylor hadn't been noticing much at school besides Suleiman for the last three weeks and vice versa. She continued chattering with her friends but grinned at the school's star soccer player as he explained his collage to Vander. Back in September, it had been hard to get the kids to socialize, as they were coming out of three years of online school. By November, it was hard to get them to stop.

As Sulieman explained that his image was of the Christmas Truce of 1914, Vander sensed an ominous presence behind him. He straightened and began to turn when a voice cut through the library.

"Vander Tourn!"

A small woman in head-to-toe yellow stood in

the doorway, pointing straight at him. He felt a little like the pronghorn they'd shooed out of the building minutes earlier.

It was never a good thing to be singled out by Loretta Lazarus.

"Hello, Principal Lazarus." He nodded politely, as though she were just greeting him first before she pointed to every other occupant in the library and called out their first and last name.

"Trying to find you around this school is like looking for a haystack in a pile of needles."

"I'm sorry," Vander said.

"That doesn't sound very difficult," Willa quipped.

"It's a *me-ta-phor*," Loretta enunciated, as though Willa were unfamiliar with the concept.

"It would have to be a really small haystack," Mateo, the popular math teacher, noted from the doorway.

"Which is what makes finding him so hard." Loretta widened her eyes at Willa. "But that's neither there nor elsewhere. I have a big announcement to make!"

"No," Vander said, knowing immediately what was coming. He thought this idea had blown over, like a good two thirds of the big ideas Loretta had.

No one heard him. By now word had spread that the principal was on campus and the other thirty-one students in attendance spilled into the library.

Vander felt the used books and musty magazine collection closing in on him.

Confident she now had an audience, Loretta threw

her arms up and announced, "We're going to throw the biggest, grandest Christmas pageant this town has ever seen!"

Blood rushed to Vander's face.

"It's going to be grand!" Loretta continued. "I can see it now." She swept a hand through the air, inviting others to envision it with her. "There will be music and trees and poignant speeches."

"Uh, Loretta?" Vander wasn't much for interrupting, but this needed to be nipped in the bud. Actually, it needed to be pulled up at the roots and burned before the idea could spread. "Not all of our students celebrate Christmas." He nodded meaningfully to a cluster of students wearing orange. "We shouldn't have a pageant."

"That's okay." Mav, who had a penchant for contradicting anything and everything, raised his chin in defiance. "Personally, I *like* exploring new ideas."

"I didn't mean—"

"That's the beauty of it!" Loretta said. "We have students from all over the world with different traditions. It's up to you to make it work." She stood next to Vander and with a gesture invited him to look at Ilsa. "Is there Christmas in the Netherlands?"

"Yes," Ilsa said flatly.

Loretta ignored her, still working the mystery-tradition angle. "Is there Christianity in Brazil?" She turned to Antonio and shrugged her shoulders. "Who knows?"

"The people of Brazil know," Luci said. "And

they gave the rest of the world a clue by erecting a hundred-foot-tall statue of Jesus."

"We have students, we have a music teacher, what more do you need?"

"We *don't* have a music teacher," Vander reminded her.

"Pish." Loretta waved away the obvious concern. "You play the guitar."

Because he had his guitar on his back at that very moment, Vander wasn't in a strong position to argue her point. Instead, he said, "I don't play in front of an audience."

"You just carry it around all day?" she asked.

"No, I—" He stopped. Trying to explain to Loretta why playing a song about linear momentum in front of six students was different from accompanying a pageant was useless. If Loretta didn't want to understand something, she wouldn't.

"It's no use pretending to be bashful," she cooed. "You're a wonderful musician."

"You've never heard me play," he reminded her.

Loretta laughed. "Don't be ridiculous. You play for the entire town every night."

Her words settled on Vander like sleet, freezing him to the spot. He made eye contact first with his coworkers, then realized all the students were looking at him as well.

He *did* play every night.

He played in the courtyard of the hotel, letting the music wash away the stress of the day. He played to relax, to center himself. He played because it allowed him to be alone, while still in the company of his friends.

It never occurred to him that anyone else in town could hear the music.

"You all can hear me?" he asked.

The small contingent of students who lived in town nodded.

Mason gave him a sympathetic smile as he said, "That's part of the reason Mom added the outdoor seating area to The Restaurant."

Loretta crossed her arms and gave Vander a look. "No need to be shy. Everyone loves it. Although if I could make a request, maybe learn a few more songs by Abba. Everyone loves Abba."

The room crowded in closer; the smell of books intensified. Vander valued his privacy. It was part of what appealed to him about Pronghorn, the vast open spaces where he could simply *be*.

"I don't like being the center of attention," he said, fully aware he was the nucleus of attention at the moment.

"Then why are you a teacher?" Loretta asked.

"The kids are the center of attention in my class," he said.

"Well." Loretta shook her head. "That's not the way I would do it."

No doubt.

Loretta continued to trill out instructions and expectations for the pageant. Vander could feel the kids getting caught up in the prospect, each idea Loretta threw out making it harder for him to get out of this.

Students from non-Christian backgrounds were excited to participate in this new experience. Students who attended church in Pronghorn were excited to have some real Christmas festivities around here for once and to learn about the traditions of others.

And somehow, he had to be the one to make it all happen.

If Vander could claim any gifts as a teacher, it was an ability to guide the focus away from himself and onto the material he was teaching and the kids as they learned. As far as friend groups were concerned, he considered himself the lichen in any social setting: quiet but colorful and essential to any ecosystem.

"Hey," Tate, the PE teacher, yelled to quiet the room. He was the loudest person Vander knew, someone who was completely comfortable at the center of attention. "It's time for fourth period. School staff will get together tonight and make decisions about the pageant. For now, everyone, get to class!"

"A decision's already been made!" Loretta reminded him, before scooting out of the library and heading off to sell a house. Or whatever she did all day as a real estate agent in one of the least populated regions in Oregon.

Students made their way from the library into the hall and to their various classes. Vander readjusted the guitar on his back and headed for the library door, head down so he wouldn't look at Loretta and accidentally yell at her.

"You okay?" Mateo placed a hand on his shoulder.

"No."

"Maybe it won't be that bad?" Willa suggested hopefully.

"It will be *that* bad." Vander looked her in the eye. "There is no way I can pull this off."

"Should we go out to The Restaurant tonight?" Luci suggested. "I mean, it's not Thursday, but you could drown your sorrows in mediocre food and flat Coca-Cola."

Vander shook his head. "Naw. Thanks, though. I think I'll go spend some time with Stet out at Jameson Ranch."

"How's he doing?" Willa asked.

"He's coming along." The old horse had been treated poorly, then turned loose by owners unable to care for him or find a buyer. Willa's fiancé had rescued the horse and let Vander care for him. If Vander's day had been bad, it was nothing compared to what Stet had been through before he'd been rescued.

Vander took a deep breath. He had to be the star of the show in class today for about ten minutes. That was how long it would take to teach the kids the song. Then he had an activity to reinforce their learning. With any luck, the song would get stuck in their heads, and they'd never forget this concept for as long as they lived. It would take ten minutes, then he could return to the place he was comfortable—on the sidelines, coaching his students.

Vander pulled the guitar around to his chest as

he paced across the hall, already strumming the first few bars to "Bust a Move" as he walked into the room.

"Who's still confused about linear momentum?"

CHAPTER THREE

HARLOW'S RENTAL SHIMMIED over the final hundred feet of gravel road. She summoned Siri, made a request and her gate swung open. The crunching, bumping and rattling ended instantly as the car transitioned onto the smooth blacktop she'd had poured for the drive on her property.

She was home.

The long drive arced around the base of Raven Hill, finally coming to a neat oval between her house and the detached garage. Harlow had plenty of food to hold her over until she could get to Lakeview for some real groceries. She could spend the rest of her time in the area without going anywhere near Pronghorn.

A shiver of frustration ran through her. She didn't need Raquel or Pete or anyone in Pronghorn to like her. But she somehow wished they knew that other people *did* like her. In her world, she was smart, funny, respected, popular even.

It didn't matter. Harlow was home now.

She bent her head to get a better look out the window. Her heart lifted. She traveled extensively, but nothing hit her quite like her family property. Nestled in a cleft in the hills, her home had an extraordinary view of Warner Valley. The expanse of sagebrush and prairie grass gave way to a string of lakes and seasonal wetlands. In the distance, rimrock rose, leading up to the long table of Hart Mountain. This private canyon had been her kingdom as a child—a place where she'd created imaginary palaces in the copse of aspen trees, made cozy nests in the rushes next to the lake and scrambled over rock formations, a great explorer discovering new territory.

Rough days at school fell away as she retreated to the family land.

Rough months as a lawyer fell away as she came home to think and rest.

The last eight months had been intense, her workload a series of crushing boulders bouncing down a steep ravine toward her at all times. She enjoyed the busy city but became overwhelmed if she didn't get out from time to time. Harlow could easily recognize the warning signs in herself: feelings of frustration, restlessness, guilt, a persistent irritability and flat mood. She'd gotten good at knowing when to pull the plug on her busy life and take a break.

In an ideal world, Harlow would split her time evenly between Pronghorn and Nashville. Much of her work could be done with her computer and video conferencing. Ever since she'd installed a satellite dish, internet was easily available at the ranch. Working for several hours, then taking a long hike before returning to her tasks was good for her.

But being regularly insulted by small-minded people with a vendetta against her for bettering herself? Not so good for the soul.

Harlow took the final curve in the drive and rolled

up in front of the custom home she'd had built after winning her first major case. She'd had to fly in a construction crew and ship in most of the materials, but it was worth it. The original family home now served as a guesthouse, and she often had visitors. Jameson Ranch was both a private retreat and a place to entertain important guests, to create the connections that would lead her to even greater success.

It was so good to be home.

Muscles in her neck and shoulders she hadn't even realized were tense relaxed as she came to the end of the drive. A sense of well-being flooded through her. Tears pricked at the back of her eyes at the joy of being back on her land.

That was when she heard the dog. A confirming but nonthreatening bark.

Harlow didn't have a dog.

She scanned the property, then groaned. Sheriff Aida Weston was sitting on the juniper-wood bench Harlow had commissioned for her front porch. A handsome German shepherd sat alert next to her.

This town. Why couldn't Pronghorn just let things be?

Harlow parked where she was, right in the middle of the drive, and swung her door open. "It's just a few cows."

"It's fifteen head of cattle," Aida corrected, like she was some kind of bovine auditor, "and they're wandering all over Warner Valley."

"That's an issue for my foreman," she said. The dog stood as Harlow approached her own front porch.

Aida crossed her arms, like a jaded detective from a 1980s cop show on cable. "From what I understand, your foreman has reached out repeatedly, requesting your guidance on a complete fence replacement."

There was truth in that statement.

Her foreman had called and emailed, but Harlow was a very busy person. The last two months had been a blur of work. Who had the time to respond to every email?

"I'm home now. I'll give direction on the fence first thing tomorrow morning." Harlow started up the steps with her little sack of groceries. She'd come back for her bags after she dislodged Aida and the dog from her property. "How'd you get around my gate?"

"I used the code."

"How did you get the—?" Harlow stopped abruptly and sighed. It didn't matter. In a small town, her private gate code was considered everyone's business.

"Do you know where your foreman is right now?" Aida asked.

"What kind of question is that?" Harlow huffed. "I'm not an employee stalker."

Aida answered her own question. "Mike's at the hospital in Klamath Falls with his wife, who is having a second coronary stent replacement after her reaction to the first. He hired an assistant, who's keeping an eye on the place and caring for your horses, but Vander already has another full-time job."

Harlow tried another tack. "Then it would be horrible for you to fine Mike for the escaped cattle, what with his wife and all."

Aida, and the dog, gave her a dry look.

Harlow sighed and sat down on her bench next to Aida. She simply wanted to come home and relax, center herself after a long, drama-filled fall. She wanted to fill her lungs with the fresh air of her home, smell the particular combination of sagebrush and prairie glass. She wanted to be alone.

Aida had the grace to look a little remorseful about the ambush. "Harlow, I know you have a lot to keep you busy in Nashville. But an escaped herd of cattle is a big deal. You're fortunate they haven't gotten into the wetlands preserve. That would be a disaster."

Harlow sat up straight. She hadn't thought about the wetlands. In addition to the how-ever-many species of mammals the attractive science teacher had been talking about earlier, the Warner Valley was home, or part-time home, to hundreds of species of birds. She'd delighted in watching their patterns as a child. She wouldn't forgive herself if her cattle had harmed any of the protected breeding grounds.

"I'm sorry." Harlow focused on Aida and told her the truth, which was probably going to get her in more trouble, but at this point, *oh well*. "When I heard they escaped, I figured it was one or two cows. I assumed this was nothing but another piece of small-town Pronghorn drama Pete or Loretta or Raquel Holms stirred up to have something to talk about."

Aida looked like she was about to object, then tilted her head in acknowledgment of the statement. "I can see how you thought that."

"Look, I'll deal with it. I'll have the fence replaced and get the cattle…herded? Is that the right word?"

Aida didn't move. She gave Harlow a long look.

"Is that not enough?" Harlow asked. "Do I need to write a formal apology?"

"There's the matter of the fine—"

"Does the state take Venmo?" Harlow reached for her phone. How much could it be? She'd just pay it and be done.

"It's not that simple. You need to make amends to your community."

"This *isn't* my community," Harlow snapped.

Aida looked up, as if surprised by the sharp words.

"Don't act like you're surprised," Harlow said. "People around here don't like me, and I don't like them. This isn't fresh gossip."

"We grew up together," Aida reminded her gently. "We went to the same church. You were a senior when I started high school. I know you like to pretend you don't have history here, but you do."

Harlow's mouth tightened.

They both had history here. Aida was a soccer star. The whole town had loved her, probably still did. Harlow was an awkward, shy child. Her love of books got her into trouble with her teachers, who either chastised her for reading in class or got angry when she'd already mastered the simple concepts they were teaching.

Everywhere she went in Pronghorn, she stepped on toes by asking clarifying questions or challenging old assumptions. She didn't want to cause trouble, but her brain loved to gather evidence and arrange it into satisfying answers. *"Because I said so"* never flew with Harlow.

The only person in town who seemed to get her, or even care about her, was Mrs. Moran. The gentle Spanish teacher had modified Harlow's lessons, allowing her to soar past the others in the mastery of her first second language.

"Is Mrs. Moran still teaching?" Harlow asked.

"Oh, yeah. She's still at it."

"Well, that's some good news, then."

Harlow remembered that Aida was engaged to one of the new teachers. She glanced at her hand and saw a simple platinum and diamond band. Aida looked happy.

Because there's nothing like levying massive fines on nice people to make for a satisfying work life.

"Can we finish this?" Harlow asked. "What's the punishment?"

"You're going to get off pretty easy because your cattle were lucky enough to find their way into the Open Hearts Intentional Community."

Harlow rolled her eyes. "So my cows are wearing orange now?"

Aida gave her another dry look. "They've been cared for."

Harlow nodded, attempting to look thoughtful. But seriously, how much actual care did cows need? She only had the herd for aesthetic purposes. When guests came to the ranch, they expected to see cattle. If she didn't have them, she looked like one of those Nashville posers who refer to themselves as ranchers, when in reality they just flew private to a large chunk of land and sat in their mansions all day long. Cattle leant an authenticity that mattered in her world.

Or rather, an air of authenticity, since she was clearly not doing a great job as a cattle boss.

"Okay, so they wandered into Open Hearts," Harlow mused. "That's not so bad. I'm ostracized in Pronghorn. They're ostracized. At least we have something in common."

Aida shook her head. "No, actually, they've started to connect with the community."

"What?"

"Seriously, ever since deciding to allow their 'emerging adults' to join the high school, there've been some big strides. Pete Sorel and Today's Moment are friends now."

"No!" Harlow gasped and grabbed her chest. If she'd had a string of pearls, she'd be clutching them. This was worse than the Christmas decor. And Aida was rambling along as though it were no big deal.

"The good news for you is the folks at Open Hearts have been kind to your animals. When I contacted Today's Moment to let her know you were in town, she told me they would prefer to deal with this situation, and I am quoting her words here, 'by getting the love involved, rather than the law.'"

Harlow sputtered out a laugh. Aida clearly wanted to laugh, too, but wasn't going to let herself.

"What does that look like? Hugs?"

"No." Aida barely repressed a shudder. "I would never legally require anyone to hug it out. They have suggested community service."

"Did they specify which community I'd have to serve?"

"Pronghorn."

Harlow narrowed her eyes and twisted her lips in a scowl.

"I figured we wouldn't be your first choice. But since the fine is more than six months overdue, the other option is ten nights in jail."

"What? Ten nights for wandering cows?"

Aida eyed her coolly. "Ten nights for the repeated offense of willful illegal grazing, refusal to respond to a summons and failure to pay a fine."

"That would never stand up in court."

"What makes you say that?" Aida asked.

Harlow folded her arms and leaned back on the bench. Nothing in particular. It was what she always said when she was backed into a corner. She leaned her head back and groaned. This was the worst. She came here for solitude and reflection. Now she was stuck with community service.

Something fuzzy nudged her hand. Harlow looked

down to see the German shepherd slip his head under her palm so she could pet him. His soulful gaze communicated understanding; this wasn't her first choice, but it did seem to be the best choice.

Harlow could not spend ten, or any, days in jail. Her reputation was everything, and incarceration wasn't a good look. She rubbed the dog's ears, and he leaned against her leg, suggesting an ear rub was always the best and first choice.

"Fine. I'll do it."

"Okay," Aida stated. "You're going to get through this. Thirty hours will pass in a flash."

Harlow was tempted to ask if the roadside garbage collection, or whatever she'd be doing, could start immediately. She'd prefer to pull an all-nighter, knock this out and return to her solitude on the ranch.

"Stop by my office tomorrow, and I'll have an assignment for you." Aida stood. The dog gave the sheriff a side-eye, suggesting he wasn't through having his ears scratched.

"Let's go, Greg."

Greg sighed, then joined Aida as she took a few steps into the yard.

The sheriff turned back. "It's not going to be as bad as you think it is. Take it from me, sometimes helping out can be exactly what you need."

"What if I need solitude and reflection?"

"Just approach it with an open mind."

A citizen of Pronghorn telling her to have an open mind? It was almost funny.

"Thanks for the tip." Harlow gave a brief wave, then watched as Aida opened the door for her dog. Greg leaped into the car, Aida pulled off the property, and Harlow was finally alone.

Wind blew through the aspen trees, shaking a few last leaves to the ground and sending them skittering across her driveway. It was only four thirty, but the light was already starting to fade.

Harlow stood abruptly, jogged into the house to drop her groceries on the counter, then headed out the back door. In the early twilight, stars winked from the deep blue sky. She breathed in the smell of sagebrush, decomposing leaves and prairie grass. *Home.*

It had been a bad day, but it wasn't the first bad day she'd shaken off in this very spot. The land had been in her family for generations. Harlow had spent her best hours as a child here. She knew every outcrop of rimrock, every stand of aspen, every deer trail winding through the sagebrush. Jameson Ranch was her safe haven.

Her parents and uncles had been at a loss as to what to do with the land when her grandparents passed away, but Harlow hadn't. She had plenty of money to buy everyone out. Her parents moved to Boise, a dream Harlow had never understood but supported nonetheless.

Harlow took long strides through the grass, quickly finding a deer trail. Every step refreshed her, bringing back the joy that inevitably slipped away during her high-tension life in the city. Tomorrow she might have to serve her least favorite community, but right now, in the twilight on her own ranch, she was free.

It was a balance. Her work in Nashville was hard and high pressure, but it was fascinating, and it enabled artists to make a fair living off the beauty they created. To do it well, she had to take time out, to revive her soul on the land. And if she held on to Jameson Ranch, it might serve others. She might be a grandma someday, retired to this beautiful place, with her grandchildren finding freedom and inspiration on the land.

Her body warmed with the brisk walk. She didn't have much time before nightfall, but she meant to explore as much as she could while there was enough light to find her way back. Harlow moved faster, rounding a stand of birch trees her grandfather had planted, heading for the stables.

She stopped abruptly.

Light shone from the riding arena.

Harlow took a few steps closer, information stacking up in her mind.

An ATV was parked next to the barn.

A man, not her foreman, stood in the center of the arena.

He was speaking with a massive horse that shuffled on his hooves as though scared.

Should she be scared too?

No. If someone had come out here to harm her, he wouldn't make a stopover to talk to a horse in her arena. Or turn on the lights.

No, this guy was nothing more than a regular

squatter. Someone who'd heard the owner of Jameson Ranch wasn't home all that often and had his mangy horse living off her feed.

Harlow squared her shoulders and brushed her hair back. She'd had about enough of Pronghorn for one day.

VANDER HELD HIS palm out flat. Stet eyed the slice of apple, then checked Vander's expression.

"Go on," Vander told him. "It's for you."

Stet nosed the apple, then pressed his velvety lips into Vander's palm and devoured the slice.

"How's that?" He laid a hand on the horse's forehead.

Stet chomped down on the treat, then for the first time, sniffed Vander's jacket to figure out where he was keeping the apple slices. Vander laughed. It had been a rough day, but this was a big win. Every small sign of trust from the horse stacked up in his heart as a victory.

This evening it had taken Vander forty minutes, and about half an apple, to get Stet in a harness and out to the arena. He'd had to calm his own emotions before he could handle the horse, so the time had been productive for both of them.

"Hey!"

Vander startled at the angry voice. Stet pulled his head back and shuffled his large feet. Vander glared in the direction of the voice, but the bright lights of the arena obscured the speaker.

"What are you doing here?" she snapped.

Spooked by the anger, Stet scrambled backward, pulling against the harness. Vander tried to relax himself like Colter had taught him to when handling a horse.

"You need to get out of this arena, immediately," the intruder barked.

"Shh, shhh." Vander ran his hand under Stet's mane, but the horse was already trying to break away. Vander planted his feet and gripped the leather harness. If Stet broke away, he'd run, and without Colter's help, Vander didn't have the skills to bring him home in the darkness.

Footsteps approached behind him, and he held out a hand to stop whoever it was. This had already been a bad day, and if Stet spooked and ran, he wasn't going to take it well.

"You're upsetting my horse," he said, as calmly as he could under the circumstances.

"Are you kidding me?" The voice was familiar.

Stet settled briefly and Vander turned around.

The beautiful, Pronghorn-hating woman glared at him. She looked as startled as he felt.

"What are you doing here?" he asked.

"Going for a walk?" she said slowly and clearly, like it was a new concept for him.

"This is private property," he informed her. He intended to turn his attention back to Stet, but she was like a supernova, fascinating and deadly.

She scoffed and threw her head back. "This is *so* Pronghorn."

"Yeah," he confirmed, turning back to Stet before he could meditate any further on how pretty she looked with a flush in her cheeks and eyes bright from the cold evening air. "This is Pronghorn. And maybe trespassing isn't the best way to get along."

"Let's back up. What are *you* doing here? And what is this?" She gestured to Stet.

Vander pulled another apple slice from his jacket. Stet nosed the treat, then seemed to settle as he ate the slice. Vander kept a reassuring hand on his flank. "My name is Vander Tourn. I'm assistant to the foreman here at Jameson Ranch. This is Stet. And you are trespassing."

Her golden brown eyes met his, and she stared at him meaningfully.

Vander's mind was blowing synapses trying to remember everything he knew about this woman.

She hated Pronghorn, she traveled with a housekeeper, she was confused by Christmas decorations.

She was in town to spend some time on her ranch. *Her* ranch.

"Let me introduce myself," she said, way too calmly. "My name is Harlow Jameson. This land has been in my family for four generations. I didn't hire you to be assistant to the foreman, but I am curious as to what I'm paying you. I'm an intellectual property attorney, and while I practice in Tennessee, I'm well-versed in Oregon law. You and Stet are trespassing."

A cool evening breeze wafted through the arena, stirring a scattering of aspen leaves across the dirt floor.

She was the owner.

And he was using her stables, and her feed, to rehabilitate what he knew was a mangy-looking horse.

Reflexively Vander tightened his grip on the reins and stepped closer to Stet.

She smiled, as though she'd tracked his reaction and knew exactly what was happening. The threat of negotiation hung in the air. She crossed her arms and walked in an arc around the horse, like some kind of courtroom lawyer.

Which she was, apparently.

The buzz of overhead lights intensified.

She couldn't demand he get rid of Stet. The horse had come so far. Sure, this might be her ranch. Her feed. Her stables, blankets, tack and grooming tools.

Yeah. She could kick the two of them out right now, and no one would blame her.

"Tell me about the horse?" She raised her brows. "How long have I been feeding him?"

With anyone else, he might try to appeal to the heart, but he didn't think she had one. Might as well stick with the facts and hope for the best.

"This is Stet."

She eyed him expectantly.

All useful words seemed to flee, leaving him with nothing more than variations on, *Please don't kick us out.* "Stet's a rescue horse. He was skin and bones when we found him and pretty skittish."

She paced, glancing up at the rafters, then back at him. "How'd the song about linear momentum go over?"

"Good."

A barn owl hooted, reminding him that night had fallen, despite the early hour. He needed to hop on the ATV and get back to the hotel.

"So you teach high school, sing to your students, work for me and rescue horses."

"Horse," he clarified. He might be in the wrong here, but he only had one offense.

"Horse." She acknowledged this with a nod. "Are you aware that my cattle have escaped?"

Vander was aware her fences were in disrepair, and the foreman had tried to contact her about a plan to fix them six months ago. He also knew that when Mike's wife got sick, he dropped everything at the ranch to care for her. It had also come to his attention that Spring Rain and Antithesis, two kids who lived at Open Hearts, had named all the cattle and considered the shorthorns lovable pets.

"I heard about that."

"Can you wrangle them back here?" she asked.

Vander looked at the horse, as though he might have the answer. Could he? Maybe. With Colter's help, he could probably figure it out. He opened his mouth to agree to the statement, but an unidentifiable urge to argue washed through him.

"If I bring the cattle back, it's not gonna do a lick of good unless you get your fences fixed."

"So we fix the fences."

"*We* fix the fences? Or do you mean I fix the fences?"

"I know how to fix a fence."

"You know how to string barbed wire?" Vander didn't want to be judgmental, but didn't it make sense to judge occasionally? The woman balked at having to shop for her own canned soup, and now she was talking about fixing fences?

"I grew up in Pronghorn," she reminded him. "We may not have run cattle when I was growing up, but we had plenty of damaged fences."

Good point.

At least one of them knew how to string barbed wire. Maybe he could get Mateo and Luci in on the job. Harlow could explain the process to the two of them, at which point he could listen in and learn as well.

Vander swallowed hard. He wasn't practiced at negotiation, but that's what this was. "So hypothetically—" Was this hypothetical? He wasn't making a hypothesis, but it seemed like something you'd say when working out a deal. "I help you with the cattle and the fences—"

She got a little grin on her face. "*Hypothetically*, I'll pay for the time. Maybe recruit some of your teacher friends to help."

"That's what I was thinking." Vander rubbed his jaw. "Then you'll let me keep Stet here?"

"You can keep Stet here for now. And keep him out of the way when my guests arrive."

"Okay."

She blinked, as if surprised. They'd come to a satisfying end of their negotiation. "Okay?"

"Yeah. This seems fair."

The corners of her mouth turned down as she considered this. It was cute. She was cute. And the negotiation, upon reflection, had been kind of exhilarating.

Not so fun that he was reconsidering asking her out for coffee and ice cream again. Not really.

She twitched her brow, as though his thoughts were appearing in bubbles above his head.

"Maybe we should leave it at that." She pulled her hands from her coat pockets and reached out to shake on the deal.

Vander grasped her hand, warm and soft against his cold fingers. Everything about her that had seemed so appealing when they first met came back into sharp focus. Instinctively, his other hand slipped in to join the party. Vander found himself holding her hand in both of his, staring at her pretty, manicured fingers in a situation that was nothing like a handshake.

"I should get out of here." He released her hand and stepped back.

She gave him a conspiratorial grin. "Before we start fighting again."

He chuckled, like he agreed with her. But he was up for another round if she was. "I'll tuck Stet in and get back to the hotel."

"The new teachers are really all staying there together?" she asked.

"We are. It's been good." He pulled an apple slice out of his jacket pocket and offered it to Stet. The horse took a step toward the apple, Vander and ultimately his snug stall.

Harlow stood her ground, like she wasn't finished with the conversation. "Have they dealt with the internet problem in town?" she asked.

"Nope." *Thank God.*

"I have a satellite dish. It works perfectly. Why doesn't the school get one? I don't know how you all can live or teach with the spotty cell coverage."

He leveled the Teacher Eye on her, a look that told students they did not want to continue down this path and discover the consequences. "Our staff looks to our forebears from the 1990s and study their ways. We make out all right."

She rolled her eyes. "Right. Because the internet is useful, helpful and modern. We wouldn't want *that* around Pronghorn."

Rebuttals tangled up in Vander's chest. Yes, the internet was incredibly helpful, but it could also be distracting and destructive. These kids had been sentenced to online school for three years. If their families could afford a satellite dish like Harlow boasted, the student sat in front of a screen all day. If they didn't, a representative from the district delivered photocopied packets of readings and worksheets once a month. The last thing any of these kids needed was screen time or anything that kept them from interacting with one another. Coming together with their peers and a dedicated teacher to discuss ideas and explore new subject matter was going well.

A little too well, as the students had been chatty since coming back from Thanksgiving break. Still, the teachers had no desire to squelch student connection by facilitating more time on their electronic devices. And Vander had no desire to live in a town where social media took the place of reasonable dialogue.

"The internet comes on about once or twice a week. That's enough."

She huffed, mumbling to herself, "Only in Pronghorn."

He experienced an unexpected desire to argue. It wasn't his style, but something about this woman got his back up. He still had a lot of questions. Where did her money come from? Why did she pour it into an area she didn't have a lot of love for? What was it about Pronghorn that she disliked so much?

And why was he inexplicably wanting to continue this conversation? It was clearly time to get out of here.

"I'll make sure this guy's settled and get out of your hair." Vander pulled out another apple slice and offered it to Stet.

"Does he need anything tomorrow morning?"

Vander looked up sharply. Was she offering to help? "I come out before school to feed and turn out the horses," he said. "I've been doing that since Mike's wife got sick."

Riding out on the ATV at dawn, working with the horses and watching the sunrise over Hart Mountain was a highlight of every day.

"I generally care for the horses when I'm home," she said. Vander's expression must have fallen because she added, "You should come out and work with Stet, though."

"Thanks. Yeah, if you're up, Mike's been having me feed all the horses and open up their turnout pens. On nice days, I'll let them pasture. Stet's not quite ready to join the group yet."

"Of course not. Are you using the upper road pasture or lakeside?"

"Lakeside."

"Got it." She waved. "I'm gonna head back."

"Yeah. I'm gonna go."

"Okay."

"Bye."

She stood for a moment longer, then winked at him. "We should get out of here before we start arguing again." Her smile suggested she didn't mind arguing, that it might even be her favorite sport.

"Agreed." He nodded, leading Stet a few more feet toward his stall, then he glanced back at her.

A spark lit her eye as she turned, then tucked her hands in her pockets and strode in the direction of her house.

The quiet murmur of nature and heavy steps of the horse replaced the spark of their debate. For the first time in a long time, Vander wasn't ready to stop talking at all.

CHAPTER FOUR

HARLOW PARKED IN front of the sheriff's office at three the next afternoon, then checked her outfit one more time. Jeans, Chelsea boots, shearling-lined plaid vest. Did it say, *Garbage collection along the highway*?

No, it was too stylish. The outfit said, *Wrongfully sentenced to garbage collection along the highway*, which was what she was going for. Cars passing by would get the message, in the unlikely event that a car should pass by.

Harlow climbed out of her vehicle into the bright, cold afternoon. Connie the cat was stretched out in the middle of the highway as always, her paws scooching a few more inches, just to make a point. Harlow shook her head, then knocked on the tastefully decorated door to the sheriff's office.

This was unpleasant, and she didn't want to do it, but the sooner she got started with her community service, the sooner it would be over.

Anticipating a *Come on in*, Harlow reached for the doorknob.

The door flew open, as though a vortex within wielded power over the portal.

"Well now, look who's finally decided to jump out of the frying pan into the home fires? The home fires *are* still burning, you know. We keep 'em burning."

Horror gave way to a sense of injustice as Harlow stood in front of the firing squad: conversation with Loretta Lazarus. Even Aida looked chagrined as the town's self-proclaimed ambassador chattered incessantly, mixing up common idioms and sending a thousand tiny insults straight to Harlow's weak spots.

Was this her community service? Did the town need someone to deal with Loretta for thirty hours? Because the eighth amendment protected against cruel and unusual punishment.

"Hello, Loretta," Harlow interrupted her. "I'm just here to see the sheriff." Hopefully Aida had been gracious enough not to tell Loretta, or anyone, about the community service.

"Oh, I know all about it," Loretta said, winking at Aida.

Winking! Who winked in a sheriff's office? Again, only in Pronghorn.

"You have some very naughty cattle, or so I hear."

Harlow widened her eyes at Aida. They might never have been friends, but did she have to throw her under the bus like this?

Aida responded with a slight twitch of her head, then reminded Harlow, "Word spreads fast around here. No matter how discreet some of us are."

That was fair. Harlow gave Loretta a dismissive smile. "I have faulty fences, and a plan to fix them." Harlow turned to Aida, creating a conversational channel that excluded Loretta. She'd have to step in front of the sheriff to get a word in. "Is this a good time, or would you like me to come back later?"

Loretta stepped in front of Aida.

"And *we* have a plan to help you make up for the destruction your cattle have wrought on our beloved community." Loretta put a hand on her heart and looked up at the ceiling, as though her small herd had done apocalyptic damage.

Harlow stood on her toes so she could speak over Loretta's head and addressed Aida, "Is law enforcement by committee a new thing around here?"

"Community service has to involve the community," Aida reminded her.

Once again, Harlow thought long and hard about the ten days in jail. She tried to picture it. A narrow bed, bars, sullen inmates, bad food. No Loretta.

Tempting.

But she could not have this on her record. No matter how painful community service in Pronghorn would turn out to be, she could not have a criminal record.

"So, trash on the side of the highway, then?" Harlow asked. "And this counts, right?" She waved her hand at the assembled gathering. "This conversation is part of my hours." She almost said *billable hours* but managed to stop herself. That said, this would have been a very expensive fifteen minutes back in Nashville.

"Oh, heavens no," Loretta put a hand on her shoulder. "Nothing so humiliating as picking up trash. You're helping with the holiday pageant."

Everything seemed to slow dramatically. Loretta's words bounced through the room, expanding, push-

ing out all breathable air. A holiday pageant? Other
people's germ-encrusted children singing off-key
for hours on end?

Not gonna happen.

Harlow shook her head, simultaneously trying to
shake out the space-time continuum so everything
was back on track.

"I can't." Harlow widened her stance, literally putting her foot down. She spoke clearly. "I cannot help
with a holiday pageant."

"Why ever not?" Loretta batted long, tangly false
eyelashes at her. It looked like a spider was waving
with half its legs.

"Because I don't want to."

"Well, you should have thought of that before
you let your herd loose to trample all over Warner
Valley."

"I didn't let the herd loose—" She knew better.
She *knew* better than to engage with the conversational black hole that was Loretta Lazarus, but she
couldn't help herself.

"Too late! The bull's out of the ballpark, as they
say."

"No one says that." Harlow appealed to Aida,
then her German shepherd for confirmation.

Loretta ignored her. "You're helping with the pageant."

"Why?"

"Because you work in the music industry."

Harlow opened her mouth to explain that she was
a lawyer, not a studio musician. She had no musical

gifts, beyond an uncanny ability to identify a song after hearing only a few chords. Friends called her the human Shazam. But that was it. She couldn't hold a tune in a bucket, and she certainly couldn't help anyone else hold a tune in any type of receptacle. If the town needed legal counsel, that would be a much better fit.

Aida caught her eye, then shook her head briefly. *Good point.* If her community service wound up being something law related, there was no chance Loretta would land herself on the correct side of a legal argument.

"You work in the music industry," Loretta repeated. "This town hosts an annual Christmas pageant—"

"Since when?" Harlow asked.

"Since when what?"

"Since when does Pronghorn host an *annual* Christmas pageant?"

"Since I say so." Loretta threw her shoulders back. If she were a barnyard hen, the action would have resulted in fluffing her feathers. She looked meaningfully at Aida. "She does know I'm the principal, doesn't she?"

Aida finally spoke up. In her defense, it'd probably been difficult to get a word in edgewise between the two of them. "Loretta is trying to revive the arts at the high school."

"Principal Lazarus," Loretta corrected her.

"Sorry, our volunteer principal is hoping to revive the arts. She thought a holiday pageant would be fun for the kids, and she's right. We have eight kids who are very excited about it. That's twenty percent of the school."

Harlow didn't *want* to like this idea, but she was listening.

"Our teachers are at capacity. Your help would be a huge lift to a staff that's done some great work this year."

"So, do you need help with song rights? Legal advice? If the pageant is free, or even donation only, it would give us a lot more flexibility. And it always blows me away how people grumble at buying a twelve-dollar ticket but will drop two twenties in the collection plate after watching kids sing—"

"Oh, no." Aida shook her head. "We need your help with the kids."

"The what?"

"The students," Loretta over-enunciated the word. "The youth. Or in Nashville, maybe you'd call them the talent."

Harlow wasn't in the habit of calling teenagers anything. She let the idea rattle around in her head. Could teenagers really be that different from country music stars?

But then, what would she realistically do for the pageant? It wasn't like she could play the piano or direct a choir.

"I'm not a musician," Harlow reminded Aida.

"But you love music. You have more real experience with what goes into a live performance than anyone else around here."

Harlow's instinct was to argue, to talk her way out of this. That was her go-to.

But a little flicker of excitement lit in her heart. She didn't want to admit it, but there it was—anticipation. Harlow had no musical talent, nor the special type of patience it took to develop it. As a kid she would have loved to participate in a holiday pageant or any type of performance. But she couldn't sing, didn't dance and was uniformly given the message that she had no charisma. No adult ever encouraged her to try out for anything, and she'd learned early on how this town reacted when you drew undue attention to yourself.

Maybe there was another young Harlow in Pronghorn, desperate to express herself among the chorus of dream-flattening silence.

"And this is the only option?" Harlow clarified.

"Given the *suggestions*—" Aida looked meaningfully at Loretta "—it's my opinion that this is the best fit."

Harlow cataloged all available information. She had to engage in community service; jail time and a criminal record were not an option. There might well be another kid like her participating, or wanting to participate, and if her thirty hours helped one kid feel like they meant something in this soul-crushing town, it would be well worth her effort.

And, if the pageant went well, Raquel Holms and Loretta Lazarus and everyone else who looked down on her would have to acknowledge she'd done excellent work. Was there anything as appealing as revenge success?

Was she going to admit there was a little piece of her heart that sparked at the idea of another run-in with the cowboy teacher? Hypothetically speaking, of course.

No, she was gonna keep on pretending the guy hadn't gotten into her head, and she definitely hadn't spent any time thinking about his dark eyes.

"All right." She nodded. "I'm in."

Something soft and warm pressed against her leg. Harlow glanced down to see Greg positioning his ears under her hand. She knelt down to give the dog a proper ear rub. It beat having to look at Loretta as she agreed to her request. Greg propped his chin on Harlow's shoulder, acknowledging she'd made the right decision.

Unfortunately, it didn't stop Loretta from talk-ing. "Now just because you live in Nashville doesn't mean you can turn this pageant into some folksy, twangy ruckus."

Harlow groaned. Loretta didn't notice.

"Remember, this is Pronghorn," she said, pick-ing a clump of cat fur off her plaid yellow jacket. "It needs to be classy."

Aida let out what started as a laugh, then man-aged to turn into a cough.

"It will be the classiest pageant this town has ever seen," Harlow promised. Because literally, how much competition was there for that title?

Loretta began batting around a slew of stipu-lations, but no one caught them. The back door opened, and a man with dark hair and bright blue eyes poked his head in. "How's it going?"

Aida and her dog abandoned them for his laughter and jovial conversation. Loretta gave him her spidery wave and mixed up a few metaphors for the occasion. He managed the volunteer principal well, but his eyes, and clearly his heart, were for Aida.

Curiosity rumbled, but Harlow let the conversation play out. People in this town were insular. She was only interesting as a source of gossip, so there was no reason to expect to be included in their happy conversation.

But strangely, after asking the dog several questions about what a good boy he was, the man walked right up to her.

"You must be Harlow. Welcome back." He held out a hand with what looked like a sincere interest in meeting her.

She shook his hand. "And you must be Tate," she said, remembering what Vander had said about Aida's fiancé. "PE teacher, right?"

"That's me. I'm here to show you to rehearsal, if—" he paused and glanced at Aida "—if that's happening."

"It's happening," Harlow admitted. "Let's get it done."

It took a minute to get untangled from Loretta, but eventually Harlow followed Tate out of the sheriff's office and twenty yards down the street to the school. He was charming and enthusiastic, putting her at ease. It wasn't until they headed up the front

steps of Pronghorn High that the memories and
sense of dread came flooding back.

As a student, she'd been given every message
that she needed to conform to her peers. Stop being
so curious and put her thinking back into the box
along with everyone else. It wasn't that her teachers had been bad people; they were overworked and
trying to operate in a system that was falling apart.
Looking back, she could see how her questions and
habit of studying up on a subject before it was in-
troduced in class would have been annoying. These
same traits helped her fly through undergrad and
law school and made her a formidable champion
for her clients. But it hadn't made her teachers' jobs
any easier.

Tate held the door, and Harlow stepped into the
entrance hall, her heart loitering somewhere near
the base of her stomach.

"Whoa." Harlow nearly tripped as her eyes were
so overstimulated the rest of her body stopped working. "Who redecorated?"

"You wanna take a guess?" Tate asked dryly.

The entrance was a cacophony of color and tex-
ture. The old wooden floors gleamed in the light
spilling in from the windows. A reading nook had
been built into a window bay, inviting readers with
soft, cozy chairs and overflowing with books. The
smooth metal lockers were now bright yellow, and
students personalized their spaces with magnets.
Above the lockers, and on every available inch of
wall, were decorative wooden signs.

These Are Your Good Old Days stood out promi-
nently over the opening to the main hall.

Choose Joy hung perilously to its nail.

Every pithy saying anyone had ever taken the
time to scrawl on a piece of plywood hung from
the walls, a hurricane of inspiration.

Tate allowed her a moment to take it all in. Then
he gestured to the signs and said, "Loretta loves a
bargain."

"She does." Harlow paced toward the wall, noticing a large, pastel bunny with Hoppy Spring!
scrawled across his belly.

"It all works, though. We've definitely had our ups
and downs, but it's amazing to be part of the experience of reviving a school."

Harlow could appreciate his enthusiasm. It wasn't
how she felt about the idea of working in a school,
but he seemed happy about it. Tate was cool. Twice
as tall and three times as loud as the person she
might have expected Aida to settle with, but cool.

"Practice is in the library for now," Tate said,
gesturing for her to follow him. "I hope we don't
have to wind up having the pageant in there. But
the acoustics in the gym are terrible, and the caf-
eteria is too small."

Yeah, there was no way they would perform in
an unsuitable venue. Harlow would find the perfect
space in town for the pageant.

She trailed after Tate, noticing more differences
in the building. The walls of the hallway were plas-
tered with student work. A series of posters high-

lighting the differences between early river valley civilizations dominated one side of the hall. On the other, student-made advertisements with titles like, *Sleep! It's not just for toddlers anymore* and *Feeling stressed? Try our patented new medication, a long walk in the fresh air!*

"Those are from my class," Tate said.

"They're great." Harlow furrowed her brow as she read an advertisement casting leafy green vegetables as the new miracle skin care routine.

"You want to see something really cool, check this out." Tate opened the door to what Harlow remembered as Mr. Carus's extremely dull science class. Harlow stepped inside to see a fascinating array of ordinary offerings from nature—a tumbleweed, willow branches, wild rose hips, a pronghorn skull, a chunk of volcanic rock—all made beautiful and fascinating by their display. One wall contained windows with a stunning view of Hart Mountain, and along the other three walls ran a brilliant seascape. Schools of fish, sea urchins, octopuses and other underwater creatures, all painted in vivid colors, sparking a sense of wonder about the natural world.

"Is this Vander's room?" she asked.

"Yep." Tate shoved his hands in his pockets. "How do you know Vander?"

"I don't know him, really. We just—"

What? Argued in the street about the merits of Pronghorn? Then I caught him harboring an old horse on my property?

Also, had he *not* mentioned her to his friends? There was no reason to, of course. But still. If she lived with five friends, she'd have mentioned him.

Not that any of it mattered at all.

But still.

"Oh, wait." Tate smiled at her. "Harlow Jameson, like Jameson Ranch."

"Correct."

"Vander said your place is stunning. He talks about it all the time."

Okay, he thought her home was stunning. Cool.

"Speaking of, let's get you to rehearsal."

"Speaking of my stunning home, let's go to rehearsal?" she asked as they stepped back into the hall. "Segue much?"

"Speaking of Vander," he clarified.

Harlow didn't take time to register his words, as music spread through the hallway like light breaking through a foggy morning. A soulful rendition of "Away in a Manger" swept away any concern or worry.

She let the music fill her, resonate within her heart. Harlow cherished and cultivated her ability to recognize the rare quality that made a song or painting or novel true art. It was the one constant through history, the reason both Beethoven and Freddie Mercury could make anyone stop and listen. It was how Jackson Pollock captivated the viewer with splattered paint, and Botticelli's Venus still spoke to the masses five hundred years after her creation.

Some artists had the ability to connect with something greater than themselves. Whoever was playing right now had that connection. But beyond that, the performer was making informed musical choices—when to draw out a note, when to upset the established rhythm and pick up the pace. He liked this song and knew it well enough to improvise in the moment.

The music wove itself into the spark of excitement she'd felt when Loretta mentioned the pageant, unspooling a ribbon of joy in her chest.

"It's pretty, isn't it?" Tate asked.

"Beautiful."

But it didn't take a scientist to predict who was on the other side of those guitar strings. Pronghorn's biggest fan was about to be sorely disappointed when he met his court-appointed helper.

VANDER LIFTED HIS fingers from the strings. He'd concealed himself in the music for as long as possible. The eight students gathered in the library looked at him expectantly. Yeah, playing holiday songs was no substitute for directing a pageant.

He was already exhausted. According to his calculations, the average teenager absorbed the same amount of energy as three adults. He'd been "on" all day. And now that Loretta had informed him his practice of unwinding by playing music in the courtyard was really entertainment for the entire town, well, he didn't know what he was going to do.

But extending his day as a teacher for another hour certainly wasn't helping.

He wanted to ride out and see Stet. Of course, he wouldn't be alone at Jameson Ranch either. He'd be tempted to go find a gorgeous woman and make up something to argue about. That wouldn't be relaxing either.

But it would be fun.

The last few notes of the song still hung in the air as Vander looked up from his guitar.

Straight into the eyes of the woman he'd been trying not to think about.

"Hi," she said, as though there was nothing at all unusual about her presence in the library.

Vander tilted his head to one side, like a confused owl. Harlow stood next to Tate, wearing an expensive-looking outfit—the sort of thing an actress would wear for an outdoor photoshoot.

"Harlow?"

"Correct. Nice job keeping my appellation in your head for twenty-four hours."

Vander noticed two sisters, Taylor and Morgan, turn to one another and whisper at the mention of Harlow's name. She was definitely the most glamorous person to ever set foot in the library.

But why was she in the library? It couldn't be good news.

Vander set his guitar aside and stood. "Is it Stet?"

"No, still Harlow," she said with a dry smile.

Vander was too tense to appreciate the humor. "Is my horse all right?"

Her expression softened. "Yes. Mr. Mangy is doing fine. He ate a big serving of oats this morning and let me pet him."

Air refilled his lungs, but then Harlow flipped her pretty hair off one shoulder and the breath flew straight out of him again.

"Then is something wrong at the ranch?" he asked.

If something was wrong at the ranch, it would get him out of this. But the only crisis he could imagine was a breach in the fence and the cattle getting out, which had happened long before Harlow got here.

"Something *is* wrong." She glanced at Tate who gave her a sympathetic smile. "But not at the ranch. I've been assigned to help with the pageant."

The words seemed to bump up against Vander's skull as he tried to make them make sense. He didn't want to be rude, but blurted out, "You? Why?"

She closed her eyes and nodded, like she expected her help to be rejected. Like *she* expected to be rejected.

"Sheriff Weston's orders. I've been sentenced to thirty hours of community service."

Vander turned to Tate to confirm this.

"It was Loretta's idea." Tate chuckled. Because saddling him with this gorgeous, maddening woman was funny? Then his friend waved and headed for the door. "I'll catch you two later. I've got basketball practice."

Vander was too absorbed in the moment to remember to wave back as his friend exited. He certainly understood the gravity of Harlow's negligence. On the other hand, thirty hours on a Christmas pageant sounded pretty harsh.

"I guess this teacher shortage is no joke," she said flatly. "You have to resort to roping criminals into helping."

At the word *criminal*, the students, already curious about the stylish woman in the room, became fascinated.

"What were you arrested for?" Mav asked. "Was it a non-peaceful protest? Did you chain yourself to an endangered tree?"

"Seriously, Mav?" Taylor Holms, one of the two daughters of Pronghorn's most opinionated mom, rolled her eyes. "People who chain themselves to trees don't wear Blundstone Chelsea boots. Was it tax fraud?"

"I bet it was insider trading!" Taylor's sister, Morgan, suggested.

The kids were now throwing out every crime they could think of, from illegally importing fruit into the state of California to being the mastermind behind a major art theft.

"Were you behind the eBay data breach? Are you stealing information?" Ilsa asked.

Oliver Sorel gave Harlow his best Ryan Gosling smile. "Stealing hearts?"

Harlow shut him down with a hard stare. "Willful, repeated illegal cattle grazing," she said.

"OMG!" Taylor's eyes widened. "You *are* Harlow Jameson."

The room erupted, gossip and misinformation flowing like lava.

Vander's gaze connected with Harlow's. What was the big deal? She put her hands in the pockets of her vest and strolled over to stand next to him.

"Everyone in this town hates me," she said. "They will literally show up at this pageant just to stare at me and judge. Which is probably why Loretta came up with the idea of me helping in the first place. People will willingly donate twenty bucks to get a look at me and feel superior."

"People don't hate you," he said.

"Uh. Yeah. They do."

Vander couldn't wrap his brain around the concept. Her words were there, but they didn't form meaning. Also, her spicy, subtle perfume was messing with him, threatening to shut down his frontal lobe. It *was* possible he hadn't heard her correctly.

"So, what's the plan?" she asked. "How can I help?"

There was no plan. His only thought walking in today was to get through it. "Do you play an instrument?" he asked.

"Nope. But I love music."

"Is set design more your thing?"

"I'm a terrible artist. I did, however, minor in art history."

"And your experience working with teenagers?"

"I was one, once." She grinned at him. "And I'm pretty good at arguing."

His gaze connected with hers. All around them

students were gossiping, some had their phones out because for whatever reason the school had a good internet signal that day. But standing next to Harlow, it felt like she transported him into her own personal bubble, created by her perfume and sustained by her smile.

A place he did *not* want to get comfortable.

"I'm gonna go out on a limb and guess you don't have any more interest in running the pageant than I do, for all you're Mr. Teacher of the Year."

"I'm not teacher of the year."

"I think you might be." She paced a few steps, sizing up the students. "You're a good teacher, but Loretta threw this in your lap, and you don't exactly have a plan right now."

"You got that right."

"Okay then. Let's get them talking. You already know what you're dealing with here, but I don't."

"Good idea," Vander admitted. "Make this about what they bring to the situation, rather than what we bring."

"Which appears to be a guitar on your part, and a proven inability to wrangle on mine."

He laughed despite the situation. If he had to be stuck here, at least his fellow inmate was clever.

"What's funny?" Taylor asked, or rather accused. She was eyeing Harlow with suspicion, as though she were somehow harming the teaching staff by existing.

Vander ignored the question. "Let's circle up, everyone. Grab a chair."

The students responded to the directive quickly, as he gave the same instructions almost daily in class, whether for a science demo or to share their findings from a lab.

Chairs scuffed against the carpet. Mav wondered why it had to be a circle, muttering something about teachers having prejudices against other shapes. Taylor fussed at Oliver until his chair was in perfect alignment.

Finally, they were in a circle.

Now what?

Harlow leaned back in the library chair and crossed her legs, her evaluative gaze working around the room. Silence fell. Harlow quirked an eyebrow at Vander, as though to ask if this was all he had.

It was.

She placed both of her stylishly clad feet on the floor and rested her elbows on her knees. "Is there anyone here from the Open Hearts Community," she asked.

Since two kids were dressed in orange and had telltale piercings at the helix of their ear, it was a pretty obvious question. But Mav and Antithesis both nodded in the affirmative.

"Any exchange students?"

Ilsa lifted her chin. "I'm from Amsterdam. Nari is from Seoul." She gestured to Nari with her thumb. "We're trying to get Sofi to join too."

"That's awesome." Harlow scanned the circle. "Looks like we have folks here from a lot of different backgrounds. But pretty much everyone in the world celebrates a winter holiday. Why don't you each tell us about a favorite holiday tradition?"

The students glanced at one another, looking anywhere but at Harlow in an effort to avoid the question.

She pointed to Oliver. "You. James Bond, whatcha got?"

Oliver made a face, as though he couldn't remember any holiday traditions. "We just have Christmas, nothing special."

"You do stockings?" Harlow asked. "Do you wake up and find oversize footwear stuffed with candy?"

"Yeah, but—well, we actually have to wait to open our stockings."

Harlow raised a brow in interest.

Oliver leaned forward, facing Harlow. "We spend the night at my Grandma and Grandpa Sorel's house. And before we can go into the living room and see the tree or the stockings, me and Grandpa have to feed the cattle." Oliver looked around the circle as he began to get deeper into the story. "It's always really cold. And Grandma gives me a thermos of hot chocolate to take with us. Then we take the tractor to get the alfalfa hay, and… You guys know my grandpa?"

Kids around the circle nodded. Pete Sorel was on the school board and an ardent supporter of high school sports.

"When we got the hay, when I was a little kid, Grandpa would always like—"

Oliver paused.

Harlow gestured for him to keep the information coming.

Oliver got a goofy smile on his face. "Grandpa would always point out 'missing hay' and tell me that Santa's reindeer had stopped for a snack."

The kids in the circle laughed. Vander had the feeling Pete Sorel probably still pointed out the missing hay, and Oliver might just let himself keep believing.

"As a kid, that's when I started getting really excited. Then we'd feed the cattle, and well, this sounds cheesy—"

The circle was now in rapt attention.

"What happened next?" Mav asked. Growing up at Open Hearts, he'd never celebrated Christmas and was clearly fascinated with this talk of reindeer and stockings.

"Well, when I was little, Grandpa would always 'find' a candy cane in his jacket pocket, like Santa had left it there." Color rose to Oliver's face. "I totally bought it as a kid. That candy cane was always the best, most delicious candy cane. Like, it tasted better because I thought it came from Santa."

Vander could imagine the old rancher, gruff and to the point, pulling out a candy cane and pretending to be surprised, year after year.

Harlow smiled at Oliver. "You still help him feed the cattle on Christmas morning?"

"Yep."

"And does Grandpa still find a candy cane in his jacket pocket?"

Oliver laughed, then admitted, "Yeah. And it's still like, the best candy cane ever."

"Aww!" Ilsa said. "That's like how my mom and I would always get up before my siblings and get the Kerststol ready."

"What is Kerststol?" Mav asked. "Does it go in the sock too?"

The traditions were all over the map. The kids from Open Hearts described their elaborate solstice festival. Nari also celebrated the winter solstice in Korea, but Christmas was a fun, minor holiday thrown into the mix in Seoul. Ilsa's Christmas traditions from the Netherlands were a source of fascination for the kids, launching a robust discussion about whether it was more practical for St. Nick to deliver presents in a boat or a sleigh.

As Mav described the feast of the sunrise, Vander noticed Taylor pull out her phone. Internet was so spotty in Pronghorn that phones hadn't been a huge problem at school, but this was not okay. He didn't want to interrupt Mav by calling attention to the fact that Taylor wasn't listening, so he turned the Teacher Eye on her. Kids could usually feel when he was looking at them, and he would indicate that she needed to put her phone away when she looked up.

It wasn't working.

Then Harlow asked Mav a clarifying question about the symbolism of limes to keep him talking.

She stood, crossed the circle and pulled the phone out of Taylor's hands.

"That's my phone!" Taylor exclaimed.

"One would assume." Harlow set the phone face-down on the table behind her. "Mav, what did you say those lime cakes were called again? They sound amazing."

Before he could answer, Taylor snapped, "You can't take my phone."

"It's rude to text when someone else is talking." Harlow's tone wasn't harsh; it was more like she was simply offering a piece of advice Taylor might not have heard before.

As the room was now silent, Harlow continued, "One time, I was in a meeting with Carly Pearce, and some guy pulled out his phone while she was talking. Her manager snatched it out of his hand and *didn't give it back*. Like, I don't think that guy ever saw his phone again."

Confused and impressed muttering ran through the circle.

Taylor scoffed. "You were *not* in a meeting with Carly Pearce. She's like a major star."

"I've been in a lot of meetings with Carly Pearce."

"Why, because you're like, *her friend*?"

Vander started to ask Taylor to watch her tone around their guest, but Harlow just laughed.

"God, no. I'm friends with her lawyer. Or one of them anyway. They brought me in for a conversation about a collaboration she's considering." Harlow glanced around the circle. "Do you kids know what I do for a living? Or is that not part of the town gossip?"

The students stared back at her, as though just now seeing her as a real person.

Harlow continued, "I'm an intellectual property lawyer, specializing in music copyright. I make sure artists get paid for what they create and don't accidentally steal the work of others. It's fascinating. And Carly's awesome. Super chill." Harlow crossed her legs and refocused on Mav. "What were you saying about welcoming the return of the sun? I have to be honest, the feast of sun splendor sounds super fun."

Harlow had completely refocused on Mav, but Taylor was still staring at Harlow. Then she glanced at her sister, who slipped her own phone back in her bag.

Mav finished up his description, and Harlow leaned back in her chair, a devious glint in her eye. She scanned the circle, and Vander could almost see the gears in her mind shifting and reevaluating, before landing on something that made her smile like she had a wonderful, awful idea.

"You all have such rich and varied holiday traditions. This is going to make for a *brilliant* pageant. We've got a lot of work ahead of us." She winked at Vander. "And I've only been sentenced to thirty hours of community service, so we need to get busy."

CHAPTER FIVE

COLD AIR WHIPPED Vander's face as he drove the ATV back to town from Harlow's place. The insulated gloves did nothing to cut the chill in his fingers. The hour with Stet had done nothing to ease the confusion roiling through his chest.

He sighed, his exhale audible over the ATV's inconsistent motor. What was it that had him so tangled up inside? And what was he going to find if he started to unravel the mess?

Three days into pageant rehearsal, and Vander didn't see any possibility for making it through to winter break. The kids were squirrelly ever since returning from Thanksgiving.

It was funny to think that three months ago, the teachers celebrated every small bit of chatter and activity. When the students first returned to in-person school, they'd barely interacted with one another. If they did, it was often a fight between students from the Open Hearts Community and the ranchers' kids. But over time, the teachers' efforts at helping the students work through their social anxiety, overcome their differences and get along had been effective. The school had started to buzz with social energy.

Then Loretta had recruited nine exchange students who added even more excitement to the mix.

By this point in the year, his students had forgotten the purpose of school was to learn. Everyone showed up to hang out, get distracted by drama and flirt with each other.

Today's biology lesson felt like trying to teach molecular structure at a twenty-first birthday party in Ibiza.

Vander turned the ATV onto the highway running through Pronghorn. Connie sat upright in the moonlight, alert to trouble. Vander was so tired he didn't even bother to park the ATV in its shed behind the hotel. He shut off the motor in front of the entrance to the courtyard, ready to head inside, eat whatever his coworkers had prepared for dinner and retreat to his guitar.

As the sound of the engine faded away, stillness settled around him. The searing frustration, lying in wait for confusion to clear, reemerged. He closed his eyes and gave in to the memory.

One misbehaving student. One reasonable consequence. Two angry, embarrassed parents.

Four hundred responses on Facebook to an unsubstantiated accusation of bullying his students in class.

He was just a student teacher at the time, without the connections or reputation to fight back. People who didn't know him judged him solely on lies spewed across social media. Words like *arrogant*, *sneaky* and *vindictive* stuck to him like resin. Job offers were rescinded. Friendships fell apart.

But he was here now, in a place he loved. In Pronghorn, if he worked hard and treated others with respect, that was how he was known. Gossip could fly in a small town, sure, but without a steady internet connection, it was a lot harder to bend the truth. If people didn't like what he was doing, and there had been a few complaints, the accusations were at least based on his actions.

Voices echoed out from the courtyard into the still night. Vander slipped the memory back into the impacted recesses of his heart. His arteries constricted tightly around the event, drawing the blood flow from the rest of his body, pushing the frustration deeper.

"There you are!" Luci admonished, stepping through the arched entryway. The others spilled out behind her—Mateo, Willa and her fiancé, Colter Wayne, Tate, Aida and Greg the German shepherd. "You made it in time for dinner at The Restaurant."

Vander furrowed his brow. They had to go out to eat tonight?

Luci tugged at his hand, urging him off the ATV. "That's what we do on Thursday, remember?"

"It's already Thursday?" he asked.

"All day long," Mateo quipped.

"That joke was tired twenty years ago," Luci grumbled.

"And yet it continues to make me laugh," Mateo said. "That's impressive on the joke's part. Real stamina in the face of negativity."

Luci rolled her eyes.

Vander *could* hang back at the hotel, tell his friends

the truth—that he wasn't up for more social activity. But he didn't want to deal with the questions, not tonight. And the rowdy company of his friends would be a distraction.

"Let's do it," he said, climbing off the ATV and joining the crew.

Vander trailed behind his friends as they walked two blocks to The Restaurant. Pressure built around his feelings, packing them tighter, gaining heft but taking up less space. The sadness would pass; he could act like everything was fine.

Greg brushed against his leg, keeping pace with him.

He glanced up at the sky. Stars lit the valley, hanging so close it seemed impossible they weren't just on the other side of the earth's atmosphere. The Christmas lights along Pronghorn's Main Street twinkled in response, like a child dressing up in their parents' clothing. He breathed in deeply, the icy air both painful and refreshing.

"How are you hanging in?" Aida fell into step beside him.

"Fine."

"I mean, are you okay with, you know, the situation?"

Vander nodded, not bothering to clarify what the situation was. Aida didn't know about his past, and whatever the present situation was couldn't be that bad.

"Aida is trying to apologize to you," Tate said, dropping an arm around her shoulder.

"No need," Vander said. There was no need to apologize or talk.

"Loretta thought you could use the help," Aida said.

Vander stopped walking. They were talking about Harlow? He wondered if she was on another hike. If she, too, thought the stars were particularly close tonight. "It's fine. After my reaction, I can see why Loretta thought that."

"You shouldn't have to babysit Harlow." Aida seemed to struggle with the words, then said, "I'm sorry."

"We're doing fine."

"I know Harlow can be a lot."

Vander took his eyes off the stars. She was a lot, but even he could admit that was exactly what the situation called for. His only concern was that she wanted to make the pageant a bigger deal than it needed to be. So long as she could reel in some of her grand ideas, her help was fine. Legitimately help*ful*. "She's cool."

Aida blinked, as though unsure how to respond to a direct, positive statement about Harlow. "She probably knows a lot about music."

"She sees a lot of shows and knows how to organize things," Vander said. "And the kids like her."

"Really?"

He nodded. There was definitely an air of rebellion in the way some kids attached themselves to Harlow. Particularly with the Holms girls, Taylor and Morgan. After Harlow had confiscated Taylor's phone that first day, then returned it at the end of rehearsal without any kind of reprimand, both girls had made an effort to earn Harlow's approval. This inspired other students to do the same. In turn, Harlow regularly asked students for their ideas, praised their work and generally treated them like adults.

Harlow was stylish and funny and a serious boss in Nashville. It was no wonder the kids took to her.

"Why is that a surprise?" Vander asked. "She's a huge help. No, help's not the right word. She's not helping, she's instigating. Harlow came up with the whole plan for the pageant."

Luci turned around and walked backward. "What *is* the plan? And I know you're upset that you're stuck doing this, but honestly, I'm super excited about it."

Vander gave a brief nod but didn't answer her question. Willa released her fiancé's arm and placed a hand on Vander's back. Willa wasn't much older than the rest of them, but her mom energy was powerful and appreciated.

"Did I tell you guys Sylvie is hanging out with Sofi tonight? They've been designing clothes and want to come up with a student-created spring line suitable for Pronghorn." Willa skillfully changed the subject, allowing Vander to rest on the sidelines of conversation.

"So something to go with mud?" Luci asked.

They arrived at The Restaurant, stepping from the cold, open night into the cozy, crowded establishment.

When they'd first arrived in town, they'd nearly gotten themselves kicked out for breaking Angie's long and complicated code of conduct. Don't pull tables together, don't try to get takeout, don't over-tip, don't undertip and whatever you do, never ever ask for substitutions. Over time, they'd learned the ropes. Now, four months in, and Angie got worried, then mad, if they didn't show up every Thursday night. Two tables were already pushed together for their crew, and patrons waved and called out greetings as they entered.

Vander paused to examine the sandwich board that held the evening's offerings:

> *Grilled chicken, green beans and*
> *mashed potatoes with chicken gravy*
> *Fried chicken, peas and baked potato*
> *with chicken gravy*
> *Vegetarian option: Peas, green beans,*
> *baked potato with vegetable gravy*

"What do you suppose vegetable gravy consists of?" Willa asked under her breath.

"Canola oil," Aida said. "I heard her bickering with Today's Moment about it last week. Angie's primary argument was that everyone was entitled to their own beliefs, and she didn't believe in serving potatoes without gravy. And since gravy didn't have a face, Today's Moment didn't have reason to complain."

"Today's Moment has never *needed* a reason to complain," Luci noted.

Angie came out of the kitchen when she heard their voices. She scolded them for a few minor offenses by way of greeting, then ushered them toward the table. Before disappearing back into the kitchen, she glanced at Vander, then patted his shoulder in sympathy. "I'm sorry to hear you have to work with Harlow Jameson. It'll be over before you know it."

Vander opened his mouth to contradict her, but Angie had already vanished into her kitchen.

HARLOW PARKED HER CAR, then ducked her head to look out the window at the light spilling from The Restaurant.

Ugh.

She leaned back in her seat.

Was she seriously going to walk into Angie's and order a meal? Half the town would be there, staring, judging. Angie would act offended she had the nerve to show up in her establishment. Then she'd be mad it took Harlow so long to show up.

Harlow ran through her mental list again.

She was out of food at home.

The store was closed. And even if it hadn't been, four days of soup, crackers and Nutter Butter cookies were honestly enough. Lakeview was two hours away, and while she could have gone any time during the last few days, she hadn't. She kept telling herself her housekeeper would arrive at any moment, even as she continued to get texts from said housekeeper explaining she was still sick.

Harlow was tempted to leave the mental list there.

But if she was going for the truth, the whole truth and nothing but the truth, well…

There was still some truth left.

Why hadn't she carved out an afternoon to drive to Lakeview? She didn't want to. She was having fun here in Pronghorn. Time on her ranch was always exhilarating. Hours slipped away in seconds as she tromped across the land and scrambled over boulders. She'd make plans to go to Lakeview as soon as she took a horseback ride or organized her Christmas decorations or hiked up to the top of Raven Hill. Time would fly by so quickly, she'd check her watch to find she was nearly late for rehearsal.

Afternoon rehearsals were only an hour and a half, but they were interesting. Okay, they were fun too. And she *had* to talk to Vander as they finished up, because they were the adults in charge. She wasn't going to be involved in a pageant, forcibly or otherwise, that wasn't perfect.

By the time they said goodbye, it was dark out, and it felt too late for a four and a half hour trip for groceries.

Also, sometimes Vander came over to check on Stet after rehearsals.

Sometimes, meaning he'd come every day.

The upshot was, she had no food at home. She was hungry. The Restaurant was the only option.

Harlow pulled herself out of the car and slammed the door behind her, the noise echoing up the empty street. She centered herself on the stoop, squared her shoulders, brushed her hair back, then opened the front door and stepped into the cloying heat.

She felt eyes on her. A ripple of surprise passed through the tables, then the room went silent.

Small town drama takes itself so seriously.

Harlow ignored the stares and stepped up to the counter. It was possible her gait could be referred to as a mosey.

"Hi, Angie."

"Harlow," Angie replied.

"Quite the cold snap we've been having," Harlow said.

Angie gave her a glare far colder than any weather pattern. "*We've* been having cold weather." Angie made sure to exclude Harlow from everything, even the wind-chill factor. "I'm sure it's always sunny in Nashville."

"It's not." Harlow fixed Angie with a courtroom glare, then glanced at the sandwich board. "What's on the menu for tonight?"

"I'd love to serve you, Harlow." Angie's tightened jaw and knit eyebrows suggested otherwise. "But we're all full up tonight. I'm afraid we don't have any tables left, and I know you're far too busy with your life to wait for something to open up."

Harlow didn't turn around to confirm the lack of tables. She held Angie's gaze and said, "Then I'll just have to settle for *takeout*."

An audible gasp spread through the room.

Angie rested an elbow on the counter and got

right up in Harlow's face. "There is no takeout at The Restaurant."

Harlow squared her shoulders. "Then I'll stand here and wait for a table. I hope I'm not a *nuisance*." Harlow took a lazy glance to her left and people immediately averted their eyes. Except for Taylor, who watched the whole exchange with interest. She gave Harlow a secret smile.

How gratifying was it to be a force of rebellion in Pronghorn?

"I'll go ahead and get your order started," Angie said. The kindness in her voice alerted Harlow to trouble.

"You've got a vegetarian option, I see. That's new." She pinned Angie with a sharp gaze. A vegetarian option suggested she'd started to serve people from the Open Hearts Community, which was a nice thing to do. Angie certainly wouldn't want to be accused of doing something nice.

"You a vegetarian now?" Angie asked.

"No, I just thought—"

"That option is for vegetarians only." She made the statement as though being a vegetarian was a biological condition, rather than a choice.

Harlow cast a quick glance at Taylor, who shrugged. Okay, there was no fighting that one.

"I'll take the fried chicken."

"I just served our last piece."

"Then I'll take the grilled chicken."

"I'd love to serve you grilled chicken, but I'm all out of peas."

Harlow glared at Angie. She was hungry. Angie had plenty of food. And Harlow was not walking away from this chess game with her queen off the table. She braced both hands on the counter and got in Angie's space.

"Then I guess you'll have to substitute green beans for peas."

Every noise ceased this time, with the exception of someone's silverware clattering as they dropped it on their plate. Everyone knew better than to ask for substitutions at The Restaurant.

The silence seemed to expand, pushing against the old wooden framing of the building as patrons watched to see who would back down first.

"I have a chair."

Everyone turned to stare, no one more curious than Harlow about who would publicly champion her. She locked eyes with Vander, who stood next to a seat he had clearly vacated seconds earlier.

He pointed, as though surprised to discover an empty seat. "There's a chair."

Harlow stacked up the facts. Vander and the other teachers were sitting at two tables pushed together, next to the front window, like Angie wanted to show them off.

The rest of the patrons were as shocked as Harlow to see Vander interfere.

Then Willa, the oldest and seemingly the wisest of the new teachers, was out of her seat. She whisked over to Harlow. "We have plenty of room."

She laid a gentle hand on Harlow's shoulder. "And plenty of food."

Confused, Harlow walked with her to the table. Vander pulled his chair out for her, and there was some shuffling of seats until Aida wound up smushed into a chair with Tate.

Vander sat next to Harlow. "You can share mine," he said quietly, pushing his plate toward her.

Harlow looked down at a meal that had barely been touched, then back at Vander.

"You can have my potatoes," Luci offered. "If you can find them. I think they're behind the wall of peas, underneath what I'm going to assume is chicken gravy."

"Thank you?"

"Thank *you*," Luci muttered, "for taking them off my hands."

"Hey," Angie barked. "What have I told you kids about sharing? It's not sanitary. It violates the health code."

Harlow opened her mouth to make a snarky remark about what else might be violating the health code in The Restaurant, but Willa spoke first. "Then maybe you can find her something in the kitchen, Angie."

Tate launched himself out of his seat. "I'll help you cook."

"The last thing I need is you in my kitchen," Angie grumbled.

"Am I the *last* thing?" Tate asked, teasing Angie

and somehow getting a smile out of her. "Or would a herd of pronghorn be worse?"

"Anyone can handle a few pronghorn in the kitchen," she scoffed, then retreated through the swinging doors.

A collective sigh of relief lowered tension throughout the establishment. Harlow glanced up to see two tables full of teachers staring at her. Who knew what Vander had told them about her? May as well be honest so they could get in on judging her with the rest of the community.

"Thank you. I'm out of food at home, and the store is closed. My housekeeper is sick. She won't be here until Saturday at the earliest, and she plans and packs all my food."

Harlow waited for the group to exchange glances and clear their throats in judgment.

Instead, Luci said, "I hate it when that happens."

"You hate it when your housekeeper is sick, and you have no food?" Mateo asked. "Because your housekeeper's been missing for months."

"I hate it when I make plans, and everything is in order, then something upsets the balance." She looked at Harlow. "It's not your fault, but you also can't get mad. The worst!"

Harlow warmed to Luci. The social studies teacher was sharply dressed, with a neat blond ponytail and tortoiseshell-rimmed glasses. There was something familiar about her. She could pass for one of the students from Vanderbilt Law School Harlow worked with occasionally, but that wasn't it.

"How's the pageant going?" Mateo asked.

Harlow exchanged a glance with Vander. He gave her a glimmer of a smile. How was it she hadn't noticed his eyelashes before? They were long and thick, drawing attention to his dark eyes with flecks of gold.

Mateo cleared his throat.

Right, the pageant.

"Pretty good. The kids are doing great."

"And what's the plan?" Luci asked.

"We've got four songs we're singing as a group, then each kid gets to pick a song to either sing as a solo or duet, and they share a personal holiday tradition. I think it's really going to come together." She glanced at Vander for affirmation, and he nodded. "The big issue is the venue."

"The library is fine," Vander muttered.

"It's *not* fine."

"It's gonna have to be."

"Are you planning on getting a construction crew in there to knock out a few walls, maybe raise the ceiling?"

Vander shook his head, like he'd done the last two times they'd had this argument.

Luci interrupted before he could speak. "How are you dealing with the whole—" she gestured broadly, indicating chaos "—religion situation?"

"Is there a situation?"

"Well, yeah. Public school, religious holiday, vast array of religious traditions."

"Oh." Harlow frowned and glanced at Vander. "The kids all picked the songs."

Vander leaned forward and addressed the table for the first time. "The choice was either to have no religious elements or to have broadly inclusive religious elements. I probably don't have to tell you the direction these kids are leaning."

"So, songs from every religious tradition of everyone who has ever lived in or near Pronghorn?" Tate guessed.

"And everyone who has ever driven through," Vander added.

"I think it's been good," Harlow said. "They seem to enjoy learning about each other's traditions. *A lot.* Although that's not without its issues. Like Mav's confusion about the mistletoe?" She chuckled, thinking back. "That kid's amazing. He would not let the topic drop, trying to figure out why a parasitic plant that once symbolized Druid vitality is used as a Christmas decoration. But I'm sure Vander already told you all about it."

The teachers stared back at her.

"You're sure *Vander* told us?" Luci asked.

"About anything?" Mateo added.

Tate lowered his voice like he was sharing a secret with Harlow. "I don't know if you've noticed this, but Vander's not the chattiest guy."

Harlow laughed.

Vander's lips twisted in a smile as he leaned back in his chair. It was fun to see how well the teachers got along and to be part of their cozy unit, even if only for one meal.

"You're right. And he's told me nothing about you all. How did you become teachers? And what brought you here?"

Vander's friends launched into spirited retellings of their journeys into education and being recruited to work in Pronghorn by Loretta. They all had vastly different stories, but the motivation was the same. They wanted to expand students' world views through learning and to help kids build futures on track with their goals.

"It's not about being a savior or the best teacher ever," Luci said. "It's about helping students develop the tools to shape and direct their own lives. You know?"

"We want them to learn how to do hard things," Tate said. "Developing the belief that you can rise to a challenge is a fundamental life skill. Grit and persistence get things done. We can help students practice taking on challenges in a safe environment."

"But everyone's challenges are different," Mateo offered. "So while Mason—" he gestured to a young man clearing dishes "—is ready for advanced calculus, I have other students who still panic when confronted with basic algebra. Much of teaching is knowing when to scaffold an activity and when to let kids approach it on their own. And to help them succeed enough so they aren't afraid of failure, because the ability to fail forward is essential."

Harlow thought she noticed Mateo glance briefly

at Luci, but the social studies teacher didn't acknowledge the look.

"Because we have a small school, we can get to know our students really well," Luci said. "We have behavior problems, but a personal connection makes them significantly easier to deal with."

"But the flip side is having fewer resources," Tate said. "Like consistent working internet."

Harlow leaned forward, completely wrapped up in the conversation. "This is all so fascinating. I feel like in my day, school was all about imparting information."

"That's important too," Willa said. "You can't speak Spanish without knowing words in Spanish. Similarly, you can't make connections in a history class unless you know some history."

"It's a balance." Vander leaned toward Harlow, his gaze connecting with hers. "One we're all still figuring out."

Harlow was about ready to suggest this team of five head to Washington, DC, and start figuring out educational policy for the entire US when Luci blurted out, "And what about you? All we know is you have great style and a super fascinating job. What else? *New York Times* subscription? Reality TV addiction? Boyfriend?"

Harlow coughed, then reddened. Technically, no boyfriend. But there was a man coming to visit her in a few weeks who sure wanted to be her boyfriend, and up until Monday, she hadn't been sure she didn't want the same.

A relationship of convenience was still a relationship, after all. And convenience was seriously underrated these days.

She forced her eyes onto Luci so she couldn't look at Vander, but she felt him there all the same. Up until a few days ago, she'd been considering a relationship with no spark because it had been so long since she felt a spark, she'd forgotten what it was.

But now? It was like she was sitting next to a bottle rocket.

"A few subscriptions, no addictions, no commitments," she managed to say.

"But lots of hot country stars?" Luci asked.

The overhead fluorescents seemed to dim. Probably because she was heading into some kind of moral underground: considering a relationship with someone who didn't thrill her while sitting next to someone who did. Harlow glanced up to see Angie at her side with a brown paper sack from the Safeway in Lakeview.

"Here's your order. To go."

Startled, Harlow glanced in the bag, then back at Angie. This was the truce. Angie had been cajoled into serving her, but Harlow needed to leave now. That was fair.

"Thank you," she said, then stood.

"You're leaving?" Luci asked.

What could she say? Her food was all boxed up, ready to go. She didn't want to be rude, but it never seemed to matter if she tried or not, she always wound up doing the wrong thing. "I should get home."

The mood at the table deflated.

Harlow accepted the bag, asking Angie, "How much do I owe you?"

"I've got it," Colter offered. "As school board president it's the least I can do since you're helping out with the pageant."

She could have easily bought everyone's meal in the room and not noticed the blip on her checking account. But Colter's offer was about welcoming her. She'd take it. "Thank you, Colter."

The rancher smiled back at her, tucking an arm more securely around Willa.

Vander stood. "It was real nice to see you here."

"Yes," Willa chimed in. "We always come in on Thursdays and would love to have you join us."

"Thank you." Harlow said. It was a platitude. She was sure Willa didn't mean it. "I guess I'll see you all around the school?"

The teachers affirmed this, but she was more focused on Vander as he stood to see her off.

"Drive safe."

"Drive safe." While not a flirtatious statement, somehow it managed to set her heart fluttering. Harlow spun on her heel and headed for the door. Raquel Holms tsked as she walked past, but Taylor gave her a sly smile of acknowledgment.

"I want those Tupperware containers back," Angie barked from over the counter.

"I'll do my best to keep from stealing your Glad products, but no promises."

Harlow passed the front counter and nearly made it to the door when Angie muttered, "Take a candy cane."

Harlow couldn't have heard her correctly. "What?"

"Take a candy cane," she snapped. "What, you've forgotten how to celebrate the season in the big city?"

VANDER WATCHED HARLOW EXIT, her head high, shoulders straight. The moment she walked out the door, voices rose throughout the dining room, talking about her.

"Dressed up like she's going to see the queen…"

"Always had to have the last word…"

"Demanding takeout at The Restaurant…"

Harlow's prejudice against Pronghorn was beginning to make a lot more sense. What were people's issues with her? Sure, Harlow had some sharp edges, but no sharper than anyone else around here.

Maybe it would help to show her a little chivalry, and he could start by getting her cattle back. Unfortunately, he didn't know the first thing about wrangling cattle. But there was someone at the table who did.

"Hey, Colter. Do you have some time on Saturday?"

Colter, who had been supportive of all the teachers since day one—including taking the time to teach Vander how to ride and care for horses—shook his head.

"No." He glanced at Willa. "No, it's kind of a big weekend."

"What's going on?" Vander asked.

Willa placed a protective hand on Colter's shoulder. "My family is coming to visit."

Colter gazed at Willa with a complicated mix of love and regret in his eyes.

"It's okay," she said. "It's going to be fine."

Vander turned to his other coworkers, but no one seemed to understand the exchange any more than he did.

"Is Willa's family...?" Luci gestured broadly, suggesting someone fill in the information.

"Part of the mafia?" Tate guessed.

Mateo furrowed his brow. "Big shots in a multi-level marketing scheme?"

"I know—" Luci batted Colter's arm "—are they really into Dungeons and Dragons?"

Colter chuckled. "No. I have a complicated relationship with Willa's brother. Or not complicated. He hates me."

"He doesn't hate you," Willa said. "You guys just have a lot to talk about."

Vander knew Colter and Willa had met and fallen in love in high school, but life had taken them in different directions until they wound up here. Something about Colter's face suggested there were memories he didn't like reliving either.

Colter stared down at the table for a moment, then nodded sharply. "Yeah. Hayden and I have a lot to talk about." He glanced at Vander, his smile back in place. "Did you need something?"

"Naw. Just some ranching stuff. No big deal."

Everyone had their issues. Vander could figure out how to herd fifteen head of cattle off a commune where they were treated like pets and back to Harlow's place on Saturday, no problem. Right?

CHAPTER SIX

HARLOW SPED DOWN the main hall of the school, running through her mental to-do list. One week into rehearsal, and she had a solid plan. This pageant was going to blow the roof off this town. It was going to be so moving, so heartfelt, so full of holiday cheer Pronghorn wouldn't know what hit it. People would laugh, cry and remember it for the rest of their lives.

And how uncomfortable would that be for every citizen of Pronghorn? They'd show up to watch her fail, then be confronted with the best holiday pageant of all times.

Perfect vengeance.

There were just a few details she needed to figure out.

Costumes, or some type of cohesion of outfits. Semiformal would work.

Decoration rather than scenery. Harlow didn't want anything cheesy or overdone. Decor should be elegant and wintery. The pageant was Christmas focused but not Christmas exclusive. Decorations should follow suit.

But decoration didn't mean anything if they couldn't find a place to hold the pageant. There had to be some vacant building in town they could spruce up. Harlow flipped through mental images of old barns and abandoned buildings around Pronghorn.

No, wait, an empty building meant no heating or lights. There was rustic charm, then there was downright uncomfortable.

Harlow peeked into classrooms as she headed toward the library. It was, as she'd come to learn, elective hour. Willa had her learners seated in a circle, involved in some kind of discussion. In the next room two pairs of students led a formal debate regarding US foreign policy. Luci watched from the back, focused and taking notes as a student made her point about tariffs. Across the hall, Mateo's room was warm and inviting, with students sitting in clusters at lamplit tables, relaxed and easy, playing some kind of complex math game. Tate's voice echoed into the hall as he led his class in a rowdy movement activity.

Her steps slowed as she approached Vander's classroom. She peeked through the open door into his art class. Students had natural objects scattered across their desks: branches of sagebrush, pinecones, a tumbleweed. They were creating soft, impressionistic images of the objects with watercolors. The room felt alive with energy and warmth. Harlow suspected kids were learning as much about the flora of Warner Valley as they were about painting.

Harlow glanced over to see Vander watching her watch his class. He waved, keeping eye contact. She mugged an impressed expression. He shrugged, like it was nothing.

Her heart pulsed against her rib cage, so light it threatened to slip through and float on over to the handsome teacher. Harlow pulled her jacket tight around her, just in case.

"Mr. V, come look at mine!" A young woman in the orange of the Open Hearts Community flagged him over.

Vander studied her painting, then crouched down so he was at eye level with the student and encouraged her to explain what she'd painted.

Harlow's phone buzzed in her bag, shaking her back to earth. The text read: See you soon! Looking forward to it.

Trey had been pursuing her since they'd met at a fundraiser three months ago. She had connections he wanted. He was nice and easygoing. Harlow knew she wasn't the most lovable person, so the offer of companionship was truly the next best thing.

She glanced back at Vander. Off-brand emotional intimacy just didn't seem all that appealing anymore.

Harlow backed out of the doorway and continued on to the library. She had a job to do. That job started with getting to rehearsal well before the students and moving the tables and chairs out of the way. If the kids saw that she took their time together seriously, they would take it more seriously as well.

Yeah, she was working pretty hard for some community service she didn't want and definitely didn't deserve. But it was all part of her plan. This community wanted her service? They could sit back and get served. She'd deal with Trey when he got here. Right now, she was too busy imagining Raquel's face as she was impressed against her will.

Harlow reached the entrance to the library, then paused. Faint a cappella music hovered nearby. Someone was singing. She took a few steps back into the hallway.

No, someone was singing *very well*.

Harlow glanced around, trying to locate the source. The song was "Wide Open Spaces," a hit by The Chicks decades earlier, sung by a clear voice, full of emotion but still attentive to structure.

The voice was coming from the stairwell.

Pronghorn High, as it had been called when she attended, had two stories. Back in the town's glory days, it was overflowing with students. As the population dwindled, the upstairs was abandoned. The stairwell had been off-limits fifteen years ago when Harlow was a student, and she couldn't imagine kids were allowed in there now.

Why was someone with a beautiful voice singing in the off-limits stairwell next to the library? Harlow had worked in Nashville long enough to recognize the sound of talent waiting to be discovered.

The double doors to the stairs were old, with paint peeling behind a Do Not Enter sign. She'd walked past these doors every day this week, and probably her entire high school career, without noticing them.

She gripped the metal handle and opened the door slowly.

A pale girl with lank, dirty blond hair stood halfway up the staircase, facing a set of multipaned windows that probably hadn't been washed in forty years. Her voice was full and rich, echoing in the stairwell. This was no coincidence.

"Hi there," Harlow said.

The girl turned around with feigned surprise, then her expression shifted. She wasn't expecting Harlow. But then again, who around these parts *was* expecting her?

"I'm Harlow Jameson. What's your name?"

The girl glanced nervously at the door. "Nevaeh."

"Nevaeh, I'm going out on a limb here, but are you supposed to be in class?"

The girl shrugged.

"What class are you supposed to be in?"

She swallowed, then glanced at the dirty windows. "English."

Willa's class, where they'd been having a formal discussion. Made sense.

"Are you waiting for a friend here?" Harlow asked.

Nevaeh shook her head hard. The kid didn't want to be mistaken for someone who had friends at school.

Harlow made a calculated guess and asked, "Have you thought about participating in the holiday pageant?"

Nevaeh shrugged again. Then glanced at Harlow. She *had* thought about participating in the pageant, and with a voice like hers, the girl clearly sang a lot and loved it.

Harlow tried to put the pieces together but was aware that she didn't have half of the puzzle. Vander would know more about who this girl was and why she was hesitant to sign up for something that she clearly wanted to do.

"Well, *I'm* thinking about you participating in the pageant. We could use a strong voice like yours."

"I can't stay after school."

"My guess is you're not supposed to skip out on your English class either, but you did."

Nevaeh's chin angled toward the floor, as though skipping class didn't present nearly the moral dilemma staying after school did.

Harlow returned to the stairwell door and opened it, gesturing for the girl to join her. "Come on, I need to set up the library for rehearsal. We can talk in there."

Nevaeh followed slowly but jumped right in helping Harlow push the library tables back and circle up chairs. Harlow pulled a chalkboard on wheels over and began to outline the schedule for the day.

But the minute the clock struck three and other kids started to filter in, Nevaeh headed for the door, nearly running over Vander as she did.

"Nevaeh!" His face lit up.

Nevaeh's reaction to Vander was palpable, as though this one teacher knowing her name made the whole world brighter.

"Are you here for rehearsal?" Vander's expression suggested there was nothing more amazing on earth than this one child joining in an after-school activity.

Nevaeh shook her head, then mumbled, "I have to take the bus."

Harlow had had enough by this point. The kid clearly wanted to stay—she put herself in a position to get caught singing—and was now pulling out some excuse about a bus? It all seemed a little manipulative, like some of the talented, sensitive artists Harlow worked with who had to be convinced on the daily that the world still appreciated their gifts.

Also, since when did Pronghorn have a bus?

"I'll talk to the school bus driver," Harlow said, striding to the door. "I'm sure it would be fine for me to drive you home."

Vander started to say something, but Harlow stalked out of the library and headed for the front of the school.

Nevaeh followed at her heels, nervous. "I don't have to stay," she said.

Harlow stopped in the flow of kids and turned to the girl. "Do you *want* to stay for rehearsal?"

The girl gave a barely perceptible nod of her head.

"Well, *I* want you to stay too. You have a great voice and were more helpful in the last fifteen minutes than anyone else around here. This is purely selfish on my part."

Harlow stormed out the front door and looked around for a bus. Kids were grabbing bicycles, some headed to the store. A group of six kids wore athletic gear and were kicking a ball around on the soccer field. Connie rubbed against Tate's leg as he argued with a student who held a basketball but was heading for the soccer field instead of the gym.

The street was completely bus-less.

Nevaeh gestured to a truck with a back bumper covered in flags from various countries, and a large American flag on a pole in the back, along with another flag she didn't recognize. Pete Sorel leaned an arm out the window.

"Let's load 'em up!" he called.

Harlow glanced at Nevaeh. "Pete Sorel's truck is the school bus?"

Nevaeh nodded solemnly. Three other students climbed into the extended cab.

Harlow brushed her hair back and approached the driver's-side window. "Hi, Pete."

He touched the rim of his hat. "Harlow."

"I was wondering if I could give Nevaeh here a ride home. So she could participate in the pageant."

Pete looked sharply at Nevaeh, then Harlow. He gave Harlow an impressed nod of acknowledgment. She didn't know what was going on with this kid, but if Vander's reaction, then Pete's were anything to go on, getting this kid involved in a holiday pageant was community priority number one.

But then Pete said, "Nope."

"Nope?" Harlow echoed.

"Nope, you can't take her home without express permission from her folks."

Harlow wanted to reach inside the cab and bop Pete on the nose. This was obviously important, the girl wanted to stay, and he was getting all legal eagle on her? "What if Vander's in the car too?"

"You're still driving."

Then he cracked a smile, an expression she didn't

remember ever seeing on Pete. She tried to remind herself this was the same guy who tucked a candy cane in his jacket pocket for Oliver on Christmas morning.

"I'll come back," Pete said. "I'll run my route, then come back for you. How's that sound, Nevaeh? I need to pick up Oliver anyway, and I may as well drop Morgan and Taylor at home since I'll be out at your place."

"Isn't that like, a whole extra hour of driving on your part?" Harlow asked.

Pete shrugged. "Kids need activities." He leaned past Harlow to address Nevaeh. "I'll stop at your place and tell your folks you're going to be late," he offered.

Nevaeh shook her head. "No need."

"It's no trouble," he said.

The girl looked decidedly nervous as she shook her head again. There might be a *need*, but clearly no *want*.

Harlow studied Nevaeh and let the facts stack up.

She expected to get caught singing. She was all in for helping Harlow set up, then got skittish about staying. When Harlow called her bluff, the girl rallied again. What was going on at home that made it difficult for her to participate in the pageant? And how much did she want this that she was willing to risk the consequences?

"You want to do this?" she asked Nevaeh quietly.

Nevaeh pressed her lips together, then the first smile she'd offered came peeking out. "I really do."

Harlow was well aware of her limitations as a human, but if there was one thing she did well in this world, it was fight for an artist.

"Then let's do it."

RUNNING A REHEARSAL with Harlow was like watching a tsunami approach from the shoreline. A sense of dread and wonder roiled within Vander as Harlow laid out her plans for the students.

What was supposed to be a few kids singing a maximum of six songs was turning into a full-fledged Broadway extravaganza. And trying to stop it would be about as effective as meeting eighty-foot waves with a ShamWow.

"Taylor, if I put you in charge of decorations, I need to be sure it will get done. It's got to be perfect. We can't mess around here."

Taylor, who hadn't taken school seriously since developing a flirtation with Pronghorn's star soccer player, squared her shoulders.

"I'm already making a list." Taylor held out her phone.

Harlow glanced at it, then nodded. "Looks good. I like where you're going with this."

"It would be easier to plan if we knew the venue," Taylor said, throwing Harlow's boss intonations right back at her.

Venue? Who says "venue" in Pronghorn?

"Believe me, venue is top priority."

Vander glanced at Nevaeh, who watched the exchange with interest. She gave him a flicker of a smile.

"What about costumes?" Morgan asked.

"Sylvie Wayne and I are working on it," Sofi said. She was an exchange student from Armenia with an artistic flair, and had already helped design the school's athletic gear and fan merchandise.

"Clothing should be simple but elegant," Harlow said. "And while we don't technically have a budget, I can throw some money at it."

"Hey, no," Vander interrupted. "I don't think we need costumes." Costumes were tricky in Pronghorn. Kids didn't have a lot of shopping options, many families didn't have the money for extra clothing and the kids from the Open Hearts Community had to be wearing at least some orange at all times. "Everyone can just wear something nice."

Harlow and her cadre of mini bosses turned on him. He could swear that Morgan gave his outfit a once-over.

"Noted," Harlow said crisply.

Yeah. Putting a stop to Harlow and her plans was a *lot* like showing up to a tsunami with a sponge and a roll of paper towels.

Vander grabbed his guitar. "Let's get rolling." He glanced at the chalkboard on which Harlow insisted on writing an agenda for the day.

Warm up was first on the list.

Harlow and her crew had certainly warmed up their voices.

He played the first riff of "Winter Wonderland." Nevaeh's face lit up at the music.

Students made their way into the circle. Vander tapped the seat next to him for Nevaeh, and she perched on the edge of her chair, keeping her eyes on the floor. Students continued to chatter. Vander switched up the tune, moving into "Frosty the Snowman," a song that had horrified him as a child in his concern about the sentient snow creature melting. Nevaeh hummed along as he played.

Harlow raised her brows at him, like she knew something about Nevaeh he didn't.

"Vander, let's warm up with a holiday song we all know," Harlow suggested.

Vander nodded. The exchange students, whether they celebrated Christmas or not, knew a number of songs from exposure to pop culture. Mav and Antithesis hadn't thought they knew any holiday songs, only to find there was a lot of cross over between traditional Christmas carols and the solstice songs they'd been taught as children.

Vander played the opening to a song that seemed like a good way to settle the kids.

"'Silent Night'?" Harlow asked, when he wasn't even two bars in.

He nodded and continued to play. Nevaeh shuffled her feet, listening as the other students sang. The song centered the group and brought them to a common purpose.

Nevaeh lifted her eyes from the carpet and joined the singing on the second verse. Her voice rose and filled the room, like she'd sung the carol a thousand times. As she entered the chorus, she lost all hesitation. Nevaeh sang as though she were alone in the center of the Warner Valley.

Around the circle, students glanced at one another, forgetting to sing as they listened. They didn't know Nevaeh and hadn't taken much notice when she stayed for rehearsal. But they were focused on her now.

By the end of the song, Nevaeh was the only one still singing. Vander lifted his fingers from the strings as the library absorbed the last few notes.

Nevaeh pressed her lips together and retrained her eyes on the carpet.

It was several seconds before anyone spoke. Vander didn't know what to expect. Would kids be jealous or dismissive? Nevaeh wasn't connected at school. Kids didn't know her, and that, he'd learned, was when people felt comfortable being rude.

It was Taylor Holms who broke the silence.

"Okay, you're amazing," Taylor stated, waving a hand in a perfect imitation of Harlow. "We definitely need a better venue if she's going to be performing."

Color rose up Nevaeh's neck.

"And costumes," Morgan added. "Because her voice is way too beautiful for us to be all mismatched."

The rest of rehearsal passed in what felt like minutes, a busy blur of music and discussion. The kids seemed even more invested, their wild ideas for costumes, lighting and *venue* growing more outrageous by the minute.

Vander didn't know how to tamp down expectations, but he had to do something.

When rehearsal ended, Harlow followed the kids out front to make sure Nevaeh caught a ride with Pete. Vander pushed the rolling chalkboard back to its place, then began stacking chairs on tables. Confusion snaked in his belly. He was grateful to Harlow for fighting for Nevaeh but frustrated that she wasn't acknowledging his desire for the pageant to remain simple.

What could he say to her to get this pageant reeled back in?

"All right." Harlow stalked back into the library. "Where are we gonna hold this thing? We've got to solve that problem before we move forward."

"Here," he said.

"Here as in Pronghorn, or here as in—" Harlow flicked her hands to indicate the room *"—here?"*

"We don't need a big auditorium," he said. "We'll push the tables back and perform in the library."

"We are *not* performing in the library," Harlow snapped.

"Well, I'm pretty sure the Pronghorn Opera Hall is booked that night."

She glared at him.

He continued to put the library tables back in place and stack the chairs. Not that there was a janitorial staff to come in and vacuum after they'd gone. Or even a vacuum. The Pronghorn parents were taking turns coming in on weekends to vacuum the one carpeted room. "There's plenty of space for the parents of these kids in here."

"In what world do you think the audience will be limited to the parents of these kids?" she asked.

Vander thought back to the soccer games, where people would come from all around to watch. He changed his tack. "Well, maybe if we hold it in the library, we can keep it small."

"We're not holding the pageant in the library."

"Why do you care?" he finally snapped. "You don't even want to do this."

She furrowed her brow, as though the question caught her off guard. Like she'd forgotten she didn't want to help with the pageant in the first place.

She brushed her hair off her shoulder. "I don't want to do this, but if I'm going to be a part of something, I'd like to do it well. I'd like the performance to be fun and moving and heartfelt. I'd like it to fill up the audience and give them a high to last all week. That's what a good live performance can do, and that's what we should strive for."

Vander opened his mouth to argue, but he couldn't come up with a reason the audience shouldn't be moved, filled up and joyful. Except that would mean having an audience.

"I'm trying to think outside the box," she said. "There has to be a space in Pronghorn where we can perform."

"Look, I hear you want to make this nice, and I do too. But my primary objective is for the kids to have fun."

She blinked. "Right. One hundred percent." She gave a half frown, like she was thinking. Then she paced in a semicircle. "But we also want the kids to rise to a satisfying challenge."

Vander narrowed his eyes.

Harlow grinned. "Do hard things! Grit! Angela Duckworth!"

Vander finally laughed, leaning against the table. "Let's set some boundaries around this pageant. Then you're not disappointed or setting the kids up to be disappointed, and I'm not the bad guy because I have to remind everyone this pageant needs to exist within the laws of physics."

"Boundaries would be great." She pressed her lips together in a smile. "Good boundaries will help me know exactly where to push."

"Harlow—"

"Come on! Let's make it magical. Let's give this town something to gossip about."

"This town is still buzzing about the possibility of Mac getting his espresso machine working one day."

"That's what I'm talking about! This town is so stuck, Mac is afraid of a common household appliance."

"Fancy espresso machines aren't common household appliances."

"They are in my household."

The confusion shifted in his chest. Harlow wasn't listening. She was making assumptions based on the information she chose to accept. And if he'd learned anything about her so far, it was that she wasn't gonna back down. The trait probably made her an excellent lawyer, but she couldn't argue an *appropriate venue* into existence.

Vander crossed the room to finish putting chairs on tables, muttering, "Next thing you'll be havin' the kids singing pop holiday music."

Harlow shuddered. "I abhor pop holiday music. Especially the weirdly romantic Christmas songs. Like, a person shouldn't be asking Santa for another person, you know?"

Vander looked up from his chair stacking. Were they agreeing on something pageant related?

"They are the worst," she confirmed. "And everywhere you go someone is playing a sappy Christmas love song and your ears are assaulted." Harlow paced to the end of the room. "I can't even pick the worst one, because they're all so bad."

"Oh, I can. 'Last Christmas' by George Michael. That song… I don't even know where to start with what makes it so bad," Vander said.

"I would have said 'Last Christmas' by George Michael, but then recently there have been all these remakes of it, which are somehow even worse. And also, why?"

"They made a second version?" Vander asked.

"There are like, thirty new versions. Where have you been?"

He looked at her dryly. "In Pronghorn. Where I have now memorized Willie Nelson's Christmas album, down to the scratches in the vinyl."

"I kind of love that album," Harlow admitted.

"I used to love that album," Vander noted.

"I can see how Mac's overplaying is problematic, but you have to give him credit for introducing music to the store. But if I were to pick a worst Christmas pop song?" Harlow drummed her manicured nails on a tabletop, a little frown emerging as she thought. "Have you heard Justin Bieber's version of 'Little Drummer Boy'?"

Vander straightened, alarmed. "You're joking."

"Oh, I wish I were."

"Justin Bieber recorded a version of 'Little Drummer Boy'?"

"That is the title of the track, and some parts of the original tune and melody are included in the recording. But one could argue the spirit of the song is so far off that the title is a mere suggestion."

Vander laughed.

"Both he and his producer should be held accountable, possibly with jail time."

"Jail time?" Vander slid the last chair onto a table and turned to Harlow. "What about community service helping with a holiday pageant?"

"See? It could be worse. You could be working with Justin Bieber's producer right now, and I can tell you that man would not be satisfied with performing in the library either."

Vander chuckled, but there was a twinge in his heart. He couldn't imagine Justin Bieber's producer was half as engaging as Harlow.

"No, all romantic Christmas songs are horrible," Harlow said.

Vander kicked the toe of his boot against the leg of a table. He felt a little bad condemning every pop Christmas song. There were even a few Justin Bieber songs that weren't that bad…

"What?" Harlow asked.

"What, what?"

"Your thoughts are super easy to read."

"No, they aren't," Vander argued.

"You're thinking about a Christmas love song you like. What is it?"

"Well…" Was he really going to admit this? He didn't have to. At the same time, he felt like he was betraying a good song if he didn't.

Harlow advanced on him, as though she had the power to reach inside and pluck the truth right out of his mind. "What is it? What cheesy Christmas love song do you actually like?"

Vander felt heat rising up his neck. This was embarrassing, but he'd rather admit the truth than let Harlow make it up. "I don't hate all of Justin Bieber's holiday songs."

"Oh." She stopped in her advance. "'Under the Mistletoe'?"

Vander studied his boots and admitted, "I like that song."

Harlow threw her head back and laughed. "I *love* that song."

"Why is it so good?" he asked. "I don't get tired of it. Every time I hear it, it puts me in a good mood, and I want the singer to spend as much time as possible with whoever he's singing about. Every time."

Rather than laugh, Harlow crossed her arms and studied the carpet for a moment. "Do you want to hear my theory?" she asked.

"Yeah. Yeah, I absolutely want to know why I love an overplayed, overengineered Christmas song by a former teenage pop star." Vander leaned up against the table next to her. She was quiet for a moment, so he nudged her shoulder with his. "Come on. I made my confession. You make yours."

She looked up, her gaze connecting with his. "I believe true art, in any form, is a combination of skill, attention to detail and what I like to think of as soul, or a spark of the divine. When someone loves an art form, they go all in, honing their skills over time. But it's only when they allow a part of themselves to merge with the music or painting or whatever it is that it becomes art."

Her words filtered through his experience and nestled around an idea. "It makes me think of watching Aida play soccer."

"Yes." She nodded, like he was getting it. "Yeah, I've seen Aida play. It's beautiful, right?"

Vander thought back to the evening Aida and Tate played a pickup game against the students. Aida had been skilled, completely focused and seemed to be playing with her whole heart. "It is."

"We see art everywhere, anytime someone goes all in and lets their heart get involved. And I can't imagine it always feels good to be an artist, right? They can be hard on themselves, and putting soul into their work has to feel pretty vulnerable."

"It does," Vander admitted. Then realized he'd lumped himself in with the artists Harlow was praising.

She nudged his shoulder with hers. "I *am* talking about you," she confirmed.

"Let's talk about someone else."

"Justin Bieber's producer?" she suggested.

Vander laughed and let himself gaze into her pretty eyes.

She widened those eyes. "This is why I want the pageant to happen in a space worthy of these kids, and the art they are creating. There are way too many *Field & Stream* magazines in here for this level of commitment."

Vander groaned. "Okay. I'll start looking for a place."

"Do we know?" She pointed toward the ceiling with her index finger. "Do we know what's upstairs in this building?"

Vander looked up. "Spiders probably. Definitely asbestos."

Harlow shuddered. "But possibly an ornate performance hall?"

"I doubt it." His shoulder brushed hers again, and wandering through cobwebs and old textbooks with her in search of a performance hall didn't sound that bad at all.

"Oh, wait." She widened her eyes at him. "Maybe that's where Mrs. Moran lives?"

"Mrs. Moran doesn't live at the school."

"Then where does she live?" Harlow asked.

He furrowed his brow. "You know, I don't know."

"I always thought she lived at the school. Like seriously. I believed this was her home when I was a teenager."

It wasn't until Harlow admitted this that Vander realized he'd been thinking the same thing. Mrs. Moran was always at school, teaching part-time, playing pinochle with the kids at lunch or working in her little broom-closet office.

He'd seen her outside the building at soccer games, but that was it.

Hmm.

"Now, she's an artist," Vander said. "The way she works with kids? It's amazing."

"The consummate artist," Harlow confirmed. "Literally, the best human in Pronghorn. Possibly, the best human ever."

"If we're talking about artists, how about Nevaeh today?"

Harlow placed a hand over her heart. "Oh. Absolutely. I mean, wow."

"She's a special kid. I appreciate you encouraging her to stay."

"Of course. I mean, with her voice? We have to have her in the pageant."

"I would want Nevaeh to participate even if she couldn't sing a note," Vander said. "This is about the process for the kids, not the product we give the audience."

Harlow gave him a side-eye. "I think the process should involve creating the best product we can." Vander opened his mouth to clarify himself, but Harlow continued, "What's Nevaeh's story? It seemed like she wanted to stay but wasn't sure if she should."

"There's not a lot of support for school at home."

"What's her last name?"

"Danes."

"Oh. Okay." She widened her eyes as though this meant something.

Vander didn't know much about the Danes family, only that they lived outside of town and generally kept to themselves.

Harlow continued, "I was in school with Amber Danes. She managed to get in even more trouble than I did, when she chose to show up."

"What did you get in trouble for?" Vander asked.

Harlow gave him a sly smile. "Trying to shape and direct my own life. A cardinal sin at Pronghorn High back in my day."

He laughed.

Harlow continued, "There's not a lot of love for public education in the Danes family. Not a lot of love for me either. Amber Danes probably dislikes me more than anyone else in town, so that's fun."

Vander didn't get it. Sure, Harlow had some high expectations, and she didn't run around trying to please everyone all the time. But she was as likable as anyone else around here.

She met his gaze and let her shoulder brush against his again, the warmth of her sweater against his jacket forging an unexpected connection. Then her mouth turned down in a little frown that he was beginning to recognize as her pondering expression.

Truth be told, he could be doing some pondering too.

Harlow stood abruptly. "So, cattle drive tomorrow?"

Vander's shoulder seemed to ice over in her absence. He placed his hand on the spot her sleeve vacated. "Cattle drive tomorrow," Vander confirmed.

"I fixed the fence in the lakeside pasture, so we can keep them there over the weekend. I have two guys coming from Mountain View on Monday to make the other repairs, and we should be set. No more escapee cattle."

"Oh. I thought we were gonna…" Vander trailed off. What was he trying to say here? He thought he and Harlow were going to string barbed wire together with the help of his friends for a fun off-campus activity?

"I got it." She pulled on her coat and gave him a wry smile. "I'm not completely inept."

Vander stared as she settled her elegant wool coat on her shoulders and adjusted the cuffs.

"That's the last word I'd choose," he admitted.

Color rose up her neck. She tucked her hands in her pockets and focused on the thinning carpet, as though letting the accidental compliment pass.

"All right then. I'll tuck in the horses tonight, so you can enjoy big Friday night plans with your friends." She waved and was out the door before he could say goodbye. Or admit that his big Friday night plan was learning how to drive cattle.

And hopefully figuring out how to extinguish this spark Harlow was lighting in his chest.

CHAPTER SEVEN

HARLOW OPENED HER front door and stepped into the December morning. Frost blanketed the ground, sparkling in the watery blue, predawn light. Warner Valley was cold and silent, waiting on the sun to rise.

Meanwhile, her heart emulated the steady beat of a kick drum as Vander strolled into the center of her yard, holding the reins of two horses. His smile broke out, the way the sun would crest over Hart Mountain within the hour.

Harlow raised a hand in greeting. "Good morning." Her voice seemed loud in the icy air.

"Mornin'," he said. "You ready to go fetch some cattle?"

Sure, she was ready to get some cattle. Not quite ready to stop staring at Vander just yet, though. He wore an insulated canvas jacket over a wool flannel shirt, along with jeans, boots and a Stetson. His smile suggested that he, too, might have replayed their conversation from the night before.

Harlow breathed in sharply, the cold air splashing through her.

Vander was attractive. She'd known that was a hazard from the start.

He was great with his students.

He was a complex, interesting person.

He was here to help her get her cattle back because he was her employee, and they'd made a deal wherein she would stable his rescue horse in exchange for his help.

Like she was ever seriously considering kicking that lovable fuzz ball out. But Vander didn't need to know that.

Harlow ambled down the front steps. "Yep. Let's do it."

Vander's fingers brushed hers as he handed her the reins. "It's a cold one."

Harlow placed a foot in the stirrup, grabbed the horn of the saddle, then launched herself onto the horse. Vander followed suit, and they headed out of the yard in the direction of the Open Hearts Intentional Community.

Harlow just needed to keep *her* heart closed.

They rode up the ravine in silence. Or not silence, really, more like companionable not-speaking. Vander's thoughtful glances, intermittent communication with the horses and occasional smile were a conversation in themselves. The activity connected Harlow and Vander in a different way than words would have. It was like being attuned to nature, where nothing was forced; you just had to be present and respond in kind.

It was a challenging ride. The horses were energized by the open terrain and wanted to run and explore. It took a lot to focus the equine energy. Harlow warmed with the activity of guiding her horse up a deer trail and around rocky outcrops.

The sky brightened as they crested Raven Hill.

"Harlow, look."

She felt a hand on her arm and turned to see Vander, his face illuminated with the rising sun. He gestured behind them to the east.

A line of deep red broadened along the ridge of Hart Mountain. They pulled up on the reins, watching as red gave way to vibrant pinks and golds, streaking across the ice-blue sky.

The sunrise was outrageous in its beauty. Color shifted and intensified, then spread into heart-moving pastels. The ordinary miracle was more audacious than any Vegas light show or Baroque masterpiece.

"I've seen gorgeous sunsets all over the world, but I'm not sure anything compares to a Pronghorn sunrise," she admitted.

Vander smiled at her. And, yeah, maybe that was on a similar level to the sunrise.

"It's real pretty here," he said, his eyes moving across her face. To his credit, the red flooding her face was probably as dramatic as the sunrise.

Harlow turned away and nudged her horse forward.

Vander was attractive and interesting and a terrible match. Meanwhile, a man who was an excellent match was sending her texts daily and would arrive in Pronghorn in just over a week.

"What are you thinking about?" Vander asked.

"Was I thinking?"

"Yeah." He pointed to her brow. "You've got your thinking face. You're thinking about something."

"Aren't humans normally thinking about something?" she asked.

"Fine, it's your pondering face."

Harlow laughed. "I was just letting my mind wander."

"You don't have to tell me what you're thinking about. But you have this kinda frown, not a bad frown it's—it's cute. And the line in your brow. That's how I know you're hatching a plan, and I wanna be prepared."

What could she tell him? *I've been thinking about Trey Tucker, a perfectly nice, completely practical man I was ready to settle for until I met you. And you are the least practical partner I can imagine. But when you look at me, I feel like I've been dipped in starlight. I feel like I shine so brightly anything is possible.*

Yeah, it probably wasn't appropriate cattle-herding conversation. She needed to get her mind off the topic, and his nowhere near it.

"I've been thinking about overnight tuxedo rentals for the pageant."

Vander scoffed. "No way."

"What's wrong with tuxedos?"

"What's *right* with tuxedos?"

"You can't just be anti-tuxedo," she said as they turned in the direction of Open Hearts, and she gave her horse a nudge. "What's the basis of your argument?"

"They look silly."

"According to whom? Tuxedos are as far from silly as you can get. If you lined up all clothing on a silliness continuum, tuxedos would be at the far end of serious."

"That's not true," Vander countered. "Anyone who has ever looked at a penguin can't think of anything else when they see a tuxedo."

"Oh, so now you're calling penguins silly? I thought you were supposed to be some wildlife-loving science teacher."

"I do love wildlife. And I love penguins because they're kind of silly."

"By that logic you should love tuxedos too."

They argued their way across the prairie, arriving at Open Hearts out of breath and laughing by seven thirty. The sun was fully up, setting tiny particles of ice shimmering throughout the sage green, creams and browns of the prairie. As they passed through the ornate entrance gate, Harlow had to shake off the idea she was doing something taboo and even dangerous.

"Gotta say, it feels so strange to actually enter this property," Harlow said. "As a kid, I was told if I got within ten feet of someone wearing orange, they'd convert me."

Vander looked up at the sky. "Yeah, there was a lot of misinformation about this place when we first got here. Has it always been that way?"

"Probably worse. When the founders of Open Hearts bought the land and moved in, the community of Pronghorn did not take it well. There were town meetings and complaints to the state and accusations of everything from environmental damage to disrupting tourism. The water rights legal battle was epic. It was bad."

"I bet. It would have been hard to accept a big group of folks with different views."

She raised her brow. "True. But it wasn't a one-way street. People living at the commune considered themselves more enlightened, more open-minded. Since they all lived together and chose not to have internet access, they continually backed up their own opinions. Rumors turned into irrefutable truths in the dearth of real information."

"Plenty of people with internet have the same problem," he muttered.

"Good point. It's a fine line."

"Seems like they've come a long way, and the townsfolk have too."

"That's awesome, but..." Harlow trailed off, her brow furrowing.

"But what? And don't say nothing, you got your thinking face again."

Harlow grimaced. "They might seriously hate me."

"I don't think they're real angry about the cattle. Probably should be, but they aren't."

"It's partly the cattle, but I also like, really infuriated some leaders in their community once."

"You? Infuriate someone around Pronghorn?" He wrinkled his brow and shook his head, teasing her. "Impossible."

Harlow laughed, but she could still feel the anger coming off the woman in orange robes, all these years later. She could still feel her own sense of injustice and iron resolve not to back down, even though she was only fourteen at the time.

She'd been outside of Mac's store, waiting for her mom, when she saw a little girl with dark hair in a strange orange outfit studying her intently. She finally said hello to the girl, and the child started to pepper her with questions about school. Harlow, being Harlow, hadn't pulled any punches. She told the girl all about the limited good, all the bad and the boring, but explained that school was essential if she wanted to get out of town.

The little girl wrinkled her nose in utter confusion and asked what was *out of town*. Harlow would never forget the baffled expression, the worried lip. She realized this child didn't fully understand there *was* a whole world out past the Pronghorn city limits.

"Yeah, hard to picture, I'm sure. I tipped a child off to a world larger than the Open Hearts Intentional Community and Pronghorn. From what I've seen, Open Hearts has loosened up a bit, but at the time they didn't take kindly to opinionated ninth graders expanding the world view of their 'impressionable small humans.'"

A chagrined smile spread across Vander's face. "It was a big step for folks to let their kids come to the school at all. Today's Moment got kinda mad at me too."

"She got mad at *you*? You're like a hero in this town."

Vander shook his head. "She did. She accused

me of 'wooing students to normalcy.' She said I was such a good teacher I was trying to convince their emerging adults of my controversial views of science."

"Do you have controversial views of science?" Harlow asked.

"Not to most folks."

Harlow laughed.

"But over time, we worked it out. Pete and Today's Moment realized their fight was having a real negative effect on the community. They're more similar than they are different," Vander said. "Probably true of most folks."

"It's just all so weird—"

"You know you're not supposed to use that word at Open Hearts," he reminded her.

"No, I mean, the way Pronghorn is changing. I never expected it."

He caught and held her gaze for a moment.

Harlow finally got it. "It's the school, isn't it?"

Vander shrugged.

"It is," Harlow said. "This community, as frustrating as it can be, wants the best for its kids. And you teachers are bringing the best in spades."

"We're just doing what we can," he muttered, clearly embarrassed but not disagreeing with her.

"No, you guys are a band of superheroes," Harlow proclaimed. "Underpaid, unrecognized, exhausted superheroes."

And she was developing a crush on the quiet one.

Harlow flipped her hair off her shoulder and examined the landscape. "Are those the famous green-houses?" she asked, pointing to a series of buildings. "The finances of the community are based on grow-ing high-end flowers, right?"

Long, modern-looking greenhouses ran in rows across the land. Through the glass, she could see a riot of colors. Steam rose from the buildings in the cold dawn. Beyond were a series of yurts and then a grand, imposing building that looked like a first-year architecture student had designed it after a whirl-wind trip through Western Europe and South Asia. A vast, well-manicured lawn spread out before the central hall.

And at the center of it all was a small herd of cat-tle looking at her expectantly.

They were wearing flowers.

"Mr. V!" a voice called out. Harlow looked up to see a young woman running toward them, wav-ing an orange scarf. Then Mav came loping along, waving as well. Other members of the community emerged from their yurts.

Harlow scanned them for a glimpse of the woman who'd been so furious with her all those years ago. The child would be in her early twenties by now and may well have taken Harlow's tip about checking out the world outside of the Warner Valley.

Today's Moment came flowing out of the cen-tral hall, her orange robes trailing in the wind be-hind her. Harlow fully expected to hear her intone a prayer. Or curse her for letting her cattle loose on their property. Or convert them both on the spot.

She raised both hands in some kind of greeting, then looked at Vander and asked, "How's the basketball team coming? Do you think we have a chance this Friday?"

Vander gave her a noncommittal "eh?"

"You think they're going to get any better?"

"Hard to imagine they'll get much worse," Vander responded.

Today's Moment folded her hands in what one might expect to be prayer. Instead, the powerful woman said, "We know Coach Tate is trying his best, and the kids seem to be having fun. He'd be having an easier time if his fiancée hadn't poached the best athletes for winter soccer practice."

"That's the truth."

Harlow's head whipped from one speaker to the other as this bizarre conversation played out. Since when was Today's Moment interested in team sports? And how did Pronghorn even have enough kids for a basketball team and a winter soccer club?

The leader of the Open Hearts Community turned on Harlow. "Mav and Antithesis are enjoying their time in the pageant and learning about the traditions of others. We appreciate your inclusivity and look forward to partaking of the joy and spirit with the greater Pronghorn community. Thank you for your work."

"Thank you for…um…sentencing me to it?" Harlow shook her head. "Look, I'm so sorry about the cattle."

Today's Moment gestured to the garlanded creatures and smiled fondly. "We've enjoyed their company."

"I should have responded much sooner, and I regret that my carelessness caused problems for you. I'm fulfilling my sentence, but can I pay for the damage they caused?"

"We don't need money," she said.

Harlow took a quick glance around at snug buildings, high-end greenhouses and paved roads. They really didn't seem to need money. But Harlow didn't have anything else to offer.

"We're grateful for the inclusion of our emerging adults and our traditions in your pageant."

Okay, *what* had happened to this community in her absence? The Today's Moment of the past would have been up in arms about a holiday pageant, and now she was letting their kids get involved and thanking Harlow for it?

Antithesis walked up to an animal and pet its nose. "Goodbye, Swisher." She patted a second animal between his horns. "Goodbye, Morning Star."

Harlow glanced at Vander and muttered, "They have names?"

"Sounds like."

Morning Star nibbled at Swisher's garland of flowers as the assembled members of the Open Hearts Intentional Community said their goodbyes to the bovine.

Harlow maneuvered her horse closer to Vander. "I don't think they're gonna want to come home with us."

The cattle stared blandly at them, completely un-inspired to head back to Jameson Ranch.

Thank goodness Vander was there. He'd know what to do.

VANDER HAD NO idea how to get these cattle moving.

With the one bar of internet reception he could get the night before, he'd managed to find a couple of articles on moving cattle. At the time, the slow-loading diagrams and text seemed to make sense, but these cattle weren't responding like he'd been led to expect they would. And they seemed to be pretty happy right where they were.

Yeah, theoretical cattle herding was a lot easier to grasp than the practical version.

Harlow glanced at him, like she could tell he didn't know what he was doing.

"Move along," he intoned, the same way he dealt with curious pronghorn.

You'd have thought he shot a cue ball into the center of the herd. The cattle shuffled on their hooves, heading in all directions, save that of Jameson Ranch. One started munching on the decorative bamboo leading up to the central hall. Another was slowly following Antithesis back to her yurt. Vander tapped his horse's flank and circled left to head off the straggler. That inspired the straggler to straggle even farther from the herd, as the rest of the herd regrouped and shuffled toward the greenhouses.

Harlow threw him a quizzical look.

The cattle were now a good fifty feet farther

from Jameson Ranch than they had been and were starting to make mournful noises. Could he make mournful noises too? Because he felt like it at this point. He was worse at this than he was at organizing the holiday pageant, and that was really saying something.

"Vander?" Harlow questioned.

"I'm just gonna…"

What? Mumble to himself and hope the cattle wandered back to Harlow's property on their own?

He raised his arms and intoned, "Get along."

Like that was helpful. It's not like the cattle were arguing.

A barely contained laugh escaped Harlow.

Vander sat back in the saddle to glare at her, but she caught his eye, and he started laughing too. He shook his head, letting her know he didn't know what to do. Her lips twisted in a smile that seemed to say, *Me neither.*

"You want help?" Mav asked.

"Nope!" Harlow said briskly, as Vander called out, "We're good, thanks."

Harlow rode her horse over to him and asked, "Are we good?"

"Better than we would be if Mav got involved." He studied the reins in his hands. "I'm sorry, Harlow. I don't know what I'm doing."

"We'll just have to figure it out together."

He looked up into her eyes. "We've been doing a lot of that lately."

She held his gaze, a flush coloring her cheeks.

Then she leaned out of the saddle and gave a garland a tug, pulling an animal along with her. The three of them, woman, horse and cow, moved a few feet in the correct direction. She glanced at Vander, surprised and gratified by her small success. Then another curious bovine began to follow her, then another. Vander circled back and barked at the cattle farthest from Harlow. They shuffled on their hooves and trotted over to the group next to her. The others slowly started to walk.

They were moving. This might not be a cattle drive so much as a cattle pull, but they were headed in the right direction.

Three hours and a lot of garland-tugging later, and they managed to get the cattle into the lakeside pasture. It wasn't big enough for a long-term solution, but the fences were mended, there was plenty of grass and sagebrush to munch on, and it would do.

Harlow and Vander dismounted at the stables and worked together as they brushed down the horses, put the tack away and tucked the animals into their stalls.

"Well. That was an adventure," Harlow said as they headed back into the midday sunshine.

"It was. Enough of one that I'm gonna ride the lakeside pasture fence tomorrow and make sure there's not one place they can breach or even think about breaching."

Harlow laughed. "I'll help."

He glanced at her to see if she was serious. She was, and also somehow even prettier after a frustrating cattle drive. She smiled as she caught him staring.

"I should get back," he said, at the very moment she suggested, "You want to come in for lunch? My housekeeper arrived with groceries yesterday."

He did want lunch. He also wanted to spend more time with Harlow. And what was the inside of her house like? Would it be all chandeliers and expensive, unidentifiable knickknacks? Would she ask him to wear fluffy blue paper slippers over his boots? Possibly a hazmat suit?

She blinked at him.

Had he done something wrong? Or had he waited way too long to respond to the invitation while lost in his thoughts?

"Is that a no to lunch then?" she asked, her expression one of practiced disinterest.

"No. Sorry, no, I don't not want lunch."

She turned a bland look on him.

Get it together, man. "Lunch would be great. Thank you."

"You sure?"

"Completely sure. I'm real hungry. Thank you."

Vander kept his focus as he and Harlow headed over to her house, determined to converse politely and not come across as a total clod. It was only a house. Harlow was a decent person. This was going to be fine. He just had to make sure not to break anything expensive or fall in love. Totally doable.

Vander batted around in his head for something to say, finally coming up with, "I like lunch."

"I'm a big fan myself," she said.

He nodded, acknowledging it was possibly the most absurd conversational topic, but he was committed. "Might be my favorite meal." He pulled his gloves off and tucked them in his back pocket. "Right up there with breakfast and dinner."

"Totally makes the top three in my book."

They approached the yard of the main house. The landscaping blended in with the surroundings, but somehow the buildings as well. Native plants were grouped together artfully, creating an inviting yard and directing his attention to the house.

Harlow led him around to the back door and almost seemed a little nervous as they headed up the steps.

Vander had imagined the house was going to be fancy. He didn't expect it to be so inviting. From the moment he walked in, the place resonated with comfort and calm. He and Harlow toed off their boots in a welcoming mudroom, then he followed her into a large game room with a pool table, ping-pong table, a dart board and neat stacks of every imaginable board game. Large windows ran along one side, and Vander could imagine Harlow's important guests enjoying the views as they shot pool and made their business deals or whatever they did.

From there she led him through a vaulted living room, light and spacious with more huge windows and white furniture strewn with cozy blankets and pillows. The one nod to someone living there was a laptop resting on a pile of papers on the ottoman.

Vander could imagine Harlow snuggled up in her blankets, using the good satellite internet she invested in to work on a case from the comfort of her home.

And now he stood in what was probably the nicest bathroom he'd ever seen, carefully washing his hands because he was worried about getting her sink dirty. Vander shook the water from his fingers and eyed the pristine white hand towel. That seemed like a bad idea waiting to happen. But if he wiped his hands on his jeans, they'd just get dirty again. He shook his hands out, waving them in the air, then blew on them for good measure.

Was the housekeeper here? Was that how the whole house stayed so clean and tidy? Vander glanced around the bathroom, as though Alice from *The Brady Bunch* was waiting to pop out of the shower to clean up after him.

Vander wandered back out and into the kitchen. He leaned against the doorframe watching as Harlow laid out crackers, cheeses, dried apricots, some very thin slices of meat, olives and other small pieces of food. She was deliberate and efficient in her placement of items, as though even when creating a lunch for herself she took care it was beautiful.

She glanced up from the artistic creation and smiled.

"Doesn't look very simple," he said.

"What's not simple about it? I pull a few things from the fridge, I put them on a plate, we eat what we want. What could be more simple?"

Vander considered this.

"Campbell's tomato soup?" she asked. "Because I have a spare can if you'd prefer."

Vander laughed. "Naw, this looks great." He glanced behind him, then through an opening into a large formal dining room.

"My housekeeper is not here," she said, keeping her eyes on the platter. "Katie has family in Lakeview. She arranges my details for the trip, comes in a couple of times to do a light cleaning, then closes up the house when I leave. Most of the time she spends with her family. It works out well."

"Does she work for you back in Nashville too?"

"Some. I'm very careful about how I spend my time. There are some housekeeping activities I enjoy, like straightening my apartment. It helps me think. So I do most of my own cleaning. But if I have a case that's kicking my butt, I hire it out. Laundry, on the other hand, is not my favorite, so I have a service do it for me."

"Makes sense."

"Katie's trying to make it as a singer. Working for me helps make ends meet for her." Harlow looked up from the olives she was carefully arranging on the tray to answer the question he hadn't asked yet. "Everyone plays or sings in Nashville. Or both."

"How about you?" he asked.

She laughed. "Almost everyone. I am not an artist."

He gestured to the tray of artfully arranged snacks. "You sure?"

"I'm sure. Very sure."

Vander leaned against the counter, hoping his posture was enough to get her to continue talking.

"I fight for artists. That's my work."

"But you could learn to play an instrument, if you wanted."

"I could, but I haven't. You know what I'm saying? Loretta could learn to stay out of other people's business, but she hasn't found the time."

Vander raised his brows in acknowledgment.

"We all choose how we spend our time. I'm really good at digging into details and coming up with a perfect argument. I love it. I'm passionate about it. I know how to find exactly what I'm looking for in a mass of information." She grinned at him. "I'm basically an attack librarian, and I'm really good at it."

Vander laughed.

"But I love the life too. I love my clothes, my high-rise apartment." Harlow spoke as though she had to defend her choices. Like she expected to be judged and wanted to head him off before they got there. "I like my work and the money I make. And in Pronghorn, there's a prohibition against enjoying wealth. So don't go thinking everyone is going to understand me or that we have more in common than we don't."

She slid the tray across the island and gestured for him to help himself. Vander was hungry but didn't want to disturb the design.

"You eat like this all the time?" he asked.

"If I possibly can," she said. "This is definitely my lunch of choice."

She set two small plates next to the platter, then served herself. She nudged Vander's plate toward him. "Go on. You're worse than Stet."

Vander reached for a plate. Why was he hesitant to accept her offer of lunch? It was partly that the meal looked too pretty to eat, but like Stet, he didn't want to get too comfortable either.

Vander reached for a fork and helped himself to a small portion, about one tenth the amount he was hungry for. He folded a thin slice of meat in half and balanced it on a cracker, then topped it with cheese, like a teeny-tiny little open-faced sandwich.

He took a small bite. Then he took a huge bite.

"It's good, right?"

"It's incredible." Vander found himself reaching for another cracker, then half the crackers on the plate. "What are these?" he asked. "And why do they taste so good?"

"These are wheat crackers from England I found in a little shop near my place in Nashville. I chose this cheese to go with them." She pointed to a soft cheese. "But it also works with the fig and pecan crisps. And this prosciutto, I swear it goes with everything."

She twisted the top off a glass bottle and poured mineral water into a tumbler.

He took a sip of the sparking water, which was somehow better than all sparking water ever served, at any time. Another bite of cheese confirmed his suspicion.

"This is the best lunch I've ever had."

"You sure you're not just hungry?"

"Starving. But this is so good." Vander piled a different slice of meat and more cheese on one of the crisps. "How do you know which ones to buy? And what's going to taste good with what?"

"I don't know. I think about it? I take my time and make informed choices. I try to curate a nice life for myself."

Vander swallowed and immediately began to build himself another tower of charcuterie. "You have excellent taste."

Harlow glanced down, looping a strand of hair around her ear as her face reddened. Like she hadn't expected the compliment and was thrilled by it. But then her expression shifted. Her brow furrowed. The adorable little frown reappeared. And Vander was so curious about that frown.

He gestured toward her brow. "You're thinking again."

She let out a laugh. "Caught me."

"I don't want to pry. But I do want to know. So—" He shrugged as though there wasn't much he could do with the situation. "Dunno what to do."

Her thoughtful frown deepened. "You really want to know what I'm thinking about?"

"That's why I'm unable to drop it, yeah." He took a sip of the fizzy water. Was it the intensity of the bubbles that made it so good? Or the slight whiff of mineral rising off it?

She sat back and crossed her arms. "I'm debating the relative merits of a relationship of convenience."

Vander choked on the fizzy water, grabbing a napkin just in time.

She tilted her head, reminding him, "You asked."

Vander tried to settle himself, swallowing hard. She had him there.

Harlow continued, her voice steady as though they were discussing buying a car, "Theoretically, does it make sense to enter into a relationship for purely practical reasons, given that both people are kind, decent humans?"

Vander took another sip of the sparking water in an attempt to look cool about this.

"Like, imagine there's someone who doesn't thrill you, and that person wanted to date and marry you and is pretty clear about it. Do you explore the option?"

Vander set the glass down heavily, then scooted it away from him. There would be no more water sipping until this conversation was good and over. He cleared his throat and forced himself to ask the question. "Do you want to date and marry *him*?"

"It would be a practical relationship."

"Is that what you want? Practical?"

"Yes, ideally." She leaned toward him, her brown hair a soft curtain framing her face. "My work is intense and complicated. If I can have the rest of my life running smoothly, that's optimal. I want to get married. I want to have kids. In theory, if there's a nice guy who could help support those goals, do I do it?"

Vander studied her face. Was this guy they were

talking about a theory or a fact? "Don't you ever do anything impractical?"

She spread her arms, gesturing to their surroundings. "This. Jameson Ranch is a masterpiece of impracticality. Flying in here, maintaining the land. It's expensive, no one in town likes me, and given the whole cow debacle, my indulgence could even harm others. But I can't give it up. I love it here so much." A wistful look passed over her face as she gazed out the window. "It's all I get, this one, wildly impractical indulgence."

"This place makes you happy, it keeps you happy," he reminded her. "That's not an indulgence."

She let out a soft laugh, like he was being silly. Vander's instinct was to shut down. To grab his hat and go. But instead of taking this disappointing turn and tamping it down in his heart, he kept his feet planted, kept the conversation running.

"In theory, does this guy...make you happy?"

She tilted her head, considering this. "For argument's sake, let's say he doesn't make me unhappy."

"Do you love him?"

"No. He's nice."

"Are you—" he gestured with his hand, then realized he was indicating the two of them. He planted his palms against the table. "Do you find him attractive?"

She planted her own palms on the table. After a moment she looked up and let her gaze connect with his. "Not really."

Vander felt himself shift. He wasn't good at communicating, but somehow he'd managed to stand here and work through a conversation where everything said was disappointing and everything unsaid had his heart feeling like a bronco rider. "You want my opinion?"

"I do. What do you surmise from this evidence?"

"Don't do it. Wait for the right guy."

A flush crept up her neck. She glanced down at the island. "Okay."

"Okay?"

"You're right. It's not enough to just like someone, in theory or in practice. It's not fair to my speculative children. I want them to have a good role model of two loving people."

"You want kids?" he asked.

"In theory." She grinned. "Although I've heard in practice they can be pretty tough."

"Then you gotta wait for the right guy." He held her gaze, knowing Harlow's right guy was never going to be him but wishing it was all the same. He gestured to the spread on the island. "You gotta find somebody who makes you feel like this lunch. Every detail is perfect—it's exactly what you want."

She laughed. "I agree. I'll wait for perfect. Meanwhile, you need a woman who makes you feel like ice cream melting into espresso."

And while he didn't figure most women would appreciate the comparison, that's exactly how she was starting to make him feel.

CHAPTER EIGHT

By Thursday afternoon, Vander had come up with a word for the complicated emotion tangling up in his chest around 3:00—dreadticipation. It was a base layer of dread, with a riot of anticipation popcorning over the top.

He was legitimately worried. Harlow kept upping the stakes of this pageant, her plans growing more elaborate by the minute. But he was also having fun. Harlow brought a sense of drama and urgency to the rehearsals. It was as though the kids knew they only had so much time in her glamorous presence and had to work hard to make the most of it.

Or was it him, trying to make the most of his time with her?

He shook his head sharply. He was gonna have to get this under control.

Harlow was an interesting woman. She was beautiful. But there was nothing about the two of them that fit together. They were impractical, and by her own admission she'd reached her impracticality limit. She didn't even live here. She didn't even *like* it here.

But he was sure gonna enjoy his time with her while she *was* here.

A burst of laughter came out of the library.

Vander gave in and jogged the last few steps down the hall.

"So I'm standing there arguing with Garth Brooks about marshmallows on sweet potato casserole and then Miranda Lambert says, 'What kind of a dog is that anyway?'" Harlow finished her story and threw her hands up, setting all the kids laughing.

It was fun to watch her shine. That was a real difference between Harlow and a lot of the women he'd dated in the past. She said what she wanted, did what she wanted and expected the same of everyone around her. She wanted to shine and encouraged others to do the same.

Vander leaned against the doorframe and crossed his arms. They didn't have to get started with rehearsal right away. In fact, if they didn't get started, he could watch her for a little longer and forget about the fact that in a just over a week he was gonna have to get up onstage and play guitar with who knew how many people watching.

"Have you met any other famous people?" Morgan Holms asked.

"I have. And it's fun. I love music, and it's exciting to be a part of a creative industry when I'm not an artist myself."

"Is it true that sometimes you have famous people out to your ranch?" Taylor asked.

"Sometimes," Harlow said. She paused briefly, then looked around at the kids. "Do you know who Wilson Range is?"

"He's that guy from the nineties, right?"

"Yes. Although, should you ever meet him, don't call him 'that guy from the nineties.'"

Taylor laughed, then scooted a fraction of an inch closer to Harlow, aligning herself with this powerful, successful woman.

"Wilson and a couple of songwriters will be out at my ranch next week, for a writing retreat and discussion of what's next, new trends, things like that."

The room silenced.

Until Mav and Morgan spoke at the same time, Mav asking, "Who is Wilson Range?" and Morgan speaking over him with, "Wilson Range is staying at your house?"

Harlow looked up and locked eyes with Vander as she answered the kids, "Wilson, after being a guy in the nineties, is an important music producer. Interpolation is a big trend right now. It's taking part of a song that already exists and weaving it into a new song. Like Kane Brown did with 'I Can Feel It.' He took part of a popular song from the eighties and wove the melody and words into a new hit. Since I specialize in copyright law, I'm a good person to have on hand right now."

The kids murmured, impressed.

Harlow winked at Vander. "And speaking of good people to have on hand, Mr. V has finally arrived. Let's do this."

"Wait." Taylor held out her hand to stop everyone, in what was a total Harlow move. "If Wilson Range is coming, are you going to invite him to our pageant?"

Harlow froze.

Vander scanned the room, trying to see it from her perspective. A ragtag mix of kids with a wide range of abilities performing in a library? Probably not what she was hoping to show her guests.

Harlow's little frown appeared, then she cast a side glance at Taylor. "That depends on what we come up with. So, let's get to work."

"OMG!" Taylor jumped up. "It needs to be *perfect*."

The dread in *dreadticipation* surfaced.

"Maybe not perfect," Vander appealed to Harlow, hoping against hope she'd back him up here. "Maybe personal is a better word."

Harlow studied him for a moment, her expression suggesting both personal and perfect would be optimum. Then she gave a firm nod. "I can't speak for my guests, but like Mr. V says, we need to start from the heart. That's where all good art originates. Let's get warmed up!"

Kids moved in all directions, finding chairs and chattering about the possibility of a former country star at the pageant, but Mav remained standing in the center of the room.

"Can I clarify something about Christmas before we start?" he asked.

Mav asked to clarify a lot about Christmas. The kid had a million questions about flying reindeer, bringing trees inside houses and why the elf sat on a shelf all day, rather than hanging out with other elves.

"Um. Sure?" Harlow tucked a strand of hair behind her ear.

"What I don't understand is the Grinch," Mav said. "What *is* 'the Grinch'?"

"*The Grinch* is a children's book about the meaning of Christmas," Harlow explained.

"Which, according to the story, is coming together as a group and singing," Vander added. "So, let's do it."

"No, I know it's a book and a movie," Mav said. "Ilsa showed me the cartoon movie on her phone at lunch today when there was internet."

"Then I don't understand the question," Harlow said.

"What is *the Grinch*? Is that his name? Or his species? Or a title he earned?"

"I think it's like a title," Ilsa said.

"But he looks different from the Whos," Mav said. "And why does he live alone?"

"Because he's a Grinch?" Harlow guessed.

"So, is there more than one?"

"No," Taylor snapped. "There's just one Grinch. He's a fictional character. Can we get on with rehearsal?"

"Oh!" Mav's face lit up in comprehension. "So he's Sasquatch?"

"No!" nearly everyone in the library shouted.

"He lives alone, is furry and green." Mav spread his long, gangly arms wide. "That's Sasquatch, right?"

"In what world is Sasquatch green?" Morgan asked.

"In what world is Sasquatch *fictional*?" Oliver added.

"Every world," Vander interrupted. He might be directing a holiday pageant, but he was still a science teacher. "Sasquatch does not exist."

"He's not green?" Mav asked, completely ignoring the fact that there was no Big Foot, no Sasquatch, no hairy creature living alone in the woods of Oregon or elsewhere. "Then how does he blend in with the trees?"

The kids groaned in frustration, picking up pieces of the argument and throwing them back at Mav. That, of course, was the last way to end the topic because Mav could argue any point, with anyone, including himself. Which he had.

Taylor checked out of the argument, doing something on her phone, but Harlow followed along, her interest growing as Mav wound his way further down a rabbit hole. It wasn't until he started quoting Mary Oliver that Harlow finally spoke up.

"Mav, I love the way your brain works. You are going to change the world someday."

Mav stopped arguing abruptly and pulled his head back, shocked.

Harlow continued, "You're always taking an argument to the next level, digging deeper, asking more questions. You'd make a great lawyer."

Mav straightened at her words. Then his expression of confidence faltered. "Wait, no, I probably can't be a lawyer. That'd be cool, though, to learn a lot and argue."

"Of course you can be a lawyer," Harlow said.

"But I'd have to go to college, right?"

"Yes. Obviously."

Mav, for the first time since Vander had met him, didn't have anything to say. He stared at the carpet for a long time.

"He couldn't live at our home," Antithesis finally said. "And you can't really follow our practices if you go away. We make a choice."

The room was silent at this revelation. Mav seemed to realize the implication of the words himself. He shrugged, like he didn't care.

"You know who should change the world is—" Mav swiveled his head, looking for his target but coming up blank. "Wait, where's Nevaeh?"

Harlow glanced around the room, noticing the same.

"Oh, sorry." Taylor looked up from her phone. "I was supposed to tell you. Her aunt Amber came to pick her up today."

Harlow raised her eyebrows. "Amber Danes, that's her aunt, right?"

"I guess so," Taylor said. "They don't come into town much."

Harlow paced in a semicircle, her thinking face on.

Vander, most days a big fan of that look, got nervous. "What are you thinking?"

Harlow checked her watch, then reached for her

coat. "Can you handle rehearsal for the first forty minutes?"

"Where are you going?"

"I'm going to pick her up."

"I wouldn't do that," Vander said.

"That's fine because you don't have to. I'm going to."

"The family—"

"Oh, I know the family. I'll be back, forty-five minutes at the most."

HARLOW IGNORED THE lump congealing at the back of her throat as she pulled onto the Daneses' property. An old, manufactured home sat at the back of the barren lot, windows boarded over or blocked with piled boxes. Extension cords snaked out of the house, feeding dilapidated trailers and no-longer-mobile homes. A range of vehicles were scattered throughout, prairie grasses growing up through some. At the center of the Danes family compound was a pile of junk: old, broken furniture, boxes, musty odds and ends.

The property was even more run-down than Harlow remembered. Her parents had been judgmental of the Danes family, clucking their tongues as they passed by on the way home from town.

Since leaving Pronghorn, Harlow had come to understand more about the isolation of rural poverty. If people in Pronghorn had been hard on her, it was nothing compared to how folks judged the Danes family. She didn't want to interfere with them, per se. But Nevaeh wanted to be in the pageant, and Harlow wasn't going to let her chance slip past. Because Mav was right, Nevaeh could change the world. They all could. And at the very least, every kid should be afforded the opportunity to try.

The sun was low in the west, threatening to slip behind the Coyote Hills at any moment, leaving them in darkness. A dog barked, its warning picked up by the wind.

A door on the nearest trailer slammed open. A woman in a ball cap, wearing a fleece jacket over a nightgown came storming out of the house.

"Hi, Amber," Harlow said.

Amber Danes paused in her advance, then laughed. "What are you doing here?"

"It's nice to see you too."

"Yeah? Well, you've seen me. You might want to pull that fancy car off our property now. The dirt sticks here."

Harlow relaxed her shoulders and gave her a bland look. "I'm popping by to pick up Nevaeh. We have rehearsal for the pageant this afternoon."

Amber leaned against the trailer. "That's funny, 'cause I just got home from pickin' her up."

Harlow paced in a semicircle. "You normally pick her up from school? Because I thought she rode the bus."

The door to the trailer opened, and Nevaeh slipped out. She moved slowly but didn't stop until she'd joined them in the growing dusk. Nervous and determined, she reminded Harlow of herself when she first got to college.

Amber heaved a sigh and muttered, "Here we go."

Harlow focused on the student, the way she'd seen Vander focus on kids. "Nevaeh, we have rehearsal this afternoon. If you want to be part of the pageant, you need to be consistent and show up every day."

"Okay," Nevaeh said. She glanced up at her aunt.

"Mr. V and I hope you'll keep with it. You're a great singer."

Nevaeh lit up at the name of her favorite teacher.

Amber snorted. "Honey, Mr. V don't care about you. He's just actin'. That's what teachers have to do these days. They gotta pretend they care."

Harlow glared at her. "You don't have the authority to speak for Vander."

"And you do?" Amber laughed. "Yeah, I bet you'd like to speak for him. He's good-looking, got a good job milkin' the government for a paycheck."

Harlow kept her expression placid and didn't take the bait. She really wanted to. She wanted to chomp down on that bait, spit it out on the dirt between them and grind it under her heel. But she didn't.

Instead, she smiled at Nevaeh, well aware that she was messing with a generations-old family dynamic she didn't understand. "Your aunt is right, neither of us can speak for Vander. But *I* want you in the pageant. You have a beautiful voice, and we could use that."

"So, you're using my niece for her talent?" Amber asked.

Seriously?

"It's a small-town Christmas pageant," Harlow snapped, well aware this was not how one of the teachers would handle this delicate situation. "What is your problem?"

"My problem is some rich lady pulling onto our property, telling me how to raise my niece. Why does it matter if she participates in your dumb pageant?"

"What are you afraid of if she does?"

Amber's gaze connected with Harlow's, and the memories came rushing back.

If Harlow had been considered a nuisance at school, it was nothing compared to how Amber and her siblings had been treated. Amber struggled with academics, and Harlow had always wondered if an undiagnosed reading issue was the problem. No one intervened, and Amber fell further behind. The same system that labeled her a problem demanded she show up at a school that didn't have the resources to help her. Her family, suspicious of the system to begin with, didn't feel empowered to reach out for more support. Harlow remembered feeling uncomfortable as a teacher called Amber out for not completing a poster project at home, shaming her in front of the class. Even at the time, Harlow understood that there probably wasn't a craft supply closet at the Daneses' house Amber could dip into for a panorama project on Bavaria.

"What are you even doing in Pronghorn?" Amber crossed her arms, keeping her gaze steady on Harlow. "You don't live here. You don't fit in here. No one in town has a single nice thing to say about you. And now you're running the Christmas pageant?" She scoffed. "Why you? Big city lawyer all fancy? Don't forget, I knew you when."

Harlow kept her gaze steady. "You're right. I don't fit in. Most people in Pronghorn would be happy to never see me again, but if that were the case, who would they gossip about?"

A slight wrinkle appeared on Amber's brow, as though a flicker of compassion for Harlow had sparked. Then she shook her head. "I just don't see why they'd want *you* working with kids."

"It's a long story." Harlow turned to Nevaeh. "Do you want to be in the pageant?"

Nevaeh glanced nervously at her aunt. "Yes." The word seemed to scrape in her throat. Nevaeh coughed, then tried again. "Yes. I want to be in the pageant."

Amber crossed her arms more tightly. Wind kicked up, plastering the hem of her nightgown to her legs.

"With your permission, I'd like to take Nevaeh back with me. Pete Sorel is running an activities route. He takes kids home after rehearsal and basketball practice."

Amber snorted. "This town can't field a basketball team."

"I'm unable to speak on that matter." Harlow dismissed the comment. "Do I have your permission to take Nevaeh back to rehearsal?"

She shrugged.

"Auntie, I want to go."

"You do what you're gonna do. But don't say I didn't warn you when it don't turn out like you hoped." At that, Amber turned around and stalked back into the trailer. A dust devil rose and danced past as Harlow and Nevaeh watched the door slam behind her.

Harlow gestured to the rental. "Shall we?"

Nevaeh took one last glance at the trailer, then nodded tightly, heading for the car. She climbed in and buckled her seat belt. Harlow was aware of other family members watching them as she pulled off the property.

Nevaeh clicked her seat belt into place, then cleared her throat. "Thank you."

Harlow startled at the simple expression. In her life back in Nashville, people thanked her every day all day long. They thanked her for her work, for generous tips at the coffee shop, for the kick in the backside they needed and she was willing to give. She didn't even notice the word anymore. But this may have been the first time anyone in Pronghorn expressed gratitude for her actions.

"Of course," she said. "I'm not gonna let our best singer go without a fight."

"I'm not the best singer," Nevaeh said.

"You are." Harlow looked both ways before she exited the property onto the empty highway. Out

of the corner of her eye, she could see the effect
her words had on the girl. Nevaeh should feel good
about her voice. She clearly loved singing and practiced extensively.

The car rumbled out on the highway. They crested
a low hill, sagebrush spreading out all around them.
Harlow reached over to turn on the radio.

"And I like you," Nevaeh said quietly. "My aunt
just gets that way sometimes. She says things she
doesn't mean."

Harlow glanced at Nevaeh, then blinked heavily
before refocusing on the road. She came out here
with the intention of showing Nevaeh that she mattered in this world. It hadn't occurred to her that
Nevaeh might think she mattered too.

CHAPTER NINE

VANDER WASN'T QUITE ready to put his guitar down. Rehearsal was over. Harlow was seeing the kids off and giving Pete a heads-up about the situation with Nevaeh. He continued to pluck at the strings, letting another melody loose.

His coconspirator in the endeavor was in full-on Harlow mode tonight. One minute planning an over-the-top pageant, the next championing one of Pronghorn's most vulnerable students. His guitar gave him an outlet, his thoughts weaving into music, gaining clarity as he went along.

"'Wonderful Tonight'?" She correctly identified the song as she whisked back into the room.

"You're good."

"At recognizing a song after a few chords? Yes. I am a master."

He chuckled. Harlow tucked her hair behind her ear and glanced at her boots. He strummed the next few bars of the classic love song. What was it about being with Harlow that made him want to play every love song he knew and ever had the possibility of learning?

Finally, he settled his hand on the side of his guitar. "I don't know what you said to Nevaeh's aunt, but thank you. We've been worried about her. You got through to the family somehow."

"Well, no one's ever going to suggest that *I* got through to Amber Danes," Harlow said. "Amber… Well, she's got her reasons for not trusting the system."

"That's not new information, but you're the first to make headway."

She twitched her shoulders. "Maybe I managed to create a space where Nevaeh could get through to her aunt."

"A little time with you, and she'll be a regular boss. She's a good kid."

"She's a talented kid." Harlow brushed her hair off her shoulder. "At present, we have one kid who can sing really well, five that can carry a tune, and three…"

"Who are enthusiastic about the project," Vander finished for her.

"That's one way of putting it." She paced a few feet. "I want this pageant to be brilliant. Like, I want us to blow the lid off this town."

Vander picked at the strings of his guitar. He understood that Harlow's relationship with the community was complicated, but avenging her childhood with holiday music didn't seem quite right. "I appreciate your…" What was the right word here? Vander wasn't sure.

And now he'd been staring way too long, so he went with, "Drive. But—"

She crossed her arms and leveled her gaze on him. "But what? Why shouldn't we make this pageant the best it can possibly be?"

Vander strummed the first few bars of "Winter Wonderland" before he put his thoughts into words. He'd learned a long time ago it was better to think before he spoke. But sometimes he thought so much he forgot to speak.

Vander unscrambled ideas into what he hoped was a coherent thread. "Sometimes it seems like you want to put on a good show just to annoy the community. You want to make everyone mad when they see you're good at this, rather than wanting to celebrate the holidays and the kids."

He glanced up to see how the words landed and was rewarded with a gorgeous, devious smile.

"That's an astute observation. Spot-on."

"We should probably think about the kids."

"I am thinking about the kids—and about their parents' faces when they have to shake my hand and thank me after the pageant." He must have looked as horrified as he felt because she laughed. "I'm joking. Of course, it's about the kids. Mostly."

Vander set his guitar aside and stood, *not joking*. "I don't like the way people around here treat you. It makes me mad. But I also know that most people in Pronghorn are good folks, and sometimes they just need to let go of old ways of thinking. We all do. I'd like to see this town give you a chance, and maybe you could give them a chance too." He kicked his boot against the carpet, the steel cap pressing against his toes as he said, "Let them see the you I see, in here. The funny, kind Harlow who shines a light on every kid and illuminates their possibility."

He could almost see the words filtering through her mind, watching her turn each one over as she decided whether or not to believe him. She didn't respond, didn't appear to be capable of responding to a direct compliment.

"I should get home." Harlow glanced at her watch but made no move for the door.

"Me too."

The library felt quiet and private, like sacred ground. It felt like the one place he and Harlow made sense together.

She pressed her lips together, then reached for her bag. "I'll get the horses tonight. You can enjoy a night off with your coworkers. I still can't believe you're all living at the old hotel."

"It's great. You want to come check it out?"

She looked shocked.

Did he just invite her over?

She squared her shoulders like she did when she needed to summon bravery, then her smile returned. "Yeah. I'd love to."

Vander nearly tripped over his own feet grabbing his jacket and picking up his guitar.

The building was silent as he and Harlow switched off the lights and headed for the main entrance. Moonlight, already bright in the sky, shone in through the high windows in the front hall, gleaming off the wooden floors, making the mismatched signs and yellow lockers beautiful in the watery light. Harlow's voice echoed off the walls, a pretty lilt like a favorite melody.

"Wow. It's cold tonight," she said as they stepped outside.

Vander glanced up at the stars sprawled across the sky. He didn't feel cold at all.

Connie trotted over from her sentinel duty in the middle of the street and rubbed up against Vander's leg. He picked her up and gave her a brief snuggle, which was the only kind of snuggle Connie ever accepted.

"Doesn't that cat ever want to come inside?" Harlow asked.

"She's been in the school a time or two," Vander said. "Mostly when she senses trouble and thinks she might be able to help."

At the mention of trouble, Connie leaped out of his arms and resettled herself in the middle of the street, watchful of any pronghorn antelope that might wander into town, or tourists.

Vander and Harlow arrived at the hotel's arched entrance and stepped into the courtyard. In late November, Luci had insisted they string holiday lights over the courtyard. The job required each of the teachers to head up to a different second-floor room and toss the strings of lights back and forth to one another in a noisy, contentious but ultimately hilarious game of catch. Their efforts had been worth it, as every night they came home to the magically lit courtyard.

"This is gorgeous," Harlow commented.

Vander nodded, opening the door to the lobby for her.

It was then that he realized his mistake.

The hotel lobby was a beautiful room, with cream-colored molding, gold trim and chestnut wood accents. The antique furniture, upholstered in spring green and pale pink, was in excellent shape. The room was so inviting that the teachers had taken it over, making a mess out of the once-elegant foyer.

The old coatrack was hung with scarves, hats and myriad outerwear. Tate, who seemed to shed sweatshirts everywhere he went, had hoodies hanging off three different chairs. Mateo's grading had started creeping across the art nouveau reception desk the second week of the school year. While Vander didn't notice it most days, right now it seemed particularly messy. Like, how did he even find so many papers to grade?

Vander trotted ahead of Harlow and picked up one of Tate's sweatshirts. He opened his mouth to apologize, but Harlow spoke first. "Wow! This is fantastic."

"It's messy."

"The last time I sneaked in here as a kid, this place was covered with dust and cobwebs and was so empty it creeped me out. I had nightmares for weeks." She turned to him, eyes shining. "This is amazing."

"What's amazing?" Luci came trotting down the grand staircase and could have passed as a character out of a 1940s romantic comedy. "It's Harlow!" she said, beaming like Harlow was the one person on earth she wanted to see at that moment. "I love your coat."

"Thank you," Harlow said. "I love your home."

"Right? Let me give you the tour."

"I thought maybe—" Vander started to speak, but what was the plan here? He couldn't ask Harlow to sit patiently while he ran through the building cleaning up their teacher clutter. Or could he?

What would be worse? Leaving her here, on her own, while he straightened up, or taking this elegant, exacting woman on a tour of the messy hotel?

He glanced at Luci, hoping she could intuit his wishes. She rolled her eyes.

"Kitchen first?" she asked Harlow. "Or dining room?"

Not helpful.

Vander tensed, standing light on his feet like he did when working with animals. The kitchen was probably a disaster. Willa and her almost-step-daughter, Sylvie, were in the middle of a Christmas cookie baking ultramarathon. But if the kitchen was home to a somewhat-greater-than-average holiday mess, the dining room, which Luci used as a staging ground for her class simulations, was far worse.

"Kitchen?" Harlow suggested.

Vander sprinted into the dining room. He could hear Harlow exclaim over the steel countertops, massive appliances and the avalanche of decorated sugar cookies as he raced through the dining room, picking up papers and signage and about a hundred piles of small items like fake gold coins, tiny doll-house dishes, itty-bitty pieces of fabric.

What was Luci even trying to teach with all this stuff?

"Whoa, whoa, whoa!" Luci's voice made him freeze, like a pronghorn in the headlights. "What are you doing?"

"Cleaning up." He gave Luci a meaningful glance, then tried to subtly gesture toward Harlow.

"You're disturbing Indian Ocean trade."

"Sorry?"

"Ugh. Seriously, Vander. You may as well be an out-of-season monsoon." Luci strode into the room. "This is the dining room. We only eat in here when Tate has planned some elaborate date for Aida, which happens way more often than it needs to. Mostly we eat in the kitchen. When it's warm out, or even not freezing, we eat in the courtyard."

Harlow spun in a slow circle, taking in the intimate tables, the floor-to-ceiling windows, the vintage hotel linens. "I love this. I love that you all live at the City Hotel."

"It's fabulous. I certainly never expected to be living here," Luci said.

"Right. Why would you have ever expected to live in a hotel in a small town you'd never heard of?"

Luci froze for an instant, then laughed. "Right, super weird expectation. Do you want to see the ballroom?"

"Yes," Harlow said. "And the answer to 'Do you want to see the ballroom?' is always yes."

"Oh, one hundred percent," Luci concurred.

Before Vander could sprint ahead to see what mess lay in wait in the ballroom, Luci took off. Harlow widened her eyes and grinned at him.

And suddenly all the messes didn't seem so bad anymore.

Luci was still chattering to Harlow as she strode across the dining room to the grand entrance to the ballroom. She opened the door and big band music came sneaking out, as though two people were dancing and didn't want to get caught.

"Seriously, you two?"

"What?" Tate's voice rose over the music.

Vander sighed and ran to catch up.

As per usual, Tate and Aida were holed up in the ballroom, waltzing or fox-trotting or whatever pre-invention-of-the-television dance they were into at the moment. Luci loved teasing them about it. Which was funny, because she'd learned to ballroom dance during her prep school education and definitely joined in anytime she got the chance.

"How many hours of dancing have you put in this week?"

"We need to get ready for our wedding dance next summer," Tate defended.

"What? Are you planning on performing *Swan Lake*?"

Harlow drifted past Luci into the ballroom, not paying a drop of attention to the argument. She slipped her hands in her coat pockets and paced through the room, taking it all in.

Vander tried to see it from her point of view. The old parquet floor gleamed in the soft light of the sconces. Gilt chairs were stacked neatly at one end; at the other end, a small dais rose. Back in Pronghorn's glory days, the dais would have held a band. Maybe not a full-size, Glen Miller sort of situation, but a respectable assembly of musicians. A balcony ran around three sides of the room, with more chairs stacked in the darkened corners. In the center of the high ceiling was a mural Vander found both confusing and compelling. He'd come in one day and lay on his back, staring up at the baroque-style fresco featuring pronghorn, sagebrush and stylized mountains, rather than the classical motifs you might find in a similar painting in Europe.

It was a pretty cool room.

Harlow spun on her heels and marched toward him. "Pageant."

"Pageant?"

She gestured with both index fingers, indicating the room around them. "Pageant. Here. This is where we do the pageant."

Vander loved seeing her so happy. While he understood she needed to work through her issues with the town rather than getting back at them with the all-time best pageant ever, he did respect that she wanted to put on a good show.

And when she smiled like that? Inviting the entire community into his home to watch a pageant he didn't want to participate in seemed like the best idea.

"Yeah. Sure."

Her face lit up, her arms reaching toward him in what might be a hug.

Then Vander remembered there were four other people who probably had an opinion on this topic, and this was their home too.

"Oh, uh. Yeah. Guys?" He looked around at his coworkers.

"I mean, it's perfect." Harlow spun in a circle, tucking her hands back in her pockets as she observed the room.

"What's perfect?" Tate asked.

"This venue, for the pageant."

"Totally perfect!" Luci said. "We could bring in a tree."

"The kids are thinking gold ribbons and natural elements," Harlow said.

"Love!" Luci agreed.

"Wait, but." Aida stepped forward. "What about… the dancing?"

Harlow furrowed her brow.

Aida tried again. "Harlow, I'm so glad you're enjoying working on the pageant. I know Vander's really grateful. But this is a ballroom."

Harlow raised her brow.

"It's where we dance. Me and Tate, and sometimes Greg." She gestured to her dog.

Harlow stared at Aida for a long moment, brow furrowed. "We're just going to do the pageant one night. It's not gonna keep running like *Phantom of the Opera*."

"I know, but—" Aida reached out and wove her fingers through Tate's.

Vander didn't completely understand what Aida had been through, but he was aware that her relationship with Tate had shifted something in her heart, and spending time dancing with him in the ballroom was healing a loss for her.

Harlow swallowed hard and took one last look around the room. Vander could see her struggling against her natural urge to argue. "Okay. Sure." Color drained from Harlow's face. "The library's fine."

An unusual silence spread through the group, the only sound low-volume, inappropriately cheerful big band music coming out of the speakers on Tate's phone.

Greg pressed himself against Aida's leg, and she ran a hand along her dog's ears as they stood in silence. "No, you know what? It's all good." Aida held her arms up, like someone made a goal. "You're right. It's one night. Why am I questioning you, Harlow? This place is perfect."

"Questioning me is the birthright of all Pronghornians," Harlow said wryly.

Vander heard her words but they didn't make sense. It seemed like she'd been told she was annoying so many times that she expected to annoy. But her request had been totally reasonable. He should have thought of it sooner and would have if he hadn't been so stubborn about keeping the pageant small.

"It was a silly question on my part." Aida closed

her eyes and seemed to gather strength like she did when trying not to argue with a ref during a soccer game. Then she looked straight at Harlow. "I'm sorry. You're totally right. This place is perfect for the pageant." Aida glanced around the room. "We can all work on the decorations."

A smile lit Harlow's face again. "I'd love that. And we can plan a schedule for the week of the pageant, so we're not all in your hair all week long."

"Let's figure it out over dinner," Luci said. "We need to get to The Restaurant. It's Thursday. Angie's going to throw a fit if we're not there by seven."

"Oh. All right." Harlow's smile fell. She tucked her hands deeper into her pockets. "Can you all let me know what you decide?"

"Aren't you coming with us?" Luci asked.

"I should get home."

"We'd love for you to come with us," Vander said.

Harlow shook her head. "You don't have to be polite."

"I'm not being polite. I'm asking you to join us because I want you to be there."

Her eyelashes fluttered down, fanning across her cheekbones. Vander was well aware he'd given away too much here, even as his heart yammered on about an invitation not being nearly enough. He tapped the toe of his boot against the parquet flooring. "Please come."

Harlow nodded, still hesitant. "Okay." She looked up and met his gaze, then raised her eyebrows. "But when Angie refuses to serve us, you all just remember, it's my fault."

HARLOW STOLE ANOTHER look at Vander as they walked the two blocks from the hotel to The Restaurant. These teachers really didn't understand what they were getting into. Angie might love them, but showing up with her in tow could throw a wrench into that relationship. It could throw in the whole dang toolbox.

Vander moved next to her, as though sensing her thoughts. His eyes were on the mosaic of stars above, but he was close enough so his arm brushed hers, reassuring her.

Yeah. This was getting to be a problem.

It wasn't her first crush on an inappropriate match, but it was far and away the worst.

Or best.

Vander looked up at Colter and Willa, as though just remembering something. "Colter, how did your meeting with Willa's brother go?"

"It went great. I mean, it was hard." He wrapped his arm more tightly around Willa. "But if Willa could forgive me, I figured Hayden could too."

"He's exaggerating," Willa said. "Hayden managed to pretend to be mad for ten minutes, then was just happy to have his best friend back."

"I don't think he was pretending," Colter said as he opened the door to the restaurant. "And I'm glad to have him back too."

The pack of them filed in. Angie's face beamed in satisfied triumph as her favorite customers entered, then comically flipped to outrage when she saw Harlow among them. The proprietress sighed dramatically, eyes roving to a table set up for eight people, not nine.

"Is this going to be a regular occurrence?" Angie snapped. "Because I'd like to know."

Willa, as unruffled as ever, asked, "Would you like us to make reservations in the future?"

Angie scoffed. "There are no reservations at The Restaurant." She started to fuss about an extra chair, which could easily be garnered from another table.

Harlow shook out her shoulders. She didn't want to ruin this evening for everyone. She'd already stolen a ballroom from a starry-eyed couple, and it wasn't even seven o'clock yet.

The teachers greeted other patrons and chatted easily with townsfolk. Harlow tried to keep herself at the center of their knot, as though somehow the goodwill folks had toward them would run off on her.

They passed Raquel Holms's table, and a boy she recognized as one of the exchange students reached his hand out to high-five Aida. Since Harlow was walking directly behind the sheriff, she paused and gave a brief nod to Taylor and Morgan.

The girls glanced at their mom, then back at Harlow.

"I love your jacket," Taylor said.

Harlow looked down at her off-white, wool and cashmere pea coat. "Thank you. It's my favorite this time of year."

Raquel sniffed. "Most folks around here would choose something a little more practical."

"Mom—" Morgan started, but Raquel spoke over her, saying, "It's just some friendly advice."

Harlow noticed Colter bristle. It occurred to her that she probably wasn't the only person in town Raquel bullied.

"Most people would prefer a lined canvas jacket," Raquel was addressing her daughters now, excluding Harlow from the conversation about her own coat. "White shows too much dirt."

Harlow knew better than to involve herself in an argument with Raquel. But knowing and doing were two very different things.

"If it gets dirty, I'll take it to the cleaners," Harlow said.

Raquel scoffed. "The closest dry cleaner is in Klamath Falls."

Harlow squared her shoulders. "You say that as though lack of access to a dry cleaner is somehow a virtue."

"I'm only commenting that around here, people are a little more practical when they get dressed in the morning."

Time to walk away.

Harlow forced herself two steps farther, then spun back around.

"This coat *is* practical. It's warm, the cut works well over sweaters, and winter white feels fresh and unexpected, particularly when January and February hit."

Raquel scoffed. "If fashion is your primary concern." She turned to her daughters. "People will judge you on your character, not by what you wear."

"That's literally the opposite of what you said last week when I tried to wear my distressed jeans to school," Taylor said.

Every fiber in Harlow's body screamed that she should not be engaging in this argument. Raquel wasn't going to admit she was wrong. Taylor and Morgan were good kids, and she didn't want to stir up trouble with their mom. The exchange student seemed nice enough, and he didn't need this to be part of his American experience.

But she was *so sick* of being muttered about and having to take it in this town. If a woman couldn't stand up for her favorite coat, what had the world come to?

Harlow crossed her arms, which was easy to do because the cut of the jacket really was perfect.

"Actually, a stylish, well-made coat absolutely matters in my line of work. When I meet people for the first time, they need instant confirmation of my success. Clothing is a language as real and eloquent as any other. It would be nice if people could read my CV and judge me on my character, but that's a lot to expect. So I dress the part of a successful woman, then I follow through with a strong work ethic and impeccable track record. This coat sets the right tone." She nodded to the little family, then headed to the teacher-table as she said, "Have a great meal."

She felt fantastic for half a second. Then out of

the corner of her eye, she saw Raquel make eye contact with Angie and mutter, "Someone around here is getting a little too big for her britches."

Frustration and hurt slowed her steps. Her inner ten-year-old screamed that this was unfair, that she shouldn't have to take this. Before she could think about what she meant to say or why she should even bother saying anything, Harlow spun back around.

The kids at the table were already mortified, and Harlow truly didn't want to mortify teens in a public setting; being a teenager was damn hard enough as it was.

And what did you even say when someone accused you of being too big for your britches?

Sorry. It wasn't very thoughtful of me to accomplish ambitious goals and enjoy my life in front of you, was it? I apologize if my success makes you feel small.

Harlow opened her mouth to speak but was cut off by a loud voice that almost sounded like a man herding cattle. "Her britches fit just fine."

What?

Harlow glanced back to see Vander advancing on the table, finger pointed at Raquel. "Her britches are plenty big enough. She's not too big for them."

The room silenced.

Color rose to his face as Vander seemed to realize what he was saying. He swallowed, then nodded, trapping himself further in a metaphor involving the size of a woman's pants. "Her britches are none of your business." Vander glanced around the room, now aware of how much attention he'd drawn to himself. "And none of mine either."

He nodded again, then pulled in a deep breath and headed toward their table.

Harlow glanced at his rapidly reddening face, then spun back to face Raquel. "Since we're on the topic, Vander's right, my britches are enormous. Huge. I can't imagine a world in which I get too big for my britches. And if I do? If I become so successful, such a big shot that I outgrow them, I will buy myself an even bigger pair, with the money I earn. So you do not have to worry about me or my britches."

Harlow marched away from the table, eyes blurry with adrenaline, blood rushing through her temples, roaring in her ears. She blinked, to make sure she was seeing what she was seeing.

Angie had pulled up a chair and was setting a place for her. Brief eye contact fluttered between the cantankerous proprietress and Harlow, then Angie stalked away, as though a little annoyed with Harlow for pulling such an impressive stunt.

Harlow carefully unbuttoned her jacket, draped it over the back of her chair, then sat down.

The teachers could barely repress their laughter. Harlow glanced across the table at Vander, who was nearly purple by this point.

"So, I have big britches?"

He shook his head. "I'm *so* sorry."

"No, don't be. I'm curious—"

"We're all curious," Mateo said, grinning at Vander. "You have a lot to say on the matter."

Vander swallowed, staring hard at his place setting. "You have the right size britches."

"I love those britches," Luci said. "Are they APC?"

"They are." Harlow winked at her. "I'd offer to loan them to you, but I think my britches may be too big for you."

The table laughed, even Vander, who still looked like he was about to bolt.

"We can't all have goddess figures," Luci said, then turned to Vander with a sly grin. "Vander, thoughts? You expressed yourself so eloquently on the topic of Harlow's britches."

"I'm sorry," he said, again. "I didn't think that through."

Harlow caught his eye. "Don't be." *Please don't be. That was the sweetest thing anyone has ever done for me.*

Colter slapped Vander's shoulder. "Thank you. Raquel needs to know it's not okay to speak to people like that."

Angie appeared with plates of food they hadn't yet ordered. Harlow craned her neck to look at the sandwich board.

"Oh, is it hamburgers with your special sauce?"

Angie paused in setting the plates down and looked suspiciously at Harlow. "That's one option."

"Can I have a hamburger?" she asked. When Angie plunked a burger down in front of her, Harlow explained to the table, "I love this sauce." She picked up a french fry and dabbed it at the side of her burger where extra sauce spilled out, then popped it in her mouth.

Everyone stared.

"What?" She glanced up at Angie. "What did I say this time? I love this sauce. You can't find it anywhere, only here."

The teachers looked baffled, then Luci lifted the bun off the top of her burger. "I guess I never thought about the sauce."

"You use Best Foods mayo, right?" Harlow asked Angie as she dipped another fry in the excess sauce.

Angie scoffed. "Of course I use Best Foods."

Harlow ate another sauce-covered fry and considered. "Best Foods, Heinz 57 and, if I'm not mistaken, a little Worcestershire sauce. Am I right?"

Angie crossed her arms. "Did you steal my recipe?"

"Did you write your recipe down?" Harlow countered. "I'm just guessing. But I'm right, no?"

Angie glanced around, like Harlow was leaking a dangerous state secret. "How'd you know?"

"Because it's delicious, and I tried to recreate it. But I can't. No one makes it like you do." Harlow was suddenly ravenous. She picked up her burger and took a bite. The others looked at one another, then the food Angie set before them as Harlow chewed and swallowed.

"So good." Harlow closed her eyes and savored another bite.

That was the final straw. Angie stomped back to

the kitchen, deeply uncomfortable and a little annoyed with the compliment.

Colter lifted the bun on his burger, examined his sauce, then looked back at Harlow. "I think you're the first person I've heard compliment Angie's food. Ever."

"And yet everyone eats here once a week," she noted.

"I thought we ate here to be good citizens of Pronghorn," Tate said.

"Sure, we can all pat ourselves on the back for that one. But I'm just sayin', people like her food, whether they want to admit it or not. And you can't recreate what she does. It all has a specific taste, I'll give you that. But it's all thoughtfully done."

Everyone looked even more confused. Harlow set her burger down and laid it out for the teachers.

"I started to catch onto Angie when I was in high school, but it wasn't until I'd eaten in several world-class restaurants that it all became clear. Angie is systematic about what she serves and how it's prepared, and everyone in Pronghorn reaps the benefits."

"I'm not following," Vander admitted.

"Take her fried chicken. You know how it's always served lukewarm?" Everyone groaned. "We all know she's back there, frying chicken as people are eating and could as easily serve it hot. But she lets it sit for a good ten minutes before bringing it out. The oil seeps into the cornflake coating, which makes the outside soft, so it melts in your mouth.

She serves fried food when it's cool enough for you to pick it up. She does it on purpose, because the experience of being able to dig into a meal right when it's served is part of the pleasure of eating here."

"You're saying she serves her chicken lukewarm and oily on purpose?" Colter asked with a chuckle.

Harlow pinned him with her gaze. "How many times has Angie served you a big plate of fried chicken, and you think, 'I can't possibly eat all of this,' but then you do?"

Colter leaned back in his chair, considering this. From the look on his face the unspoken answer was *every single time.*

Harlow continued, "And then there are her pairings."

"Her pairings?" Luci asked.

"Right, she's real specific about what goes with what. Like peas are always served with something fried. Corn with the baked options. She never serves a chocolate dessert with chicken or fish. That's why there are no substitutions."

Everyone at the table stared at her.

"She puts a lot of thought into it, because despite her demeanor she loves her community. I mean, she hates me, fine, whatever. But she does all of this—" she gestured to the food "—out of love."

Vander's gaze connected with Harlow's. "So she's an artist?"

Harlow grinned back at him. "Yeah."

At that moment, Angie tromped back out of the kitchen with a small metal bowl. She glanced around the room surreptitiously, then set the dish in front of Harlow and stalked away.

Harlow glanced into the bowl.

Extra sauce.

She swiveled to face the counter, and her gaze met Angie's.

The woman lifted her chin, daring her to say thank you. "I don't want to have a bunch of leftovers sitting around in the fridge," Angie grumbled as she disappeared into the kitchen.

Harlow felt eyes on her. She squared her shoulders, only to find people were smiling. She caught Mac's eye, and he gave her a friendly nod. The teachers had accepted her without a hitch, joyfully folding her into their group.

Harlow dipped a fry into the sauce. Vander grinned at her.

Let them see the you I see.

Maybe Vander was right—she and Pronghorn just needed to see, and share, the good in each other.

CHAPTER TEN

SATURDAY MORNINGS WERE supposed to be refreshing. But it was pretty hard to feel refreshed after tossing around all night long, trying to talk yourself out of catching feelings for a woman.

Vander grumbled as he pulled on a flannel shirt and headed out of his room. When he first arrived in Pronghorn, Saturday meant a lazy morning with his guitar in the courtyard, the music blending with the voices of his friends as they enjoyed a rest after a frenzied week of adjusting to their new jobs.

By October, Saturdays meant soccer games. Like everyone else in town, or anywhere near town, Vander traveled to watch their eclectic team take on opponents all over southeastern Oregon.

But now, in the heart of December, he awoke with a roiling mix of emotions, topped off with a terrible night's sleep.

Vander buttoned the flannel over his T-shirt as he made his way into the kitchen. Luci was already up because she was Luci, and she was always up before everyone else. Did she ever really sleep?

"Happy Saturday!" she called. "One more week before winter break."

Vander grunted in response.

She glanced up at him over her tea and toast. "What's that expression for?"

"What expression?" Vander tugged at the 1950s-era percolator coffeepot.

"The moody, grumpy, science teacher expression that says—"

"Are we out of coffee?" he interrupted.

Luci eyed him coolly. "What's wrong with you?"

"Nothing. I thought we had coffee."

Luci pointed a neatly polished fingernail at the grocery list next to the fridge:

Coffee
Saltines
Sugar cubes

"What do we need sugar cubes for?" he asked.

Luci gestured to her teacup.

Because you can't put regular granulated sugar in tea?

"Are you still worried about what you said at The Restaurant on Thursday?" she asked.

"No. I'm not worried." Vander picked up the tin of Folgers coffee and lifted the lid to confirm its emptiness. "I'm horrified. I know how ridiculous I sounded."

"Vander, it was adorable. *You're* adorable with Harlow."

He wasn't adorable, he was foolish. Harlow had been very clear. She wanted a practical relationship, with a practical guy who fit into her world. Her life was in Nashville. He wanted to settle here, raise kids here, let his roots run so deep he could flourish in any storm.

He had as much chance with Harlow as Stet did at making the Kentucky Derby.

"Welp, you're grumpy, and lack of coffee isn't helping ungrump you. Go down to the store and grab some instant. I'm going to bake scones, so by the time you get the coffee and have a cup, breakfast will be ready."

He didn't think anything had the power to ungrump him, but as he stepped into the cold, letting the bright, icy morning air into his lungs, he did feel a little better. It was a gorgeous morning, with snow predicted for the afternoon. Was Harlow already up and out for a hike? Was she replaying his words the same way he was?

He glanced in the front window of The Restaurant. Angie eyed him as he walked past.

Yeah, he really hadn't left much to the imagination when it came to his feelings about Harlow.

Vander trotted up the two steps onto the narrow wooden porch of the store and opened the front door. Mac's record player was spinning some old John Denver, the sleigh bells on the doorknob an accompaniment as Vander entered.

He looked up from under his hat to offer a wave to Mac and froze. His hand was still raised in greeting, eyes fixed behind the counter where a beautiful woman stood patiently at Mac's side. Her brown hair caught the light from the window behind her, falling in waves over the shoulder of her warm cinnamon-colored wool coat.

"So I click this into place?" Mac asked, adjusting a metal portafilter into the espresso machine.

"Just like that," Harlow encouraged him. "You got it."

"And now I press what?"

"This button here. The one on the end."

A hiss of steam blasting through ground coffee obscured John Denver's "Christmas for Cowboys" momentarily, as the aroma of espresso filled the room. Vander was stuck to the spot, staring along with Harlow and Mac as rich, dark liquid filled the tin mug.

A bright smile spread across Mac's face. "Look at that!" he cried. "We made espresso."

"We did." She beamed up at the merchant. "Go us!"

Mac lifted the cup to sniff the drink. "How do we make it a latte?"

Vander leaned against the doorframe, watching the exacting woman help an enterprising Boomer come to terms with an espresso machine.

A relationship with Harlow was impossible, impractical.

But right now, it felt like the only thing that made sense.

"Hello there!" Mac called out, noticing Vander. "You come in for espresso? Because we've got our first cup right here."

Harlow startled, like she didn't mean to get caught

helping Mac. Then she blushed, and any last argument he had about why he shouldn't let himself fall for her slipped away. His feelings caught and roared to life. He was done fighting.

She gave him a shy smile and tried to roll her eyes, as though helping Mac was no big deal.

Vander didn't look away as he walked up to the counter. "This is sure neighborly of you, Harlow," Vander said.

She flipped her hair off her shoulder. "Purely selfish on my part. I wanted a good cup of espresso."

"You have an espresso machine at home," he reminded her.

"But no ice cream."

Vander gazed at Harlow, willing her to read his thoughts as they rose to his consciousness, one after the next.

I caught you helping.

You look real pretty in that sweater.

I like you.

"You want to try the first cup?" Mac offered, still so focused on his success he didn't notice the air crackling between Harlow and Vander.

"You want me to have the first cup?" he asked. "Shouldn't that go to the mayor or something?"

Mac and Harlow exchanged an alarmed glance. Mac lowered his voice and asked, "You mean Loretta?"

"No." Vander reached out and grabbed the cup. "Nope, that is not what I meant. I'll be the first to try." He raised the cup in a toast and took a glorious sip. The smooth brew had more caffeine in it than anything he'd had in months, making him feel like he could float off the ground. Or at least he was going to tell himself it was the espresso.

"What do you think?" Mac asked.

"Hmm, rich, complex, a little nutty—" he gave the cup a thoughtful gaze "—it's Harlow's coffee all right."

Mac laughed as Harlow tried to snatch the cup away from him, but Vander evaded her grasp, stepping back.

"See if I ever make you another cup of coffee," she teased.

He took a second sip, gazing at her from over the rim. *I hope you do.*

Harlow blinked, momentarily caught off guard.

"You want a scoop of ice cream in that?" Mac asked.

Vander glanced at the cup. It didn't need ice cream, but it sure sounded good all the same.

"He wants ice cream," Harlow said, grabbing the scoop. She opened the case and procured a perfect ball of chocolate caramel. Vander held out the cup to her, and she winked at him as she released the ice cream into the cup.

Ice cream and espresso, two things folks didn't normally put together, but worked real well when you did.

Harlow turned to Mac. "I need to grab a few things. Why don't you make two more practice cups, then we can work on how to use the steam attachment for a latte?"

"Who am I gonna serve it to?" Mac asked.

Harlow peeked out the window. "Today's Moment and Pete Sorel are talking out front. I bet they'd be willing to try a free sample."

"You think she drinks coffee?" Mac asked.

"You think he drinks fancy espresso?" Harlow countered. "It'll be good for each of them to try something new."

Harlow dipped out from behind the counter. Vander could barely keep his head on straight as she drifted toward him.

"What are you in for?" she asked.

Vander gestured with his thumb over his shoulder, forgetting the common word for flat salty things that were like bread, but not.

"The uh." He held his hands out in an approximation of the size of a box.

"Fishing tackle?"

Vander shook his head.

"Postcards?"

He laughed.

"Miming lessons?" she guessed. "Because you need them, I have no idea what you're talking about."

"Salt cracker. Salty crackers." Vander wanted to kick himself with both feet, but that would land him sprawled out in the middle of the aisle. *What is the word?* "Saltines," he finally spat out. "I'm picking up saltines."

Harlow had to know she had him off-kilter, but

who wouldn't be at this point? Vander tapped the toe of his boot against the floor, then gave up trying not to stare.

"It was real nice of you to give Mac a lesson on the espresso machine."

She waved the compliment away. "I didn't give him a choice, per se. It was more like an intervention."

Vander glanced over her shoulder to where Mac was approaching the machine with a furrowed brow. "I think he appreciates it."

Harlow shrugged, even as color rose to her face again. "Let's get your salt crackers. And I'm giving in and grabbing another sleeve of Nutter Butters, since I'm in Pronghorn."

"It *is* the holidays," he reminded her.

"It is. And I'll go cold turkey on the peanut-shaped cookies come January."

Vander chuckled and grabbed a second sleeve to share with her at the next rehearsal.

"Hey, can I ask you two questions?" Harlow kept her eyes on the aisle ahead of them. Since she'd probably asked him well over a hundred questions, with no express permission granted, it seemed like an odd request.

"Sure. Ask away."

"Did you see this?" She pointed to a display of jewelry. "Who made this? Mac's not talking."

Vander glanced at the handmade turquoise jewelry. "Is that what you wanted to ask me?"

"No. But do you know? Because it's stunning."

She picked up a bolo tie and held it up to him. "You could pull this off."

"Would I have to wear a nice shirt? Because I don't know if I could pull that off."

She rolled her eyes and set it down. Her fingers lingered next to a pair of long silver earrings with a turquoise inlay. They'd look so pretty against her brown hair.

"Would you look at that?" Mac's voice interrupted his thoughts. He held a cup aloft. "Coffee! Again."

"You should probably pay for your groceries before he gets too deep into barista mode," Harlow said with a lowered voice. "Who knows how long you might get stuck here."

Vander purchased his instant coffee, saltines, sugar cubes and Nutter Butter cookies, although he wasn't sure how much instant they'd drink any more with espresso two blocks down the street. Mac asked him to take samples out to Pete and Today's Moment as he commandeered Harlow's attention for his latte lesson.

Vander took his time delivering the coffee to the surprised but curious town guinea pigs on the front stoop. Then he returned, continuing to wander the aisles, waiting for his two questions from Harlow. The sounds of John Denver singing, milk foaming, of Mac getting frustrated with the process, and Harlow's encouraging comments created a hum in the background. Vander drifted toward the turquoise display.

He'd never really looked at jewelry before. In the past, girlfriends had sent him screenshot images of large, glittering things without explanation. He was supposed to know what to buy. He was supposed to know where a relationship was going and purchase jewelry to move it in the correct direction.

This jewelry didn't make him nervous. He was drawn to the rich turquoise stones, the delicate and purposeful silver settings. He bent down to further examine a ring with a square stone veined with black. It'd look so pretty on Harlow as she gestured for one of the students to hurry up.

But then again so would the necklace with the asymmetrical stone. Or the bracelet with a line of turquoise set against a silver webbing.

Heck, Harlow could even pull off one of the bolo ties.

"That is definitely a latte," Harlow proclaimed.

Mac eyed his creation, then took a sip. "It's good." He furrowed his brow. "I'd say it's every bit as good as the Pony Espresso in Tumalo."

Harlow gave a firm nod. "I think we can safely take down the Maybe you've got pinned on the espresso sign out front."

Mac beamed at Harlow. "Do you want to do the honors?"

"You want me to take down the Maybe?"

"You earned it," Mac said, already turning back to the machine and starting in on another cup.

"Yes. Thank you, Mac. I'd be honored to remove the Maybe." She glanced at Vander. "You want to join me? Document the moment where espresso becomes a fixture in Pronghorn?"

He let his gaze connect with hers and nodded. Very interested in heading back into the cold Pronghorn morning and taking down a sign that said Maybe with a beautiful woman. Or anything else she asked of him.

The rattle of a door hitting the wall as it opened shook Vander out of his trance. Loretta stood in the portal, hands on the hips of her yellow stretch pants. "What's this I hear about espresso? And why wasn't I invited?"

Out the window Vander saw Angie charge out of The Restaurant to investigate. Aida opened the door of her office and peeked out. Meanwhile, Loretta headed straight for the counter, ordering a peppermint mocha Frappuccino, extra hot.

Because who wouldn't order an iced, blended drink extra hot?

"You want me to stay and help?" Harlow asked.

"No, you go on and get about your day. I've got this covered." Mac turned to Loretta. "I have espresso, lattes or the house special, which is a shot of espresso with a scoop of ice cream. What can I make you?"

Vander followed Harlow out onto the stoop, where Pete and Today's Moment had a lot to say about the espresso. Harlow was confused by the praise, but Angie admonished them to leave her alone. Finally, the three of them headed into the store to watch Mac work his magic with the machine, leaving Vander and Harlow alone.

"You had a couple of questions for me?" Vander asked as they headed around to the side of the building together.

"Oh. Right." Harlow glanced down the street. She did not appear to be on the verge of asking one, let alone two questions. "Hey, are you coming out to see Stet later today?"

Vander came out to see Stet every day. This didn't seem like the type of question you give someone an advance warning of.

"I was planning on it. That okay with you?"

"Yeah. Obviously."

She bit her lip. They arrived at the side of the building and Harlow paused in front of the Maybe sign.

"You know what's weird?" she asked.

"Nope." *Other than you asking me if you can ask me a couple of questions, then not asking them.*

"Luci seems super familiar to me. Like, I know I don't know her, but I feel like I know her."

Vander nodded, unsure of what to say. He did know Luci, and that was about all he had on the subject.

Harlow put her hands in her pockets and spun around to study the signs that had accumulated along the side of the store. The original Pronghorn Supply sign was followed by Established 1921, then the ice cream sign and finally finishing with Espresso.

A spark lit Harlow's eye as she reached up and

snatched the Maybe off the wall. "Did I just posi- tively influence this town?" she asked.

"You've been doing that for a while now," he re- minded her.

She pressed her lips together, color rising to her face as she studied the maybe sign. "Well, that's done." She took a step back. "I guess I'll see you around."

"What did you want to ask me?"

"Yeah. Okay." She gazed down Main Street, her brow furrowed when she caught sight of Connie stretched out in the middle of the highway. Then she squared her shoulders and flipped her hair back. "I was wondering if you wanted—" She took a breath, then seemed to lose her nerve as she asked, "Do you want to help me cut down a Christmas tree?"

"That's it? That's the big question?"

"It's *a* question I wanted to ask you, yes."

Vander gave her a softer version of the Teacher Eye, one that called her out for not telling the whole truth.

"What? I could use the help."

He did not have her mind-reading abilities, but there was no way she'd danced around the question of a Christmas tree for the last thirty minutes. "I'd love to. Just let me know when."

"Great." She nodded, meeting his eye like this was a totally reasonable conversation. "Thanks."

He held eye contact, urging her to ask him the second question. The real question.

She glanced down at the Maybe, then back at him.

"Espressoooo!" Tate's voice startled the two of them out of the moment. The PE teacher loped down the street. "I'm stoked! High five, Harlow!" He held up his hands for a double high five.

Harlow laughed as she slapped his hands.

"Why are you bellowing?" Aida stepped outside of the sheriff's office, Greg at her heels.

"Because I'm in love with you, it's almost Christmas and Harlow got the espresso machine working." He held his long arms out wide. "Is that not worth a bellow?"

Aida shook her head as she crossed the street to join them. "Harlow, I apologize if my fiancé has irreparably damaged your eardrums, but we're all pretty excited about the espresso."

By now Luci, Willa and Mateo had heard the news and were heading to the store, along with everyone else in town.

Harlow glanced at Vander. If public derision had been hard for her, public adulation seemed to make her even more uncomfortable.

"I gotta get out of here," Harlow announced, taking a step toward her rental car. "Nice to see you all." She waved the maybe sign and turned away.

"I'll uh, catch you later then?" Vander asked.

Harlow paused in her stride. "Yeah. Hopefully. If I'm out by the arena."

He held her gaze, reminding her that she hadn't asked the real question.

She held up the Maybe sign with both hands.

He folded his arms, calling her bluff.

Harlow blushed, then slipped into her car before anyone else in town could show her a spark of appreciation.

"You gonna join us for espresso?" Tate asked him.

The rest of their crew had arrived. Vander glanced at his friends, then tapped the toe of his boot against the sidewalk. "I could actually use a little help picking out something."

"How many espresso drinks could he possibly have learned how to make?" Luci asked.

Vander grinned, despite himself. "I'm not thinking about espresso."

CHAPTER ELEVEN

HARLOW'S HEART WAS jammed up in her throat by the time she pulled into the drive. How was she so nervous around Vander today? But also so comfortable at the same time? That totally shouldn't be a feeling, but somehow it was. And how was *he* feeling right now?

Besides hopped up on espresso.

She didn't know what had come over her this morning. She just woke up and decided to drive into town to help Mac figure out the espresso machine. It was as if the moment Vander pointed out her good qualities, they started bubbling to the surface.

But then she'd gone and set herself up to ask him two questions, which were more like two dates she wanted to ask him out on. The tree was a lesser deal. He was willing to help her, and that wasn't unreasonable for an assistant foreman. Then again, there was no implication he'd be on the clock for their foray into the woods.

And she still hadn't asked him her real question.

Harlow entered the house through her mudroom. When she'd had her home built, she intended it for her someday-family, the kids she would bring back to the area for two weeks at Christmas and a month every summer and let run free on this land as she had.

But she didn't have a family, nor any prospects of

one, no matter how warm and melty Vander's smile made her feel. What she had, and needed to focus on, were four very important guests heading her way in a few days. Harlow clipped along the back hall, into the kitchen, mentally running through her list. The pantry, freezer and kitchen were stocked. Katie would bring in a few fresh ingredients, but other than that she had more than enough food for her guests. She'd finish indoor Christmas decorations this weekend. Katie would drop by to help her with a deep clean the following Monday.

Harlow pulled up the calendar on her phone, the neat grid of dates and tasks calming her. She had this under control.

Everything was finished, except for asking Vander if he wanted to join her Nashville guests on their first evening here. She'd have to miss rehearsal that night, but Vander could come out afterward. He wasn't exactly the party type, though. There was no real reason to invite him. She didn't *need* him there.

Even if she kinda felt like she did.

Harlow opened the notes app on her phone and began to type.

Reasons for inviting Vander Tourn out to meet my guests:
He's cool.
Wilson and the others would like him.
Vander might get a kick out of meeting a once-famous musician and some Nashville types.

It wouldn't be the worst thing for Vander to see me among people who know about my work and respect me.

Harlow stared at the neat sans serif lettering. Then she finally added the truth.

Because Vander is my partner in crime. Or partner in rehabilitation. Our skills and interests balance each other. If there was a buddy system, any reasonable adult would match us up. We work well together. We play well together.
I like him.

Harlow stared at her words, then flipped her phone upside down. The tiny sip of espresso she'd had at Mac's was like rocket fuel, intensifying this impractical crush.

That was all this was, a crush on a seriously attractive man. Just a crush on a kind, gifted, musically inclined teacher who checked all the boxes she never knew she had.

Harlow paced in a semicircle. Images of Vander's smile resonated in her mind: when he discovered her helping Mac, when she scooped ice cream into his espresso, when she caught him staring.

Ugh. This was not how she needed to spend her Saturday.

She had work to do, and her frontal lobe desperately needed a break from scrambling for ways to make this unworkable relationship work. Harlow headed for the living room where her laptop and the paperwork for her latest case were waiting. She flopped into her favorite chair and pulled a cozy blanket over her knees.

Out the window she could see a poorly maintained ATV pulling up to the stables.

She'd get over Vander. Or maybe she wouldn't. Maybe there would always be a little piece of her heart attached to this wonderful man. But right now, there was a young woman back in Nashville who had fallen prey to a predatory producer, and Harlow wasn't gonna let that snake get away with it.

Harlow grabbed her computer and reread several documents. Abigail, a singer-songwriter on the rise, had signed a contract with a producer who went bankrupt before she was able to record anything. The young woman wanted the rights to her music back, but the producer had held on to them, saying she was planning on being back in business in no time. Four years later, the producer was no closer to being back in business than she had been at the time of the bankruptcy. Harlow's concern wasn't so much that Abigail should be able to record the eight songs she'd signed over, although she wanted that for her. Harlow's big concern was that as Abigail gained popularity, the bankrupt producer could sell the rights to her songs to the highest bidder. It made Harlow furious to think about a fake producer making a dime off a starry-eyed musician.

Harlow burrowed deeper into her documents.

The light in her living room shifted as the sun headed west.

The rumble of a motor caught her attention. Harlow's head jerked up from her computer, ears assessing the noise, lest it be the teacher's ATV.

This was ridiculous. What, was she worried he would leave before she had the chance to invite him to meet her guests?

Or that he *wouldn't* leave before she got up the nerve to invite him?

Harlow tapped her fingers against the arm of her chair, staring out the window.

Enough. She needed to get out of the house and get something done today.

No, you know what? She was going to cut down her own tree, with her own ax, on her own. The last thing she and Vander needed was to be out walking in a winter wonderland, preparing for Christmas together. She'd chopped down Christmas trees with no help in the past, and she could do it again this year.

Harlow set her computer aside and launched out of her chair. She grabbed a coat and stalked into the cold sunshine, popping into her garage for an ax. The path behind her home, up the hillside was a blur as she marched on, scrambling over rocks, finding a deer trail and finally making her way to a small grove of fir trees.

Soft clouds rolled in above, and a lone flake drifted to the ground. Yeah, good call on her part. This setting was way too romantic to risk with Vander right now.

Harlow studied the tree options, appreciating the natural beauty of the trees' irregular limbs, but still looking for something that wasn't completely wild. Also, looking for one she could haul back on her own.

Which one would Vander pick?

Ugh. No. It literally didn't matter. They weren't a couple. He might not ever even see this tree.

Harlow scanned the grove and landed on a nice full fir. She judged the height. Nine feet-ish? She could drag it back on her own. Probably.

No, definitely. She had cut and wrangled a tree back to her house by herself the last three years in a row. Just because she had a mad crush on a musician cowboy teacher didn't mean she suddenly needed her own personal arborist running around taking care of her holiday tree needs.

Harlow pulled the ax back and swung at the base of the tree. A satisfying thwack rang out. She pulled back and swung again. The tree started to tip. Harlow stood back and reevaluated. Had it grown a little in the time between picking it out and starting to cut it down? Or maybe it seemed larger at this angle. Harlow pulled the ax back again. She was warm from the hike and the lumberjack action. She swung the ax, and the tree tipped. She swung again, the soft branches swaying as the tree fell with a soft crash on a bed of fir needles.

Harlow stood back, breathing in the cold air, staring at her felled tree with pride.

And trepidation.

Because lying on its side, the tree appeared to

be a little more than ten feet tall. Technically, way more. Snow continued to drift from the sky, still a flurry but with no signs of stopping.

Harlow examined the tree from several angles, one bad idea for getting herself out of this situation popping into her head after the next.

She didn't know how long she'd been there when the low timbre of Vander's voice, calm and full of reassurance, rumbled.

Harlow spun around, really not wanting to be caught in the middle of what was rapidly starting to look like a very big mistake. Through the trees, she saw a flash of his canvas jacket, of a cautious horse. Vander had Stet saddled up and spoke as he led him into the clearing.

Harlow set her ax down carefully, not wanting to make a single noise that might spook the horse.

Vander was gentle, radiating confidence as he spoke. He stopped walking on the other side of the clearing and was so focused he didn't notice Harlow and the monster tree she'd felled. He ran a hand down Stet's muzzle. Then he placed a foot in one of the stirrups. Stet shuffled, but Vander reassured him, then lightly sprung onto the horse's back.

Stet was uneasy for a brief moment. Vander leaned toward the horse's head, still speaking calmly. The animal took a cautious step forward. Vander rubbed his neck and encouraged him. Stet took another step, then seemed to realize that he was now helping Vander. The skittish horse lifted his head, transformed with confidence. He strode forward into the clearing with purpose.

Harlow's hand slipped over her heart. This was what Vander was meant to do, help students and horses and overly wound-up intellectual property lawyers find their way.

This was where he was meant to be. On this land, with her.

Vander glanced up and saw her, and a dazzling smile lit his face. She pressed her palm more firmly against her heart, feeling the pressure of the beat against her hand.

Stet continued toward her, the sense of purpose putting a spring in his step. Man and horse came to a stop next to Harlow, sending her thoughts and plans scattering.

"Nice work!" Harlow said to both of them.

Vander beamed at her as he swung down from the horse. He didn't need to speak; she could feel his joy at Stet's progress.

She ran a palm down the horse's nose. Stet nudged her hand, and she gave him a scratch under his mane. Vander stood very close to her, silently celebrating this massive victory. There really were no words, just warmth and joy and connection on a snowy afternoon.

"Thank you for letting him stay," Vander finally said, his deep voice sparking a pull in her belly.

"You do know I was never going to kick him out?"

"I know that now. Didn't know then." Vander kicked the toe of his boot against the ground. "What are you up to?"

"I was working on a case."

"With an ax?"

Harlow looked down to see the ax at her feet. "Oh. No. I was taking a break to chop down a Christmas tree." She gestured behind her. "That Christmas tree."

The expression on his face transformed as he registered the massive tree lying flat behind her. It had definitely doubled in size.

"I thought we were gonna do that together?"

"Oh. Yeah." What was she going to say here? "I didn't want to bother you."

A light, cold snowflake fell on her cheek, like a kiss. Then another. Vander stepped closer to her, the snow falling in a light flurry around them.

"It's never a bother, Harlow. I was looking forward to it."

Harlow pressed her lips together, scrambling for an excuse other than *I was looking forward to it, too, and that scared me.* "You're just so busy."

"I'm not too busy to help you put up a tree."

Snow began to fall in earnest. Each flake landed silently, but all together they created a soft chorus as they hit the earth. Harlow tucked her hands into her pockets and turned away from Vander, away from a conversation she didn't know how to have.

To the east, Warner Valley spread out beyond them, the snow gently falling on every living soul, from the most cantankerous citizen of Pronghorn to the most unassuming jackrabbit snug in her den.

"I love snow," she said.

"It's pretty." Vander wasn't looking at Warner

Valley or the snow or the rapidly expanding Christmas tree. He was looking at her. "Everything around here is."

Harlow swallowed, then gestured toward town. "What is it you like so much about Pronghorn?"

Vander held his hand out, palm up and gestured to their surroundings and Stet with an expression asking, *What's not to like?*

"No, I mean the town."

He nodded, his expression shifting. He turned his attention on Stet, as though worried he might be giving away too much. "I guess I was getting away from something, when I moved out of Eugene. Then I got here, and it felt right."

He fell quiet, the soft snow and Stet's exhalation the only sounds.

Harlow let the silence stretch out for as long as she could. Which wasn't very long. "You realize those two sentences, for a person who loves information, were unfairly tempting."

He chuckled. "Yeah. Sorry, you're right. I'm not good at talking about things."

He glanced at her, and she was reminded of Stet. What type of human behavior had Vander seeking refuge in this place?

"You can trust me," she said.

HE GAZED AT HARLOW. Snowflakes touched down on her cheeks and nose, as though even the frozen particles of water were drawn to her. Engaging with the citizens of Pronghorn had taken extraordinary grace and courage on her part. It was inspiring. She had been vulnerable in his presence, and he needed to man up and do the same.

"I do. I do trust you." He turned to face her more fully. "You want to know the story? It's kinda ugly."

"Uglier than young Harlow? Because she's some competition—"

"Don't say that," he snapped. Then he softened his voice. "Don't ever say that. I bet you were a beautiful child."

"I'm just joking."

"Joke about something else." He bent his head slightly so he was looking directly into her eyes. "You're beautiful."

Harlow blinked, like the words didn't fit in her worldview. "Um. Thank you?" She flickered her hand in between them. "Let's put a pin in that topic. What happened that led you here?"

He turned away, rubbing Stet's muzzle. "I, uh, I always wanted to be a teacher. I like kids. I like science. The work is fascinating. I can't think of anything more important to do with my time on earth. I really can't."

"You all have helped to reshape my views on the profession," Harlow said. "It seems like all I ever hear in the news are the negatives."

"There are certainly challenges, but they shouldn't get all the airtime. Anyway, I worked hard for this job. Grad school was expensive and challenging. My girlfriend of three years broke up with me because she didn't think I'd make enough money as a teacher to support a family."

"Seriously? There was literally someone short-sighted enough to break up with *you*?"

Vander caught her eye, his smile barely concealed. And yeah, maybe that came out a little stronger than she intended, but he'd take it.

"She did." Vander nodded. "Meanwhile, I'm thinking going into education is the best way to support a family, because I considered social, emotional and intellectual support, not just money. I thought being a teacher would help me be a better dad someday."

"You're going to be an incredible dad. She missed out."

"I don't mean to suggest she was all bad or a mercenary. She just didn't think teaching was a practical career," Vander said. "But we had some good times. She used to love it when I played guitar."

Harlow waved her hand in dismissal. "Everyone loves it when you play guitar. I'm not giving her props for appreciating what any basic mealworm could recognize as extraordinary."

Vander laughed. "We weren't a great fit anyway, and this issue solidified what I think we both already knew. So I did it. I walked away from a relationship. I got into the education program at the University of Oregon and paid for it myself. I got a practicum teaching placement in a great school with one of the best science teachers in the district. I was on my way."

His words faded. This was where the story started.

"Did it not go well?"

"Uh." He blew out a breath. "No."

Snow continued to fall. He needed to get Stet tucked in. Harlow's hand came to rest on his back, gently encouraging him to continue.

Vander pulled in a deep breath of the icy air. "I was doing pretty well, learning from some of the best. That whole department was amazing. The kids were great. I learned what good teaching looks like and was encouraged to put my own spin on things. Then, one day, it just...blew up." The cold intensified as Vander slipped further into the memory.

Harlow rubbed his back gently.

"I caught a kid copying a lab report. She'd taken a picture of someone else's work and had it up on her phone as she filled in her answers. I walked over and asked her to put her phone away, and it was right there on the screen. I handled it the way I was taught to. We looked at the academic integrity policy together, and I told her I wouldn't accept the assignment. It was worth five points. *Five points*."

Stet pricked up his ears, swiveling his head to look at him.

"The energy in class was a little weird the next day, but I didn't think about it. The day after that—" He shook his head, then forced himself to continue, "The day after that, the principal pulled me from class. Looking back, I can see that he was reactive. He didn't handle the situation well. He sat me down in front of a computer and Facebook was open on the screen. The principal pointed at it and said, 'Can you explain why these parents think you're out to get their daughter?'"

Vander closed his eyes but kept talking. "I just stared at it. I thought it was some kind of joke, and then it...it wasn't. The girl's parents accused me of bullying, said I didn't like their daughter or any of her friends from day one. There were all these pictures of me, looking grumpy in class. Frowning or standing with my back to a kid. This student had taken all these pictures."

Vander felt heat on the back of his neck, even as the snow continued to fall. Harlow and Stet moved closer, helping lift the memories from him.

"The thing that was hard, and is still so hard, is that I didn't dislike that kid. She made a bad decision, and again, we're talking about five points. But rather than learn about the consequences of cheating, she learned that if you don't like a teacher's decision, you take it to social media and vilify a man who was trying his best."

"I'm so sorry," Harlow said.

"It was a nightmare. Here I was on my way, working toward my dream job. And these people just made things up. They lied. I have my faults. I'm not great at communicating, and I get pretty stubborn, but I'm not a bully."

"How did the other teachers react?"

"They were amazing. Looking back, I'm still so grateful. The science department rallied around me. Most of the students didn't even care—they liked my lessons. But among the parent community, the accusations welded to my reputation."

He glanced over his shoulder, as though the accusations were a physical presence, following him throughout life.

"I wanted to be in a community where people would know me and judge me for who I am. If they don't like me, that's fine. I'm not for everyone. But I want to be judged on actions I actually take, you know? I wanted to live somewhere where people saw me day after day and based their opinions of me on observation, rather than speculation."

"So you found Pronghorn."

"Or Pronghorn found me." Vander studied the valley for a moment. "I went to a job fair, and this woman in bright yellow—"

"Oh, no."

"She called me over." Vander's wry smile returned. "Loretta said, 'You there, with the eyes.'"

Harlow laughed.

"She could have been talking to anyone at the job fair. But you know Loretta."

"Oh, I do."

"I sat down, and she described Pronghorn—"

"I can only imagine."

"And I thought, that's the place for me. And it is. I love it here. I loved it the moment I got off the bus. Here, if I do good, every day, that's how I'm judged. And sure, rumors get started from time to time. People get spooked, like horses do. But if I respond with my best, that's how I'm known."

"I'm glad you found your home," Harlow said. "I'm glad it's here."

He turned to her, serious at first, then a spark lighting his eye. "Me too."

An abrupt chortle came from Stet, followed by his nosing around Vander's jacket for an apple slice.

"You should get this guy tucked in," Harlow said.

"You gonna let me get in on the tree action, now that I've told you my sad story?"

Harlow blushed. He knew exactly what had led her out here on her own. She had to be as confused by their growing connection as he was.

"I'd love your help. This tree turned out to be a little bigger than I thought it was."

"What were you gonna do when you chopped it down?" He maneuvered himself to see the length of the tree. "Try to argue it into the house?"

"You've never seen me in a courtroom," she reminded him.

Vander laughed, then gazed at her. "It's gonna look great. Your house will be perfect when your crew arrives from Nashville."

"Yeah, speaking of—" Harlow sounded like she was going for off the cuff, but her tone failed her. She sounded very much on the cuff.

"Speaking of…" Vander unzipped his jacket and reached into the breast pocket. "I thought you might want to show off the best of Pronghorn while they're here."

"Oh, I'm not taking them to Angie's."

Vander laughed, the sound quickly soaked up by

the accumulating snowflakes. Never mind that she might actually be serious. He pulled a small package wrapped in brown paper out of his jacket.

"I was thinking more about something you might wear." He held out the gift.

Harlow gazed at it, then up into his eyes. "What's this?"

"Open it."

Harlow's hands were shaking as she unfolded the simple craft paper wrapping to find a pair of what Vander, Luci and Tate had decided were the most exquisite turquoise earrings on display. They were perfect ovals, set in silver hanging on a long dangle. The whisper-blue stones had dark veins clouding the edges, and small pockets of gold webbing. Each stone was different, but the two were expertly paired.

"These are stunning." Harlow gazed at them, then at Vander. "I love them, thank you."

"I thought they'd be pretty on you."

A flush crept up her cheeks. She stared hard at the earrings, then cleared her throat. "They'd be pretty on Pete," she noted.

Vander laughed, but he kept his eyes on her face as she slipped them on.

"Do we have any idea who makes them?"

"Loretta?" Vander guessed.

"Definitely not Loretta."

"What about Mac?"

"Or maybe Angie?"

She laughed, then pulled her hair up. "How do they look?"

Vander gazed at her. "Stunning."

Harlow's breath caught. She held his gaze as she released her hair. "Vander, I'm throwing a party for my guests on the night they arrive. Do you want to come out and meet everybody?"

He smiled. "Yeah."

"You want to come to a party?"

"With you, yes. What time, and what can I bring?"

"Okay." She nodded to herself. "Great. Come on out after rehearsal on Wednesday. You don't need to bring anything, other than your guitar."

"I can't wait." He glanced up at the snow falling from the sky, then at Stet. "I should get this guy back to the stables. Any thoughts on how we're going to get this tree to your house?"

"I have a sled, and you have an ATV. Will that work?"

"Sounds like a plan." He grinned at her, enjoying making plans as they stood in the meadow of this winter wonderland. "It's gonna take me some time to get Stet settled, and I'll bring the others in while I'm at it. Then meet you back at your house to grab the sled?"

"Perfect." Harlow took a few strides toward the house. She slipped her hands in her pockets, then spun back around.

Vander's smile widened. "Thanks for inviting me to your party, Harlow. I thought you'd never ask."

CHAPTER TWELVE

INTELLECTUALLY, HARLOW UNDERSTOOD that *"thanks for inviting me to your party"* was not the most romantic line. But wow, did it send chills down her spine. Maybe it was those eyes Loretta had so astutely claimed for Pronghorn.

Harlow glanced at Vander from across the library as he worked with Ilsa to pick up the tune of a Dutch carol about St. Nicholas. He held eye contact with her and smiled.

And just like that, a tiny library stuffed with *Field & Stream* magazines became the most romantic place on earth.

A horn blasted from the gym across the hall, signifying the start of a basketball game. For all Harlow's heart was concerned, it could have been the swell of strings in a Viennese opera house.

Vander had the tune now, and Ilsa sang. A bright smile lit her face as she had the undivided attention of everyone's favorite teacher.

Harlow let a fantasy spin. Vander, in the warm spotlight of a cozy Nashville venue. A packed house, an audience wrapped up in his music. Vander's gift illuminated for everyone but directed at her.

"Harlow, can you come check this out?" Sofi asked.

Harlow spun around, tucking her hands in her

pockets. "Whacha got?" *And for that matter, where are we? And what are we doing here?*

Sofi gestured to a colorful poster spread out on one of the library tables.

"Oh, yes. Fabulous! Your posters are gonna pack the house."

Sofi beamed as Harlow enthused the virtues of her poster. That the entire town would come even if their only advertising was a Post-it note in the front window of The Restaurant didn't matter. Sofi had created a gorgeous, stylized illustration of all the kids in the pageant, with holiday decorations representing their different traditions.

"It's stunning," Harlow said. "It sets the tone for the evening. People need to be prepared to have their socks blown off."

"I made these to go with it." Morgan held her phone up for Harlow and scrolled through a series of social media posts. Each one featured an action shot of a different student as they rehearsed. They were fun images, somehow capturing each kid's contribution. Ilsa had a sly grin on her face. Oliver was confident and hamming it up. Morgan had caught Nevaeh midsong, eyes closed, caught up in the music. The image sent chills down Harlow's spine, just as Nevaeh's brave, soulful voice would send chills through the audience.

"Love!" Harlow proclaimed. "Lovity-love-love. You guys are amazing."

Taylor held out her phone for Harlow. "I did one with you and Mr. V."

Harlow perched on the edge of one of the library tables and took the phone. Taylor had captured Harlow as she laughed at something Vander said. Her head was thrown back laughing and he gazed at her over his guitar, delighted to have made her laugh.

It was an image of two people falling in love.

Harlow stared hard, trying to wrap her brain around what she was looking at. Was she falling for Vander? Was that what this feeling of being swept up in a fabulously pleasant hurricane was?

"Are those my mom's earrings?"

Harlow startled at the words.

Taylor took a step closer and examined the turquoise.

Harlow instinctively put her fingers on the pendants. "They were a gift."

"Right," Taylor confirmed. "Mom's selling them at the store."

Harlow pulled an earring from her ear and stared at it, then back at Taylor. *Are these? No...*

Taylor gave an affirming nod, but Harlow still had to clarify. "Your mom makes jewelry?"

Taylor rolled her eyes. "Please don't tell me she still doesn't have her name on the label?"

"There was no label." Harlow struggled to keep up. Raquel made something beautiful? Raquel had a talent besides gossip and mean-spirited comments?

"Ugh! Morgan—" Taylor called her sister over. "Mom still isn't putting her name on the jewelry."

"Are you serious?" Morgan pulled out her phone. "I'm texting her right now."

"Wait, can we back up?" Harlow rolled her hands toward her chest. "Raquel makes jewelry?"

"Isn't it great?"

"Yes," Harlow said. "It's fabulous. I would literally buy out the whole display at the store, except—"

"Except you're not supposed to buy too many things at one time at the store," Morgan intoned the Pronghorn rule.

Harlow laughed.

Taylor continued, "Our mom didn't even want to sell her stuff, but we finally convinced her that if she sold what she made, she could use the money to buy more supplies. I set up a website for her, and mostly she sells online."

"But we were like, it's the holidays," Morgan said. "Put some in the store."

"Our mom is afraid if she advertises her jewelry, people will think she's drawing undue attention to herself. That she's—"

Morgan grabbed Taylor's arm and made meaningful eye contact with her sister.

Harlow looked at one girl, then the next. She lowered her voice and asked, "Is she afraid of getting too big for her britches?"

"Yeah," Morgan said, as Taylor nodded, adding, "Exactly."

"Well, her pieces are amazing. And considering I'm already on your mom's list, I'm going to take the initiative to blow her cover. But for now, let's finish up our work here. I know you're all anxious to get to the basketball game across the hall."

It still felt so weird to think Pronghorn had a basketball team. As with the elusive Sasquatch, Harlow wanted to believe but was still awaiting confirmation.

"We're terrible," Morgan said. "But the games are super fun."

"And we're all going, so you have to come too," Taylor said, pointing first at Harlow, then at Nevaeh. "You're coming, right? Everyone will be there."

Nevaeh worried her bottom lip. "I have to ride the bus home."

"Pete will be at the game. Like, that's Pete's *thing*, and he'd probably rather wait to take you home after the game," Morgan said. "And anyway, we can give you a ride. Antonio, our exchange student, is playing. Come on! It's fun."

Harlow studied Nevaeh. She was pretty sure the girl's concern about attending the basketball game had nothing to do with how much fun she may or may not have there.

"If you want to stay for a little while, I can take you home when you're ready," Harlow offered, hoping Nevaeh knew she was ready to fight for her.

Nevaeh's gaze connected with hers. Resolve solidified in her eyes, letting Harlow know she was ready to fight for herself. "I can go."

Harlow gave her a nod of acknowledgment. "Perfect. Now, let's see if Mr. V and Ilsa are ready for the rest of us."

The last twenty minutes of rehearsal was a noisy blur. Their singing was accompanied by the sounds from across the hall: a glitchy popcorn popper and people chatting in the gym, socializing and cheering loudly. At six o'clock, kids stampeded out of the library, headed for the game. Another horn blast and the groan of a crowd confirmed there was something like basketball happening across the hall.

Vander walked toward her. "You coming?"

"My presence was commanded by Taylor and Morgan. Are *you* coming?"

"Luci saved us bleacher seats and took the liberty of making you a sandwich." He grinned at her. "They're waiting on us."

Us. She liked the sound of that. Harlow flipped her hair over her shoulder. "Then let's go."

By *everyone*, Taylor meant every single human in town. Plus Greg, who wore a yellow T-shirt with Coach Greg in bright orange across the back. Ranchers, commune members, Angie, everyone was there, watching the Pronghorn Pronghorns get destroyed by Adaline.

And all those heads turned as she walked into the gym. If she wasn't exactly on Vander's arm, she was right next to it. People greeted both of them, giving friendly waves before turning back to the game. No cutting looks, no commentary on the practicality of her coat, only a few greetings, then a collective groan as someone from the other team scored, *again*.

"That's two more points for Adaline!" a familiar voice rang through the bullhorn. "Where I'll remind you there's a nice piece of property for sale, a double lot in town with a charming fixer-upper."

"Who put Loretta in charge of announcing the game?" Harlow asked.

"Loretta put Loretta in charge." Vander nodded to Tate, but the PE teacher was too busy trying to explain something to the players.

The kids listened politely but didn't seem to be taking the loss too hard. One of the players held up a hand for a high five as Vander walked past.

"How you liking basketball?" Vander asked him.

The boy shrugged. "Eh? It's okay."

"Antonio, focus," Tate snapped. Then he breathed in through his nose and out through his mouth. "You had a nice play in the first quarter, and I'm glad you're taking a break from soccer to try basketball. But presently, I need you to focus."

The buzzer sounded, and the players spilled back onto the court. A clump of rowdy students stood in front of the bleachers, all doing some sort of dance cheer together.

A tall exchange student with a soccer jersey that read Senegal maneuvered himself next to Taylor, prompting a big grin from her. Morgan tugged Nevaeh into the center of the group, and the two sisters and the exchange student taught her the dance. Nevaeh's face lit up, and then she *giggled*.

The sound pierced Harlow. She stopped in her tracks, feeling like the Grinch Mav had so many questions about, with hearts reflected in her eyes as she watched the others weave this shy girl into their friendships.

Harlow wasn't the only one who noticed. Beyond the clump of students, a few rows up in the bleachers, Raquel sat alone and upright. She watched with a look of unadulterated pride on her face as her daughters included Nevaeh in the fun.

An unexpected conclusion settled in Harlow's mind. With all the information she'd gathered since coming home, and the experience of directing this pageant, there was only one verdict. She liked most people in Pronghorn just fine.

Raquel had her faults, as did Loretta, and Pete and everyone else around here. But so did she. Maybe being part of a community was choosing to look past the rough edges and through to the heart of her fellow Pronghornians.

"You coming?" Vander asked, his lips close to her ear.

"Yes, just taking it all in."

He placed a hand on the small of her back, leading her to a set of steps up the old wooden bleachers. "The teachers sit over here."

Luci and Mateo were squabbling about something. Willa laughed with Colter as his daughter tried to sell them another piece of the Pronghorn merch she and Sofi had created.

And sitting right next to Vander's crew was a frail, white-haired woman, cajoling the ref to give someone named Cece another chance at making a basket.

The elderly woman smiled as Harlow approached. Harlow's heart did a double flip. *Mrs. Moran!*

Harlow felt seventeen again, greeting her favorite teacher the same way she had for four years in high school Spanish, *"Buenas tardes, Señora Moran."*

Mrs. Moran's beautiful, time-wrinkled face broke into a bright smile. *"Buenas tardes*, Harlow. It's been a long time."

Harlow felt the same way about seeing Mrs. Moran as other people did when meeting rock stars. But unlike a rock star, Mrs. Moran reached out to pat her arm, the peach-colored, hand-crocheted sweater soft as it brushed Harlow's wrist.

"I've been wondering when I might see you. Are you having fun with the pageant?"

Harlow glanced at Vander. A whole lotta fun. "I am. How's teaching?"

Mrs. Moran waved her hand. "It's an adventure. Now, there's a rumor going around that you fixed Mac's espresso machine."

"I didn't fix it—" Harlow started, but Vander interrupted, boasting her up.

"I caught her giving Mac a lesson on how to use it. She's the town hero now."

Harlow tried to wave away the compliment, but Mrs. Moran wasn't having any of it. "She's always been a champion for others," she said. "Even in high school."

"I was a pest," Harlow responded. "No need to sugarcoat it. Vander's seen me at my worst."

"You weren't a pest. You were curious. You have

been sticking up for others your whole life. And if you stepped on a few toes along the way, I imagine those toes were in the wrong place to begin with."

Harlow rolled her eyes but warmed at the praise. Just as she had all those years ago when Mrs. Moran saw superpowers where others pointed out flaws.

The older woman glanced at Vander, then back at Harlow with curiosity. "I'm glad you made it back this year. A holiday pageant and some good coffee are exactly what this town needs."

Luci waved at them from two bleachers up. "You guys are super late! I need someone to distract me as we lose. Mateo just keeps telling bad jokes."

"You seem pretty distracted," Mateo noted.

Harlow gave herself another moment in Mrs. Moran's warm gaze. She wanted to tell her how much her kindness had meant to her in high school. How she'd kept up with her Spanish all these years because she didn't want to walk away from the gift Mrs. Moran had given her. She wanted to tell her favorite teacher that she owed much of her success to the fact that as a kid, she was able to see herself through Mrs. Moran's eyes, as someone who was smart and curious with big things to offer the world. But in the end, all she was able to say was, *"Es bueno verse."*

It's nice to see you.

Mrs. Moran patted her hand again. *"Sí, siempre es agradable verte."*

The horn sounded. "Two more points for Adaline!" Loretta sang brightly through her bullhorn.

"I hate to tell you folks, but this may be the monkey that breaks the camel's back. Things are looking down for Pronghorn."

Harlow sputtered out a laugh. "How does she manage to mess up every metaphor? It's like she's trying."

"Maybe she is." Vander leaned a little closer to her. "Maybe she stays up late planning her attacks on the English language."

"That's not funny," Willa snapped from where she sat behind them. She held out a basket. "Eat your sandwich."

Vander took a sandwich for himself and handed one to Harlow. While he and his friends regularly cooked nice meals for themselves, big, outrageous sandwiches remained a favorite.

"Harlow's has extra mayo," Luci said, leaning over to make sure Vander had it right.

Of course he had it right. Harlow was an exacting woman, and if he was going to run her off, it wasn't going to be for forgetting something as simple as mayo.

"This looks wonderful," Harlow said, lifting the top slice of bread. "Turkey, lettuce, pickled onions, cranberry sauce, what's this cheese?"

"Sharp cheddar," Luci told her.

"Wow." She grinned at Vander. "This is a treat."

"It's no charcuterie board," he reminded her.

She held eye contact. "Sometimes it's good to try something different."

It took a lot of self-control for Vander not to pitch his sandwich aside and kiss her right there.

Because technically, kissing would be different.

It was taking a lot of self-control not to spill his heart out every five minutes. Their conversation Saturday had shifted something for them. Telling her about the past had lightened his burden. The attack on his character had become an unfortunate situation that he'd weathered, a situation that brought him here, next to this woman at a small-town basketball game, with a truly phenomenal sandwich.

The horn blasted again, shaking Vander out of his thoughts.

"That's halftime, folks! With a score of twenty-four to three, I'll remind you our team is on a downward spiral, like a Whirlpool dishwasher. But the real estate market *is* in an upswing right now. You gotta buy before the bull market is out of the barn!"

"Stop," Willa said under her breath. "She has *got* to stop."

The Pronghorn team, which would have been beside themselves if they were losing a soccer game, headed toward the locker room joking and laughing. Tate had always placed student experience over winning, but Vander could tell his friend was trying hard to keep his spirits up as his team tanked.

Fans overtook the floor, shooting free throws and chattering. Parents gave in to the lure of popcorn and lined up at Angie's old, mostly functioning popper.

Harlow widened her eyes at Vander from behind

her sandwich. "This is fantastic. Thank you for including me."

I always want to include you.

She held his gaze as she seemed to read his thoughts, a blush creeping up her cheeks.

"Hi, teachers!" Taylor trotted up the stairs and planted herself next to Harlow. "Can we start school late tomorrow?"

"No," Willa responded.

"But everyone's at the game!"

"Absolutely not," Luci said.

"What if we—"

"I think that's a no," Mateo said, kind but very firm.

Taylor sighed dramatically, then leaned across Harlow and spoke to Vander. "Mr. V, did Harlow show you the social media post I made?"

Vander swallowed hard. "I don't do a lot of social media."

"You should get an Instagram account."

"I'm *not* getting an Instagram account."

Taylor held out her phone to show him the image. Vander took it, prepared to be as kind and firm as Mateo when he explained that she would not be posting any pictures of him on social media.

Then he saw the picture.

Well, okay. No one was even going to *notice* him. Not with Harlow shining like a diamond, garnering all attention in the shot.

"Do you not like the picture?" Taylor asked, turning the phone so she could study it. "I thought it was cute."

Vander scrambled to keep himself from grabbing the phone back.

"We don't have to post that if you're not comfortable." Harlow's hand came to rest on his back. "You kids have done such a great job with advertising—"

"No, it's great," Vander said. "I love it. Go for it."

Harlow gazed at him, the question clear in her eyes.

"If our goal is to pack the house, that'll do it," he said.

"Is that *our* goal now?" she clarified.

Vander shrugged. "Not my fault the show is so good. That's on you." He tried to hide a smile as he muttered, "You're the one who's all determined to fill the audience with joy."

Harlow's laugh rang out, just as it had when Taylor snapped the picture.

"Two points!" an accented voice called from the court.

Taylor turned around to where Sulieman was celebrating a basket, loudly, in her direction. Taylor slipped her phone back in her pocket, then headed out on the court.

Harlow watched the kids for a moment, then asked quietly, "You okay with that picture going up on Instagram?"

He shrugged. "I'm never gonna love social media. But you're right, they've done a great job with promotion."

"And you're okay with all the promotion too?"

"Like I said, it's not my fault this pageant is gonna blow the roof off this town. That's all you."

Harlow held his gaze. "I think you need to grab a little of that credit for yourself, Mr. V."

"Naw. I'm good."

Luci leaned down and put her face in between theirs. "Harlow, I'm gonna admit it, I really want to meet your famous people."

"Oh, absolutely," Willa concurred. "Colter and I have been coming up with ways we could accidentally run into them."

Harlow laughed. "We'll figure something out."

"I was thinking, if you had some kind of math-related emergency, I could have an excuse to stop by your place," Mateo said.

"What does a math-related emergency look like?" Luci questioned.

"Maybe an obtuse triangle? It's never *right*."

They all groaned.

"So wait, who's coming again?" Luci asked.

"Wilson Range, former nineties star who is now a music producer."

"I loved that band when I was a kid," Colter said.

"You still love that band," Willa reminded him.

"Wilson's daughter, Carol, will be here, along with her songwriting partner Maria Doyle. I'll invite my housekeeper, Katie, out for a few gatherings, to get her name out there again as a singer. And then Trey Tucker, who makes his living as a studio musician but is an aspiring singer-songwriter. Wilson thinks he's the next big thing."

"Trey Tucker?" Luci mused. "I like that name. Is he cute?"

"What does it matter if he's cute?" Mateo muttered. "And what type of a name is Trey Tucker anyway?"

"A fake one." Harlow's thinking frown appeared, and just as Vander was really starting to let himself enjoy it, she said, "And…yeah. I guess he's cute. He's kind of an issue I need to solve."

Vander didn't like the sound of that. A fake-name guy Harlow thought was cute and an issue…?

Wait.

"Hypothetically," Vander started cautiously, "is this that guy—?"

Harlow glanced back at the court. "Yeah. He wants to date me."

Vander nearly choked on his sandwich. Relationship-of-convenience guy was coming? He thought they'd dismissed that theory.

"What do you think of *him*?" Willa asked.

"I'm not interested. But we are a golden match by Nashville standards. He's pretty brilliant when it comes to interpolation."

Vander couldn't remember what interpolation was, but he didn't like the idea that this clown was good at anything.

"You can see how someone adept at using previously copyrighted work would want someone like me in his corner. And I guess I look decent enough,

I'm well-connected, and I don't have any dreams of fame. I would never steal Trey's limelight."

That was ridiculous. Harlow stole all the light. No one could think about looking elsewhere when she was in the room. Or rather, she was the source of light. And like the sun, she shone on others so that they could grow too.

"So, yeah. He's been a little persistent about all that. In his mind, a relationship with me would be a pleasant business transaction, what he hopes would be a partnership of mutual benefit. It happens all the time, all over the world, and always has." She paused and studied her hands. "I know now it's not what I want, but I don't fault others for entering into similar relationships. There are a lot of famous marriages that started out this way and turned out fine in the end."

The color drained from Colter's face. "Please tell me Faith Hill and Tim McGraw are not a marriage of convenience."

Harlow laughed. "I've never met either of them, but by all accounts they are truly in love."

Colter wrapped his arm more tightly around Willa and kissed her cheek.

Vander stared hard at the court. Obviously Harlow was a musician's dream date; she was anyone's dream. Smart and clever with a huge heart. She wanted the perfect charcuterie board lunch of a partner, and he was more like a can of Campbell's soup.

"Have you heard from him recently?" Willa asked.

"Uh, yeah." Harlow looked uncomfortable. "He's texted a few times."

"What did he say?" Mateo asked, then glanced at Vander.

"I dunno. Smiley face, Christmas tree, celebration emoji."

"Are you kidding me?"

Everyone turned to look at Vander. Had he said that out loud?

Luci raised an eyebrow and looked meaningfully at Willa.

Apparently he had.

"What did you write back?" Willa asked, at a more reasonable volume.

"I think I liked the text? Honestly, I can't remember. It's not a big deal. I called him a few days ago to clarify what our relationship is and isn't going to be, but he never picked up."

"You should tell him you have a boyfriend," Willa suggested.

"I can deal with it head-on," Harlow said. "It's going to be awkward, but whatever."

It was going to be awkward.

Vander would be there the first night they arrived, to witness all the awkwardness. He'd have to sit in the same room with that guy while he droned on about how good he was with interpolation while Harlow—

Wait.

Vander straightened, then gazed at Harlow.

He *was* going to be there. She'd taken her time

getting around to the invitation, but she'd specifically asked *him* to join her guests. She wanted him there.

"It doesn't have to be awkward," Vander said.

Everyone looked at him.

"I'll be there. So if you wanted to tell the guy, you know, that you're interested in someone else, I could be that guy. I mean, of course you can handle it on your own. I'm not saying you can't. But if he's gonna be there and be persistent, you may as well make it easy on yourself. You could tell him you're interested in me or you want to see where we're going. Or, you know, if it's simpler, tell him *I'm* your boyfriend. Or whatever…"

Vander trailed off. Everyone was staring at him.

Willa cleared her throat.

"Is that the longest he's ever spoken?" Mateo asked.

Vander glared at his friends, then turned back to the court. "Just sayin', I'll be there anyway. Happy to help."

He could feel Harlow's gaze on him, smell her perfume. And he knew she was smiling as she read his thoughts.

Let me be your man, just for one evening. We can be practical for one date.

Harlow's shoulder bumped his, and she didn't move away. "Thank you." He glanced at her, and the cute little frown emerged. "You know, that might actually be an efficient way of handling the situation."

Luci cleared her throat. "One should try to be efficient, whenever possible."

Vander wanted to glare at her, but that would mean taking his eyes off Harlow, and she was smiling again. "It could also be really fun."

He grinned back at her, relishing the connection. "That's what I was thinking."

A long evening pretending to be Harlow's boyfriend would be a lot of fun. And maybe he could do a good enough job that he could convince her they were worth the effort.

CHAPTER THIRTEEN

IT WAS A sticky point of etiquette: Could you host an important welcome gathering while loitering by the door listening for an old snowmobile?

If the last forty-five minutes were any indication, the answer was a resounding, *Yes, you can!*

Harlow had managed to spend the better part of the last hour hovering between the living room and the foyer, keeping an eye out for her fake boyfriend. Fortunately, her guests all needed to impress one another. As they arrived, she put the wheels in motion, making introductions, sparking conversation topics, then she stood back and let it happen. Her job was to laugh at jokes and redirect conversation so no one got caught somewhere awkward. Tonight would set the tone for the work to come over the next few days.

Carol and Maria would see how well they were able to work with Trey, in the hopes that his of-the-moment talents could revive their illustrious songwriting career. Trey would impress Wilson, getting himself in the running for a solo album. Katie would charm everyone, ask for nothing and have her name on their lips as they returned to Nashville.

And Harlow would keep the snacks coming and make sure all their great ideas were legal.

A knock sounded at the door. Harlow sprinted

across the pine flooring. Less than a second later the doorbell rang, as though she might not have heard the knock.

Fling is the only suitable word for what she did to the door.

Vander was gorgeous. He wore his regular Levis, worn in naturally, rather than bought distressed and ripped. He'd cleaned his boots and wore a pearl snap shirt she was willing to bet was on loan from Colter. Best of all, he had his guitar slung across his back.

"Hey." Vander grinned at her, then kicked the toe of his boot against the threshold.

"Welcome, my boyfriend Vander Tourn. You're looking very handsome."

His smile grew wider. He leaned across the threshold and brushed his lips against her cheek, very close to the earring he'd bought her. Her heart expanded rapidly, knocking other organs to the side and threatening her respiratory system.

He kept his face next to hers and spoke quietly, "You look beautiful."

And she was supposed to keep breathing after that?

Vander reached inside his jacket. "I brought you some mistletoe. In case you needed a parasite symbolizing Druid vitality."

Harlow laughed. "Thank you. I actually already hung a sprig in the living room."

Vander looked over her shoulder with a sly grin, as though he were scouting a way to get her under it.

"Who's this?" Wilson's voice boomed from across the room.

Harlow slipped her hand into Vander's. She took a brief moment to let her gaze connect with his, then turned to her guests. "This is my boyfriend. Vander Tourn."

The reaction was swift and dramatic. Maria and Carol swooped in with questions. Wilson was loud and gregarious, but with wrinkle to his brow suggesting he would reserve judgment of the new guy. Trey rolled his eyes, like Harlow was throwing up roadblocks for fun, and Vander was just another hurdle he'd have to get over before having his own personal intellectual property lawyer.

It all went down pretty much as expected.

The surprise was Vander. He shook hands, chatted and laughed with her guests. A lot of people might have been nervous meeting Nashville insiders, but it struck her that Vander had nothing to gain from these people. He didn't want to attach himself to the famous or wealthy; he was here solely to help her out.

"Whatcha got goin' on over there?" he asked, gesturing to a long table.

Harlow and Katie had set it up with a slow cooker of rich hot chocolate and big white mugs at one end, then lined both sides with marshmallows, candy canes, cinnamon sticks, fresh ground cardamom, nutmeg, orange zest, bourbon, Irish whiskey, white chocolate sprinkles, dark chocolate sprinkles, caramel sauce, maple syrup, Junior Mints, whipped cream and every other ingredient anyone has ever tried to put in hot chocolate.

"It's a cocoa bar."

He pulled his head back. "You taking a few cues from Tate?"

"Actually yes, it was his idea. How'd you know?"

"Lucky guess. Where's your cup?"

"I haven't gotten there yet."

He held eye contact for a moment, then bussed her cheek again. "I'll get it for you."

"That's sweet," she said.

"It's gonna be." He grinned, then nearly ran over Trey on his way to the hot cocoa. "Sorry," he said, then gave Trey the same interested look he would offer a student in his class. "How do you fit in around here? Are you a musician?"

Trey bristled. "Harlow didn't mention me?"

"Naw. We've mostly just been wrangling kids and cattle. You play guitar?"

If he were any other man, she might be worried that Vander would get into it with Trey at the party. But a public brawl wasn't exactly his style.

Harlow perched on the edge of a sofa, across from Wilson and his daughter. She tried to direct the conversation back to the music industry, but Carol asked, "Where did you get this stunning tree?"

Harlow glanced across the room at Vander. "You want to tell the story, or should I?"

He rubbed his shoulder dramatically.

"I'm sorry," she said again.

"It's all good." Vander sat down on the sofa next

to her and handed her a cup of cocoa. A quick glance suggested his approach to the bar had been *enthusiastic abandon.* He turned to Carol. "I'm assistant to the foreman here at Jameson Ranch. And last weekend I was working with my rescue horse when I came across a gorgeous woman with an ax, trying to cut down a massive tree—"

"I wasn't trying, I'd already cut it down."

"Without a solid plan for getting it into the house."

"I'm not the first person to misjudge the height of a tree."

"Is that how you guys met?" Trey asked. He pointed to Vander. "You work for Harlow?"

"No." Vander was still rubbing his shoulder, and Harlow was tempted to take over for him. "Not exactly. I work here, but we met in town. Harlow was distressed over a bunch of Christmas decorations, and then attempted to change the personality of a cat."

"That cat is going to get itself flattened."

"I'm just saying no one wins in an argument with a cat. Not even you." He rested his arm along the back of the sofa, over her shoulders and turned toward her, as though creating a separate room for the two of them.

"Was this before or after you started working for her?" Trey asked, again drawing focus to Vander's status as her employee. While it was technically true, it definitely didn't play into their relationship.

Or fake relationship, or whatever this was.

"After. And we didn't really get to know each

other until Harlow started helping with the holiday pageant."

"Wait. Stop." Maria held her hands out. "You're helping with a holiday pageant?"

Carol pattered her feet against the floor. "That's adorable!"

Harlow groaned. Vander had let the cat out of the bag, and she probably wouldn't have a lot of luck trying to argue it back in.

"Oh, my gosh, I love Christmas pageants. Is it like the cutest thing ever?" Katie asked.

Harlow pressed her lips together. "These are high school students. Personally, I think they're adorable. But it's not like little kids. They're a handful."

Vander settled his arm more firmly around her shoulder. "Harlow's great with the kids. We've had fun."

"You're doing the pageant together?" Wilson asked.

"But your job is here," Trey qualified, "as her ranch hand."

Vander leveled the Teacher Eye across the room at Trey. "My profession is teaching. I teach science at the high school in town." He turned back to gaze at Harlow. "I help out here because I love it."

At the word *teaching*, her guests quieted. Trey widened his eyes at Wilson. Harlow, too, had been judgmental when she'd first met Vander and learned about his profession. She'd learned a lot in the last few weeks of the power and meaning of his work. Her guests hadn't had the same experience.

"Oh, my gosh," Maria broke the silence. "Teaching is like my fantasy career. Whenever I'm stressed out, I think about going back and getting my teaching degree."

"Seriously?" Harlow asked.

"I do. I think it would have been a good choice for me." She looked at Vander. "It seems like a really nice life."

"I like it."

Wilson leaned forward. "That's what I was studying before I left college, education."

"Dad, I didn't know that," Carol admonished.

"I was going to be a history teacher and coach football. That was the plan."

"What happened?"

"Well, the band took off, and I dropped out. But sometimes I wonder what it would have been like."

Trey hovered on the edge of the living room. "Yeah, must be nice to get off work at four o'clock."

"You get off work at four if you get in by 6:00 a.m."

"I bet you're like one of those super teachers, who work all day and night, anything for the kids," Maria said. "Like that woman in *Freedom Writers*."

Vander shook his head. "The average teacher burns out in five years. Or less. You can't go into it thinking you're gonna save everyone and change the world in one trimester. I knew some people like that who didn't make it through their practicum. It's not sustainable."

Vander had now spoken more in a social situation than Harlow had ever witnessed. He pulled in a breath, and Harlow wondered if he was about to shut down. Instead, he leaned forward, his elbows on his knees as he addressed her guests.

"Everyone does it differently. I look at my co-workers, and we all have real different ways of doing things. But if you believe the information or skill you are teaching is valuable, and that the lives of the kids in front of you will be better for knowing it, you'll do what it takes. After that, good teaching is about being flexible in the moment but doing your best every day."

Her guests were leaning forward in their seats, rapt with attention. Even Trey looked interested.

"Here we have certain challenges. There are a lot of conflicting community expectations, a lack of funding. The internet only works about a third of the time, and we have one set of old Dell computers. Rural poverty and absenteeism are real here. That's a hard combination. Behavior problems pop up anywhere you've got a mess of teenagers, but it's a lot harder to deal with when you've got a class of thirty-eight kids, rather than eight." He glanced out the window, then back at Harlow. "Every school has its challenges, but every school has kids who deserve to learn. That's a pretty big responsibility, and all I can do is work at it, day by day."

He smiled at Harlow, reminding her that she was doing the same work as she completed her community service by helping with the pageant. She let herself soak in the moment, then realized it was dead silent in the room and everyone was staring at Vander.

Vander seemed to realize this wasn't prime party behavior either. He glanced at Wilson. "What do you do for a living?"

VANDER WAS MORE than ready to slip into the background. If he had his druthers, he'd spend the rest of the party watching Harlow shine. Maybe glare at Interpolation Guy a few more times, just to be clear. But mostly he wanted to stare at Harlow.

And he would if people would stop asking him questions. He tried to respond to questions about himself by redirecting the focus to Harlow. She wasn't kidding when she said she was a star back in her world. These people loved her and appreciated all she did and was. He could also see that she didn't like being the center of attention any more than he did.

"I'm sorry, could we go back to this pageant thing one more time?" Carol shifted closer to him. "You said it's an interfaith pageant."

"That's one word for it," Vander said.

"How do you handle that?"

Vander chuckled. "I mostly just watch Harlow handle it. She's the director. She's amazing, bringing out the shy kids, helping the kids who want to be center stage all the time focus their energy."

"I bet she's great."

Harlow squeezed his hand, a sweet way of saying *knock it off.*

Vander ignored her. "Yeah, and then there's her growing cadre of mini bosses. Harlow delegates the organizational tasks so the kids can have experience putting something like this together. Everywhere you go, there's a group of Pronghorn kids making lists and throwing out orders like Harlow does. It's awesome."

Carol placed a hand over her heart and glanced at Wilson. These people cared about Harlow too. Maybe they'd seen what he saw, that this time in Pronghorn had been good for her.

Harlow stood, and his entire left side went cold. How had he ever kept warm in the past, without Harlow right next to him? And how was he going to feel after her guests left and their fake dating was over?

Unless he could use his time as a temp to leverage this job into a full-time gig.

She returned to the room and deposited his guitar in his lap. He met her eye, silently asking if this was her way of getting him to shut up and stop bragging about her.

It was.

Vander settled himself around the guitar. He didn't intend to play. It was nice to have the instrument, though. A shield of sorts.

Harlow engaged Wilson in a conversation about the summer concert circuit. Vander plucked a few notes of "Here Comes the Sun" in response. Out of the corner of his eye, he saw her smile as she recognized the tune.

His fingers and body reacted to holding the instrument without conscious thought. A song slipped through his mind, into his fingers and through the guitar. Harlow relaxed next to him. Everyone else faded away as he drifted further and deeper into the music, unaware of the conversation between guests.

Unaware when conversation stopped, or of others falling into the music with him.

He felt Harlow's eyes on him. He held eye contact as he morphed the tune into "All I Want for Christmas Is You."

She rolled her eyes, breaking contact.

That was when he realized no one else was talking and everyone was staring at him.

Vander set his guitar aside. "I should get home."

"No!" all of the women in the room said in near unison.

"We'd love to hear you play some more," Wilson said.

Vander chuckled. He wanted to explain he hadn't meant to play at all, that he was sorry for stopping the conversation, that he didn't play in front of other people. Harlow's hand came to rest on his shoulder, and Vander stopped worrying about explaining anything.

Then Trey grabbed a guitar and sat across from Vander. He had a different expression on his face— less derisive, more interested. "You want to play that last riff again?"

Vander strummed five bars of "All I Want for Christmas." Trey played with him, then departed from the established song into something new as Vander continued with the Mariah Carey classic.

The music was fun and modern. Trey nodded as they played, and Vander had to admit it sounded pretty good.

"Can we try it again?" Trey asked as they came to the end of the song.

"Sure." Vander started from the top, and this time Trey broke off sooner, and a whole new tune emerged in the process. It was cool. Vander had never played with anyone else like this. It was both creative and comfortable.

Wilson nodded along with the music, a smile growing across his face. "Sounds good."

Vander wasn't sure how long they played together or when notepads came out and people began to brainstorm lyrics. The only thing that stuck with him was Harlow's smile as he connected with her friends over music.

"I'm not gonna break this up—" Harlow rose from the sofa "—but is anyone interested in dinner?"

"What time is it?" Vander asked.

Harlow checked her watch. "A little after nine."

"It's that late? I gotta get back."

"Nooo!" Carol cried. "More music."

Vander chuckled. "Naw, I've really got to get back." He glanced at the watch on Harlow's wrist. "Whoa. How is nine thirty 'a little after nine'?"

"It's not *that* late," Trey said.

"Maybe not for you all, but it's way past teacher midnight. I'll have a room full of kids at eight o'clock tomorrow."

Wilson stood and held out a hand. "It has been a pleasure to meet you. I hope we'll see more of you."

"We'll see you at the pageant, right?" Maria asked.

"Um. Were you invited to the pageant?" Harlow countered.

"You can't direct a holiday pageant and not invite us!" Maria said.

"I don't know if—" Harlow started to justify her noninvitation, but Vander ran his hand across her shoulders. She pulled in a deep breath and considered Maria's request.

"Are you telling us we can't support kids?" Carol asked. "That seems unfair."

The others laughed, but Vander knew how vulnerable Harlow felt about the pageant. "It's gonna be great," he reminded her.

She smiled, and Vander had the sense that everything was going to be great, for all time and forever.

Then he caught Trey watching them. Vander was actually starting to like the guy. He could see why Harlow might have thought dating him wasn't the worst choice. But all the same, he had a strong desire to show Harlow what the best choice might look like.

Vander placed his hand along her cheek. Because they were fake dating. And he should give her a fake kiss goodbye. He glanced up at the ceiling to make sure they were under the mistletoe.

Close enough.

Her gaze connected with his, and nothing felt fake at all.

Vander leaned forward for what was supposed to be a light brush of his lips against hers. Her perfume seemed to fill him, loosening connections of reason and good sense.

He readjusted his hand on her cheek and brushed his lips against hers. The soft kiss set the room spinning, shifting his world view. Vander was vaguely aware of Harlow's guests, of kissing this beautiful, powerful woman right in the middle of everyone. He heard someone say, "Aww!"

Or it might have been his heart.

Vander dropped his hand from her cheek and stepped back.

Harlow closed her eyes.

The kiss was overkill. They'd said nothing about kissing.

Time to leave.

Vander waved at the group. "'Night! See you all around Pronghorn."

He took long steps toward the door. Harlow followed him, and Vander braced himself for her reaction. He set his guitar down and pulled on his jacket as Harlow came whipping into the foyer.

"I'm sorry," he said softly. "I was trying to be authentic, and I got carried away."

Harlow advanced on him. She rested her hands on the lapels of his jacket, pausing only briefly before she wound her fingers through his hair and brought his lips to hers. Soft, warm and sweet, Harlow kissed him.

Everything that didn't make sense about their relationship scrambled around him, rearranged, until Harlow became the only thing that did make sense.

Vander wrapped his arms more tightly around her, pulling her flush against him. He tipped his forehead to hers and whispered, "Can I see you again?"

Her smile lit her face, lit the world. "Yes. I'd like that."

"You want to run a dress rehearsal with me tomorrow night?"

Harlow laughed. "I can't think of anything more romantic."

She stepped back, her bright eyes an invitation for another kiss that he really should decline. He had to get home. She needed to get back to her guests.

"Good night," she said, then reached out for his hand.

It was a very good night.

He wound his fingers through hers and cradled her hand in both of his. His eyes slid shut as he pressed her fingertips to his lips. "Good night, beautiful."

Then he slipped out into the bracing cold. Moonlight reflected off the snow-covered landscape, Vander's heart echoing back the wonder and beauty of this perfect night.

"OH, MY GOSH, HARLOW!" Carol cried as Harlow reentered the living room. "That man—"

Katie fanned her face dramatically. "The way he looks at you!"

"Did you see his face when he was playing the guitar and looking at Harlow?" Maria asked.

"His face when he was looking at Harlow all night long," Katie added.

Harlow wanted to bat away their swooning, but that was hard to do when she, too, was swooning. She gripped the back of the sofa to keep herself upright.

What had happened there?

She'd given in to the urge she'd had since watching him mosey out of the hotel the first day they'd met.

"Well done, Harlow. He's smart, kind and a hell of a guitarist," Wilson said.

Harlow grinned, glad "Uncle" Wilson approved of her choice. Now she just needed to figure out a few, tiny little logistics. Like how to convince him to move to Nashville.

"Thanks for bringing him out," Wilson continued. "I'm assuming he and I will have a chance to talk later this week?"

Harlow glanced up in confusion. Wilson was definitely an avuncular figure in her life, but he wasn't in a position to vet her boyfriends. No one was. "Um…?"

Wilson paced to the picture window overlooking the valley. "My gut tells me to sign him on the spot, but I've been around long enough to ask a few questions first."

Harlow landed back in her living room with a

thump. "I don't know if Vander is interested in pursuing a career in music."

The room went silent. She may as well have walked into Angie's restaurant and asked for gluten-free options.

Trey, always on the lookout for the next opportunity, looked truly baffled. "Isn't that why you invited him out here?"

"No," she snapped. "He's my boyfriend. I wanted you all to meet him."

The second part of the statement was true anyway.

"Well, you certainly have good taste," Carol said.

"I do," Harlow accepted the compliment. "We established that a long time ago."

"Harlow." Wilson tilted his head down and to the left. "Vander is very talented. And most people, whether they admit it or not at first, want fame. It's natural. I'm sure he's open to a conversation."

"Especially if *you* ask him," Katie said, setting everyone laughing.

Harlow pulled in a deep breath.

This wasn't what Vander wanted. If he didn't like social media getting a hold of his reputation in the city of Eugene, opening himself up to scrutiny from the entire world probably wasn't going to fly.

But what if he did want it? He could come to Nashville with her. She could introduce him to all the right people. He could be one of her clients, and she would fiercely fight for the protection of his creativity.

Because that was every man's fantasy? A woman to protect him from theft of intellectual property.

She glanced at Wilson, who was watching her carefully. If Wilson Range got behind Vander, he could go all the way. She could unleash these feelings into something that made sense. He could share his extraordinary gifts with the whole world, not just with Pronghorn.

But she was getting ahead of herself. So much of her communication with Vander was her reading his body language, him reading her facial expressions, a smile, a nudge, a tap on the arm. What the two of them needed now was a conversation about facts, expectations, plans. Feelings. Harlow felt a rush of excitement. This was one negotiation she couldn't wait to get into.

CHAPTER FOURTEEN

"WHERE'S HARLOW?" Taylor asked.

"She's coming," Vander promised. He took another look toward the door of the ballroom. He was as impatient as the kids and probably wasn't hiding it much better than they were. He tried to refocus on the positive. "Looks good in here. You came up with a great plan, Taylor," he said, gesturing to the decorations. "And, Raquel, thank you for your help."

"Well, it certainly took us long enough," Raquel said. "I had no idea it would be such an ordeal to get a stepladder in here."

Vander ignored her self-deprecating chatter. "It looks great. It really does. Thank you, Raquel."

Raquel waved the compliment away and took a step back. "I didn't really do that much."

Raquel had arrived at the hotel to start decorating at 7:00 a.m., before the teachers even left for work. She brought more of the pine and juniper garlands like the ones she'd created for Main Street, these interlaced with dried flowers and tiny strands of sparkle lights.

From there, she'd proceeded to interrupt classes all day long as she asked for a hammer, a stepladder, for someone to adjust the heat. When Willa asked her to wait for the bell before interrupting class, she reminded them that when *she* was a teacher, she was always grateful for her volunteers.

But the end results were stunning. Garlands wound around the balcony railing and framed the doors. Rather than a traditional Christmas tree, Raquel and her daughters had arranged willow branches into the shape of a fir tree, and decorated them with gold ribbons, lights and more natural elements. But what really struck Vander were the tumbleweeds. Raquel had taken the dry bundles of brush and threaded them through with sparkle lights. These hung from the high ceiling on long gold ribbons like chandeliers.

She had help, of course. Once school let out, watching Raquel try to boss Luci, Willa, Sylvie and her girls around had been pretty funny. But the end results were due to her hard work, and it was stunning. He wasn't going to let her off the hook.

"You did the whole thing, and it looks real pretty. I know Harlow's gonna love it."

The confusion wrestling across Raquel's face was almost comical. She didn't want to draw attention to her contribution but was clearly proud of her work. She didn't want to admit that Harlow had done something good for the community either. But by the way Taylor and Morgan followed her around and planned their law careers, Raquel had to know what a good influence she was.

"Well. You and Harlow have certainly worked hard enough on this pageant." She swallowed hard, then admitted, "My girls are having a great time."

"You might want to tell Harlow that," he said.

"I wouldn't want to make her uncomfortable."

On cue, Harlow appeared at the door, her hair and coat dusted with snow, her cheeks pink from the cold. "Hey, sorry I'm late. Wow! This looks amazing."

Vander loped across the room but managed to put on the brakes before folding her into a hug. Or a kiss.

She bit her bottom lip. "Hi."

"Hi."

"Do you have time to talk after rehearsal today?" she asked.

He held eye contact and nodded slowly. "I do."

"Perfect."

"Or I should say I have time, provided you get to the point a little more quickly than last weekend when it took you five hours to ask me two questions."

She swatted at his arm, but he caught her hand, holding on for a moment before releasing it.

Harlow tucked her hands in her coat pockets as she spun around and took in the decorations. "This looks amazing. It's stunning. OMG, the tumble-weeds!"

Vander took Harlow's shoulders and turned her to face Raquel.

"This is stunning," Harlow repeated. "What genius is responsible for this? Taylor, did you make these?"

Vander gave Harlow a nudge toward Raquel.

Harlow shot him a *why are you nudging me?* look.

He nodded to Raquel.

The color drained from Harlow's face as she took his meaning. "You did this?" Harlow asked.

"I helped," Raquel said. "And I don't know why it's so hard to get a stepladder around here—"

"Wait." Harlow held out a hand to silence her, eliciting a huff of indignation. "You must have done the decorations in town too."

Raquel twitched her shoulders. "Someone needed to. That doesn't mean I have to go boasting about it all the time." She looked at Harlow, then did a double take as she noticed her earrings.

"Raquel, I know you made these earrings."

Raquel huffed and blustered and rolled her eyes, but then finally managed to say, "They look great on you."

"They'd look great on anyone. Your jewelry is gorgeous." Harlow's ability to find the artist in everyone inspired Raquel to straighten her spine. Harlow continued, "I'm sorry. But I think you may need some new britches."

"Oh, stop it."

"No," Harlow said. "I'm not going to stop it. These are fabulous."

Raquel tilted her head to one side briefly. "I was pretty pleased with that pair." Then she seemed to catch herself. "I just don't think people should go around tooting their own horns all the time."

"A little horn tooting is not gonna kill you, and it might even help pay for your girls to go to college."

Raquel crossed her arms, then glanced at her daughters, fiercely trying to repress the pride welling inside her. "They are pretty good students, if I do say so myself."

"They are great students, and great *people*. Also, I need three bolo ties, a lavalier and two pairs of earrings. When can you hook me up?"

Raquel finally cracked a smile. "Harlow, you just can't let things be, can you?"

"I cannot. Sorry. Let me know when you need to go pants shopping."

Raquel waved her hand in dismissal.

"Seriously, I know some places where you can get some pretty big britches."

"If you have any hopes of me filling your outrageous order, you need to stop right now. This is a small town, and you're not the only one looking for a bolo tie."

Harlow dramatically clapped both hands over her mouth, her eyes still shining mischief at Raquel. Pronghorn's most opinionated mom shook her head and muttered something about Harlow's sanity, but her smile didn't slip.

Vander had a feeling Harlow would be offered her choice of bolo ties for purchase first thing tomorrow morning.

"Okay!" Harlow clapped her hands. "Final dress rehearsal. Let's get it done."

Kids untangled themselves from groups and re-assembled in other groups like a flock of swifts in the fall, magically sensing where they were supposed to be.

It wasn't until the final shuffle was finished that

Harlow noticed the glaring absence. "Where's Nevaeh?"

"She wasn't at school today," Vander said.

"Should I be concerned?"

"Her aunt called in, which is a first," Vander explained. "She said Nevaeh had a headache."

Harlow checked her watch. "I can run out and pick her up, but that would get us started late. We could ask Pete to go pick her up."

Vander shook his head. "If she's not at school, she's not allowed to participate in after-school activities."

"Really? That's a thing?"

"That's a thing."

"And we're going to follow that rule?"

"Yes."

Harlow sighed. "Fine. I mean, she's solid. She'll be brilliant tomorrow night." Worry played across her brow. Then she raised her chin and glanced around at the kids in attendance. "Let's do this! We've got one shot tomorrow, and I want it to be perfect."

As much as he had never wanted a full-blown, over-the-top holiday extravaganza, he had to admit, this one was extraordinary. Harlow and her mini bosses had created the perfect evening. They sang together as a group, individually and in pairs. Students shared their holiday traditions; some of the stories were funny, some sweet and all of them heartfelt. As the final rehearsal wound toward its end, Vander couldn't help but be incredibly proud of their work.

He'd never imagined pulling off anything like this, but here he was, playing music onstage with a group of kids, having the time of his life.

Falling for a woman so different from anyone he'd ever imagined loving.

"Okay, this is Nevaeh's number—"

Harlow was cut off as Taylor said, "She is literally so good. Like I can't even."

"Right?" her sister concurred.

Vander gazed Harlow. She'd helped Nevaeh find her voice and connect with her peers. Harlow held eye contact with him, reminding him he'd had his part in Nevaeh's journey too. They'd done all of this together.

Vander glanced at her lips. She wanted to talk after the rehearsal, and he did too. He also had high hopes of finding some more mistletoe.

"Mr. V, you're going to sing, right?"

Vander snapped out of his thoughts at Mav's voice. "I'm not gonna sing—"

"You have to!" Ilsa said. "It will make the pageant."

"Everyone wants to hear it," Mason said.

"What would I sing?" Vander asked.

"Literally anything," Taylor said.

"A lot of people enjoy Abba," Mav noted. And while the kids laughed at his call back to Loretta, Vander got the feeling that Mav wasn't entirely joking.

Harlow turned on him with a grin. "Please?"

That was all it took. A bright smile from the

woman he was falling in love with, and he'd play every love song in the books.

He gazed back at her. At this point, was there anything he wasn't willing to do for her?

THE LAST NOTES of "Winter Wonderland" filled the room, and still no one moved. The kids were as mesmerized by Vander's performance as she was. No one even wanted to applaud because that would mean the song was over.

He had an incredible gift. Wilson was right. Harlow felt like she owed it not only to Wilson and Vander to help him pursue this gift, but to the world.

Vander looked up from his guitar, then at the students on either side of the dais who were staring at him in stunned silence. "Isn't this where you all come back onstage, and we invite the audience to sing the final song with us?"

The kids sprang into action, filing onstage to take their places. Tomorrow night they would invite the audience to join in the final song, and Harlow could imagine everyone on their feet in the hall, singing together. Filled with joy and goodwill.

Her holiday pageant was perfect.

Harlow burst into applause. Tonight, she was the only one in the audience, but if she could clap for all of southeastern Oregon she would.

"Great job!" she cried. "That. Was. Spectacular. This is the greatest holiday pageant ever, in the history of holiday pageants, which I feel like is super old. We rocked it."

The students buzzed around the room, packing up but not really wanting to leave. They were caught up in the magic they'd created, and Harlow didn't blame them for wanting the feeling to last.

She did, however, want them to leave.

"You sure you don't need any more help?" Taylor asked.

Harlow met Vander's eye. Rehearsal had been over for a good twenty minutes, and the kids still lingered, amped up with the knowledge that the pageant was going to be fabulous. She was also amped up but for an entirely different reason.

"We're good," Vander said.

"See you tomorrow!" Harlow waved at the girls. They slipped out of the ballroom, and the door fell shut behind them.

She was alone with Vander.

No words were spoken, but a lot was communicated as Vander crossed the room to her. His gaze ran to her hair, across her face, to her earrings and settled on her lips. He glanced down and kicked the toe of his boot against the parquet flooring.

"That went well," she said.

"It did."

"Thank you for agreeing to sing. People are going to love it."

He shrugged. "People are gonna love the whole thing. The kids really stepped up under your leadership. I think you got your revenge."

She laughed. "Just when I don't need it anymore."

"You mean that?"

"Yeah. I mean sure, I can be stubborn about things, but I'm not stupid stubborn."

"No, but people around here were treating you unfairly. It took a lot of courage and grace for you to give Pronghorn a second chance."

She held his gaze. "You made that a little easier for me."

He reached out and took her right hand, then her left. His rough fingers slid along hers and he smiled. "How are your houseguests doing?"

"They're having a great time." Harlow paused. She felt a little trepidation about bringing this up. But she knew Wilson, and the next time he saw Vander, *he* would bring it up. She didn't want him to spring it on Vander, then have him say no as a reaction. "Wilson would like to talk to you further."

He tightened his grasp on her fingers. "About my intentions toward you?"

He took her breath away. Literally gave her one smile, and she couldn't breathe…nor was she particularly interested in breathing. Just kisses.

"About *you*."

Confusion rearranged his features. "What does he want to talk to me about?"

"About coming to Nashville. Recording a demo."

Vander threw his head back and laughed. The bright sound filled the room.

She tugged at his hand. "I'm not being funny. I'm serious."

He looked into her eyes. "I'm not interested."

Disappointment rattled in her chest. She tried again. "You have a gift, Vander. You should share it."

He stared down at the floor. His eyebrow twitched, like she'd annoyed him by pointing out the obvious. That one subtle movement threw off her confidence.

Did they not have the type of friendship where they could encourage each other to take risks?

Or maybe he didn't want an excuse to come visit her in Nashville. Maybe this was just a holiday flirtation to him?

She pulled in a short breath and tried to redirect. "To be clear, I'm not talking about us, I'm talking about an opportunity for you."

He dropped her hands, a ribbon of confusion flexing across his face. "I don't want that opportunity."

"What would you say to Nevaeh if she didn't want the opportunity to go to school?"

"That's a totally different situation. I don't want to get onstage and have people judge me."

"But isn't that what teaching is?"

He scoffed. Harlow gave in to her urge to argue. If she was going to be hurt, fine, she could at least be right in the process. "I don't understand your hesitation here. One conversation with Wilson couldn't hurt."

"It could hurt." He placed a hand over his chest, as though it already did. "I work twelve-hour days as it is."

"I know, but—" Harlow stopped herself before she could suggest he might be able to give up teaching if a music career worked out. He was an incredible educator, she couldn't forget that. "Okay. Sorry. I'm sorry I brought it up."

That was a lie. She wasn't sorry she brought it up, rather deeply disappointed by his reaction. Her imagination had taken this…whatever it was about a hundred steps further than Vander had. She was trying to find a way their two worlds could fit together. His first response was to laugh, his second was to get annoyed.

Vander slipped his palms under hers, cradling her hands once again. Hope launched under his gaze. His voice was soft but final as he said, "I can't be someone I'm not, Harlow."

"That's not what I was suggesting."

"What are you suggesting?"

She gazed into his beautiful eyes, willing him to read her thoughts like he'd done so many times before.

I want you to be part of my world too.

He readjusted his grip on her hands.

Harlow drew in a breath. "You are a talented musician. Last night was magical. You and Trey playing off one another as Carol and Maria brainstormed lyrics, I was spellbound."

Vander's eyes softened, and she smiled at him. He seemed to finally get it.

"What if that type of creativity could open up a new life for you?"

His expression fell. Harlow recognized her mistake instantly, desperate to press rewind and swallow the hurtful words.

Before she could apologize, Vander raised his chin and asked, "What's wrong with this life?"

Harlow's throat constricted. Vander studied her face as though searching for her answer. Then he dropped her hands and ran his fingers through his hair.

"Nothing is wrong with this life," she said. Or lied, again.

"Because I've been pretty happy here, and I'm not looking to get away from Pronghorn."

Right. He wasn't looking to leave Pronghorn, leaving them with zero options for the future. "Okay. Clear. Forget I said anything. You do you. Good night." Harlow turned for the door.

"Hold on there." Vander caught up with her, then took her hand.

Which made her cry, which made her mad.

"Don't cry," he said. "Please don't cry."

This was *so* not how she wanted this conversation to go.

"I don't understand what's happening," Vander said. "I don't want to pursue a career in music, and that shouldn't be a big surprise."

"That's not what this is about."

"What is it about?" The panic in his voice sparked the tiniest flame of hope.

Harlow blew out a breath. *What is it? It's about my stupid fantasy life. It's about me thinking this relationship could go somewhere.*

Instead she squared her shoulders and flipped her hair back. She stuffed every emotion back down, like she'd learned to do as a child in this unforgiving tiny town. "I just thought it would be fun to see you in Nashville every once in a while. If that's not you, it's not you. Sorry I brought it up." She dropped his hand and headed for the door.

"You're going back to Nashville?"

VANDER'S HEART SCRAMBLED in his chest, desperate to get to Harlow before he messed this up irrevocably. They'd been talking, then they were arguing, and now she was crying. He got so tangled up he didn't know where this was going, but he was desperate to fix it.

He tried again. "You're going back for good?"

Harlow stopped, but she didn't turn around. Her voice was almost steady as she said, "That's where I live."

"But I thought—"

He didn't finish the sentence. What had he been thinking? That she was going to ditch her career and move back to a town that had never provided enough opportunity for her? No, he never expected her to leave her life for him. He didn't *want* her to, Harlow was doing important work in Nashville.

But, well, she had pretty good internet out at her place. Some people did work remotely.

"You thought what?" she asked.

Her back was still to him, but she'd opened a door to more conversation. He needed to slip in, say the right thing and not leave mud all over the place.

"I thought we were gonna try…this."

She tucked a strand of hair around her ear, the turquoise in the earrings he'd given her catching the sparkle lights strung above them. Her shoulders rose and fell as she pulled in a breath. "And what would that look like?"

Words like *ranch* and *music* and *mistletoe* bumped through his skull, but he knew those concepts weren't the basis of a good relationship. Not the practical type of commitment she was hoping for anyway.

Vander took a step toward her. He had to find the words, but the more panicked he got, the harder it was to speak.

What *would* their relationship look like? He knew what it would feel like—freedom and possibility. But maybe she already had those things in her life. He didn't ever want her to think she had to make herself smaller to fit in his world.

Harlow finally turned around, her face composed, her armor back in place. "Look. I'm sorry. I'm way overemotional, and I'm not expressing myself well. We both know we're not a good fit, so let's just leave it at that."

He didn't know anything like that. Maybe they weren't an obvious fit, but from their work on the pageant, he felt like they were the only fit. "So, what...what are you saying?" Did she not want to even try? He'd been falling in love and was ready to figure this out. And now she was ready to walk because he didn't want to have a conversation with her producer friend?

"I'm saying good-night." Another tear slipped

down Harlow's face. She folded her arms tightly around her chest, like she was holding herself together.

"I don't want to say good-night." He wanted to wrap her in *his* arms, kiss her, play the new verse he'd written to "Winter Wonderland," inspired by dragging a massive tree back to her house.

"Let's drop it for tonight." Her voice was flat, even as she had to swallow to get the words out.

"Harlow, no. I'm not going to drop it." Frustration flared in his chest. He might be having trouble finding the right words, but she didn't want to talk at all.

"You should get some rest." She reached up and ran her fingers along her earring. "You're playing tomorrow, and then you have the solo, and I know that's a big ask. I'm going to leave. We can talk tomorrow after the pageant."

You have the solo.

That was what mattered here. His music, her friends, a packed house. Vander gazed at Harlow. He took in her expensive coat, her shiny hair, the polished leather boots.

Was she expecting him to narrow his life to fit in her world? Did she just want a musician on hand, her own personal artist to follow her to Nashville and impress her friends?

Maybe that was all she'd ever seen in him, the music.

And that finally shook the words out of him.

"Actually, no. I'm not gonna sing in the pageant. This is about the kids, not me."

Harlow's brow furrowed. "The kids want you to sing."

Wow. Good to know now, rather than later when he was even more tangled up in love with her. All she wanted was the tiny slice of him that fit in her world.

If she didn't want all of him, she wasn't getting any.

"No. I'm good. I give this community a lot. These kids get my best every day." He turned away, straightening a row of seats that didn't need his attention. If he had to get up there and play guitar in front of the community tomorrow as he accompanied the kids, he was not gonna force himself to sing. Not for Harlow or anyone. "I think everyone can live without one song from me."

"But, Vander—"

"But what?" He stared at her. "I think I have a little more to offer this world than my guitar."

She blinked, like maybe he might have hit a nerve. She glanced at the dais, the sparkle lights around the room giving off a soft light in the warm glow of the chandeliers.

"I don't like being in the spotlight, Harlow."

She shook her head, incredulous with the non-revelation. "Because you wouldn't want to draw undue attention to yourself. Classic Pronghorn," she muttered.

His vision blurred. This felt so unfair. She was picking and choosing what to focus on, like a student snapping pictures of him and posting them online, out of context. He couldn't control the narrative. "Not every problem has its roots in Pronghorn." He pushed a chair into place, bumping another and messing up the already even spacing of the row.

She scoffed in disbelief, shaking her head. "Okay, Vander," she said, sarcasm rolling through her words. "I'll try a little harder with Pronghorn, how's that for you? Because *my* best doesn't seem to be near enough for you."

"You know that's not what I meant."

The legs of a chair got caught up with another, Vander's frustration compounding the problem. He spoke without thinking, just a desire for her to understand the disappointment roiling within him. "Why are you even here? If you dislike this town so much, why'd you agree to the pageant?"

"I was sentenced to it because my foreman, and assistant foreman, couldn't keep my cattle in their pasture."

Her words rang out through the ballroom, her anger and hurt and willful misunderstanding of his intentions filling the gorgeous space.

"That's not fair." Vander ran his hands through his hair. Nothing felt fair. Harlow plucked meaning out of his words, while he could barely get a sentence out. "This is all so complicated—"

"It is complicated," she snapped. "*I'm* complicated. I don't know why I even try with this town." Vander attempted to interrupt her, but she continued, "You take everything I have to give, no thanks, no understanding of what I've accomplished. Nothing. Just a reminder that I don't belong."

"I didn't say that."

"You don't have to."

Her gaze met his, all the hurt and shame of her childhood raw in her eyes. Everything she was afraid of was communicated in that moment: not having community, not being loved unconditionally for who she was, not being worthy of such a love.

Then she blinked, severing the connection.

"This was never going to work," she said, more to herself than him. "I'm gonna head home. You have the pageant under control, so I'll leave you to it."

Desperation clawed in his chest. She couldn't miss the pageant; she couldn't walk away like this. He opened his mouth to speak, but the pain in his chest made it impossible to get out the words she seemed to be waiting for.

Finally, Harlow sighed, tears now falling freely. "It's probably best if we don't have to see each other again. It's easier that way. More practical." She offered him a sad smile, one last chance to stop her.

The emotions compounded in his chest, layered so tightly he couldn't separate the love from the pain.

Then she brushed her hair back and walked out the door.

Leaving Vander trapped in his head, trying to find the right, or any, words to make her stay.

CHAPTER FIFTEEN

"BYE! HAVE FUN!" Harlow waved at her guests as they piled into the luxury van with the Squatch Watch logo splashed across the back. She'd hired a service to take them on a Sasquatch expedition. It was a fun, gimmicky sightseeing tour, something she generally did with her guests. They'd be pleasantly entertained, see some local sights and, most important, they would be gone all day.

Looking for Sasquatch was just a hook, but if you paid extra your guests "found" the elusive Bigfoot.

Even if every Oregonian knew Sasquatch lived up the Mackenzie River and only showed himself when he wanted to.

She closed the door, watching the van roll away. When it was good and gone, she finally allowed the tears to fall, blurring her vision as she made her way to the sofa and wrapped herself in a soft blanket.

She had really blown her chance with Vander. Top notch self-sabotage.

And here she was, stuck in this perfect room. Everything chosen with care. Her perfect, curated lifestyle on display for no one.

Then Vander, with dreamy eyes and dust on his boots, had showed up and changed everything.

Harlow pulled a sleeve of Nutter Butters off the table and fished one out of the package. She stared at the peanut-shaped cookie for a minute, then dropped it on the table.

Was this what misery looked like? Disinterest in cookies.

Harlow ran her fingers through her hair, pulling at the roots, forcing herself to focus on the source of pain in the hope that that might help her move forward. She constructed this roadblock with Vander. She could own that. She didn't know how to love someone who lived here when her life was in Nashville. And rather than let this play out for a month or so, or heaven forbid, have an honest discussion with Vander, she picked the one thing she knew he didn't want to do and let that be the proof of his feelings.

So yeah, that turned out as expected.

Unexpected, was how little he had to say on the matter. How he reminded her that she didn't fit in. How she was something he could let go of so easily. She was mad at herself for pushing the argument with Vander, but she did have a point. It wouldn't kill him to step out of his comfort zone and let his talent shine. It was the same ask he had of his students.

A fresh wash of tears splashed cold on her cheeks. Maybe she *was* meant for a relationship of convenience, because pain like this was not something she was interested in feeling ever again.

Harlow wiped her tears with the corner of the blanket, then stood. This was ridiculous. It was one o'clock, and she hadn't even put on shoes yet.

She needed to face the truth. He wasn't feeling

what she was. She'd fallen for a gorgeous cowboy, a soulful musician, a brilliant teacher. And while she could forgive herself for her feelings, she was annoyed that she'd let herself imagine he was the one.

Vander wasn't going to work out for her, and that was too bad because she really liked him. But she wasn't a broken-heart girl. She was supposed to fall for a man like Trey. Or if not fall for him, like and respect him enough to be half of a power couple with him.

Harlow gazed out the window, trying to imagine standing in a flurry of snowflakes with Trey, the cold flakes landing with a soft hush as they gazed out at the valley.

Trey talking nonstop about the one time he met Luke Bryan and how Luke said he liked his style.

Ugh. No.

Just, no.

Tears welled up again, the pain splitting her heart fresh and new. Harlow perched on the arm of the sofa and covered her face with her hands. She was never going to get this right. She *wanted* unconditional love, she wanted to be family for others. But she didn't fit anywhere.

Harlow grabbed the edge of the blanket and pulled it over her as she curled back up on the couch. She closed her eyes and nestled into the pain she didn't want to acknowledge.

She didn't know how long she'd been there when the slow whine of an overworked motor slipped into her awareness. The snowmobile.

Harlow launched from the sofa and ran into the foyer, pausing only a half a second to acknowledge that she was wearing sweats. Okay, fine, she was wearing a cream-colored Eres ribbed lounge set, but still.

Harlow threw open the door to find…not Vander.

A small blond woman in argyle stalked past her into the house.

"Hi…?"

"You and I need to have a serious conversation," Luci said, then gave Harlow a once-over. "Are you wearing cashmere joggers?"

"I am."

"You look amazing. Also, please stop breaking Vander's heart. It's killing me."

Harlow blinked. "Um…?"

Luci strode into the living room, then picked up the soft blanket and draped it over the ottoman.

"Seriously—" Luci settled in a chair and folded her hands "—what did you say to him?"

"What did *I* say to *him*?"

"Oh. I see. This was mutual stupidity then, was it?"

Harlow gave in and flopped onto the sofa. "Is Vander upset?"

"Is he upset? He's been playing morose heartbreak music for the last twenty-four hours. Mateo is making homemade mac and cheese with barbecue beef on top."

Harlow furrowed her brow. "What relevance does Mateo's cooking have to this situation?"

Luci waved her hand. "It's a thing. My point is, you are amazing, and Vander isn't the best communicator on earth. And right now, he thinks you don't want to ever see him again. Can you think of what you may have said that led him to believe that?"

"Something along the lines of 'I never want to see you again.'"

Luci crossed the room and sat down on the sofa next to Harlow. She carefully placed an arm around her shoulder.

Harlow buried her face in her hands, as though she could hold in the tears, hold in the disappointment. Her voice cracked as she said, "It's not going to work."

"If you don't work at it, you're right, it won't."

"We're too different."

"In some ways, sure. You're like a highway, blasting your path through the world. Vander is more of a river, powerful but in a quiet way."

"So we're never going to work," Harlow confirmed.

"Rivers and highways *always* go together. Seriously, who taught you human geography?"

"The point is, I don't fit anywhere, with anyone. I love my work in Nashville, but I have to come home to this land to refresh. I love it here, but it doesn't matter what I do. I'll always be a misfit."

"Harlow, that's simply not true. Yes, your success makes other people uncomfortable sometimes. That's life. But you are the first to shine a light on other people's gifts."

"It's different with the kids in the pageant. I fight for artists, and if I hear a voice like Nevaeh's, I'm going to champion it. And Mav is meant for a career in law—I'm not gonna pretend I can't see it."

Luci shook her head. "I'm not just talking about the kids. Everyone jokes about Angie's cooking, but you're able to pinpoint what it is about her food that everyone actually likes."

Harlow swallowed, then nodded. Okay. She did *a* good thing.

Luci continued, "And you made a point of encouraging Mac's entrepreneurial spirit. And let's not even forget your willingness to call out Raquel as an artist. You shine so brightly, and yeah, it's intimidating. Like, right now I feel like I need to replace all my loungewear."

Harlow gave her a look. "Do you actually wear loungewear? Or lounge?"

"Well, no. But I keep a set all the same." Luci wrapped her arm more tightly around Harlow's shoulder. "My point is you are a lot. And Vander is so tangled up in his feelings for you he can't express it or figure out how a relationship with you could work. His reaction was just that, a reaction."

Harlow wanted to believe, but the logic was a little shaky.

"If he's not expressing his feelings, how do you know he has them? Because from my point of view, I interpreted his feelings as more than they were."

Luci leveled a look at her. "If I hear 'Yesterday' by the Beatles one more time, I will smash that guitar."

Harlow gave a dry laugh, even as she reached for Luci's arm to signal that no one, other than Vander, should ever touch his guitar.

"Seriously, I'm here to help you. But I'm also here because I cannot hear that song one more time."

Harlow tucked a lock of hair around her ear.

Luci continued speaking, "Vander wants to be loved for who he is—a brilliant, caring introvert who happens to have a few musical gifts. I suspect you do love him for who he is."

Harlow let the words sink in. What was it about Vander that drew her? His kindness, his powerful, gentle spirit that did so much good in the world. She was attracted to the part of him that didn't want attention, that was quiet in a very loud world. Music was a part of him, to share as he chose. Vander wanted to rescue horses, be a science teacher and a dad. And if Harlow were honest, those were some seriously attractive goals in a man.

"He's really playing 'Yesterday'?"

"When it's not Bruno Mars's 'When I Was Your Man.'"

Harlow smiled, blinking back tears. "That's kind of cute."

"Says the person who does not live at the hotel. Seriously, it's making me hate the Beatles."

"You're not allowed to hate the Beatles."

"Then do me a solid and put an end to this." Luci stood and tugged at her hand.

Harlow remained on the sofa. "It's all so complicated. My life, and this town, and I have these

guests. The idea of showing up at the pageant…
I don't know. I get so tired of trying sometimes."

Luci readjusted her grip on Harlow's hand. "Me
too."

The words shook Harlow out of her own thoughts.
What was it Luci got tired of trying to do?

Luci seemed to feel her curiosity and raised her
chin. "But then again, what else are we gonna do?"

Harlow gave in and let Luci pull her off the sofa.
"I'm not going to the pageant, though."

"Ugh! Then why am I even here?"

"Because you care?" Harlow guessed.

Luci perched on the arm of the sofa. "Of course,
I care. But you remember that conversation we had
two seconds ago about how hard it is to try sometimes? Particularly when I'm trying to help a very
private man who can't hear me over his guitar and,
forgive me, a super stubborn lawyer who's good at
arguing."

Luci pulled off her tortoiseshell-rimmed glasses
and retrieved a shammy cloth from her purse, rubbing at an offending smudge. There it was again,
the satisfied concentration that made her seem so
familiar.

Harlow studied Luci's jaw, her cheekbones, the
slight ski jump to her nose, the dimple that occasionally flexed in her left cheek.

For the first time she noticed the slightest line of
darker brown at her part. Luci's summery blond hair
was such a part of her look and seemed so authentic, it hadn't occurred to Harlow that it was dyed.

She glanced at her ears and saw the same, tiny bit of darker hair growing out.

And an almost imperceptible scar at the apex of her ear.

"Luci—"

She looked up and locked eyes with Harlow. The memory rushed back as though it happened yesterday. A little girl in orange, staring up at her with curiosity as Harlow explained the world outside of Pronghorn.

Harlow raised her hand and touched her own ear at the same spot. Luci read the gesture, then slid her glasses back on, obscuring the child with the big questions. She held eye contact with Harlow, then said quietly, "Vander is not the only one who appreciates his privacy."

They stared at each other for a long moment, then Luci glanced out the window. "I'm really glad I've had the chance to get to know you. You are as fabulous as I always imagined you'd be."

Their phones pinged on the coffee table, breaking the connection.

"The internet is amazing around here," Luci said, reaching for her phone. Harlow didn't move. "Don't you want to see who it is?"

"Vander doesn't use a cell phone," Harlow reminded her.

"Right, and he's too busy being a bummer." Luci glanced at her phone, as though she and Harlow had never shared a single connection about their past. Then her face fell.

"What is it?"

She turned the phone so Harlow could read a text from Willa.

Nevaeh didn't show up for call at four o'clock. When I reached out to the family, I was told she was sick and not coming. Does Harlow know anything more?

Harlow stared at the text, then grabbed her own phone to see a similar message from Willa. She straightened and brushed her hair off her shoulder. "I need to get dressed. I have my faults, but if there's one thing I know how to do, it's fight for an artist."

"Mr. V?" Mav appeared at Vander's elbow, seemingly out of nowhere. *That kid.* "Where am I supposed to go when Ilsa sings her song?"

"I told you," Taylor snapped. "You exit off the dais and stand behind the tree."

"But I can't see from behind the tree."

"This isn't about you." Taylor threw her arms up "Ugh! Where's Harlow?"

The question of the hour.

Vander never really thought she wouldn't show up. He'd had a hundred doom-and-gloom thoughts over the last twenty-four hours, but none of them included her missing the pageant she'd worked so hard on.

What had he thought? That he could be so hurtful, and she'd somehow intuit he never meant any of it? That if he was sad enough, she'd feel it and come solve everything?

Okay, given her talent at doing just that, it wasn't a completely unreasonable expectation. What he hadn't figured into the equation was what *he* needed to do here. He'd beaten himself up for fighting with her, well and good, but that wasn't moving them forward.

The producer was trying to make money; that was his job. Most people would have jumped at the chance, but Vander never had been most people. And Harlow wasn't like anyone he'd ever met either.

Right now, he had a choice. He could sit and sulk, or he could take action and fill the audience with joy and love and give them a high that would last a week, like Harlow wanted for these kids. Even if it was gonna require some multitasking, which was not his finest skill.

Vander approached the dais. "Mav, you have to stand behind the tree while Ilsa performs. You're too tall, and you'll block the audience's view."

"But I like watching her song. It's pretty."

"You listen to a song," Taylor reminded him. "You don't watch it."

"I can watch a song if I want to."

"Mav." Vander rested a hand on his shoulder. "You can watch the song from the side, all right?"

"Fine."

"And where is Nevaeh?" Taylor checked the watch she'd taken to wearing, in emulation of Harlow. "She's the star. She should have been here forty minutes ago."

Vander swallowed, then glanced around the room. Nevaeh's family had called her in sick again today. Oliver was hamming it up, trying to get Antithesis's attention. Mav was, once again, questioning the use of reindeer for sled transportation, saying that flying sled dogs would be more practical.

Could this get any more chaotic?

"Helllllo, Proooonghorn Players!" Loretta's voice came booming over her bullhorn.

Yes. Yes, it could get more chaotic.

"Loretta, you're early," Vander noted.

"Well, I'm singing a big finale, of course."

The room silenced. The pageant was beautiful, down to the last detail. Every song, every speech, every moment carefully orchestrated.

"Nope," Vander said. "No way."

Loretta looked shocked, then confused.

"You can't sing the finale," Vander said. "Because I am."

CHAPTER SIXTEEN

HARLOW WAS DRESSED, made up, hair done, fabulous boots on and out the door to go get her star performer.

Just as her guests pulled up.

Her guests.

How had she forgotten that one, tiny little detail?

Harlow stared at the midsize passenger van, trying to make sense of what she saw.

The side window rolled down.

"We found him!" Wilson cried, pointing to a person in a Sasquatch suit waving jovially from the second row.

"Did ya now?" Harlow managed a smile.

The tour guide, wearing Realtree camo with an embroidered patch reading Squatch Watch over the pocket, winked at her. That's right, she *had* paid for the deluxe package.

"Amazing. Hey, I need to—"

"And we're taking him to the holiday pageant!"

Harlow turned a questioning look back at the driver/tour guide. He pointed to the bright red sign reading:

Tips! Never expected, always appreciated.

Oh, no.

"We thought the kids would get a kick out of it."

Oh, no, no, no, no.

Harlow closed her eyes. If the unspoken rule around here was don't draw undue attention to yourself, showing up at a holiday pageant with a nineties country star, four other Nashville insiders and Sasquatch was a major offense.

She'd worked so hard with these kids, taken what was supposed to be her vacation and filled it with teen drama, helped to create a beautiful show all to make this town see her for who she was. All of that would pale in comparison to bringing fake-Sasquatch to the pageant.

Inside the van the tour guide was handing out Santa hats. Squatch put his on at a jaunty angle.

Harlow squared her shoulders and brushed her hair back. This wasn't about her. It never had been. By now, most people in town saw her for who she was—hardworking, caring and generally over-dressed by Pronghorn standards. There would always be some people who thought she was showing off when she slipped up and used fancy words like *pasta* rather than *noodles*. But there were people in Nashville who misjudged her too.

And right now, there was one citizen of this town who needed the limelight, and Harlow wasn't about to let that girl miss her chance.

Harlow took determined steps toward the van. "Then I guess it will be Bigfoot's first Christmas." She opened the door and climbed in. "We do need to make one little stop along the way."

The van headed down her drive and out onto the

gravel road. Clouds overhead dissipated, and moonlight streamed across the valley.

The mood in the car was jovial, until she directed the driver to turn off onto the Daneses' property. Even Sasquatch grew quiet as everyone took in the collection of dilapidated trailers and mobile homes on blocks.

"Where are we?" Carol asked.

Trey gazed at the old pile of wooden furniture and junk at the center of the property. "And why?"

Amber Danes was out of the house before the van came to a full stop. The door to the trailer slammed behind her, echoing across the property.

Harlow climbed out of the van and carefully slid the door shut.

"I have had just about enough of you, Harlow Jameson." Amber launched herself down the steps.

"You and everyone else around here."

"I'm not joking. Nevaeh's sick. She's not going to some pageant so everyone in town can feel sorry for her and you can look like you're savin' her."

"No one in town feels sorry for her. This isn't about saving anyone. It's about putting on a good show."

"It's about you." Amber pointed at Harlow's chest.

"It's about the kids."

The hinges on the door groaned in the cold, quiet night. Nevaeh stepped into the starlight, then descended the steps and headed toward the van. Her voice was quiet but steady as she said, "Auntie, I want to go."

"Harlow's just gonna get your hopes up," Amber snapped at her niece.

"Where else should her hopes be?" Harlow's voice rang out in the icy air. The door of another trailer opened, and a couple in their forties stood in the doorway, a dog barking behind them.

"I want to go to the pageant," Nevaeh said, louder, planting her feet wide. "And I'd like you to come too."

An elderly man appeared outside of the original home on the property, then a woman, presumably his wife, followed. "What's this about a pageant?" he asked.

Amber glanced at the couple, then back at Harlow. "I don't give you permission to drive my niece in that van."

"What kind of legal action do you propose if I do?" Harlow asked. "Are you her guardian?"

Amber's expression moved from one of panic to anger. "Don't think you fool me, Harlow." Her voice was low and perfectly clear to everyone on the compound as she spoke. "You're just some rich lawyer from the city who never fit in around here. You're no better than me. You think you can walk onto our property and get our girl's head full of dreams?"

The rest of the Danes family had now gathered in the watery light. They stared at Harlow and examined the van with curiosity.

"You're right." Harlow nodded, accepting the truth as Amber saw it. "That's exactly who I am and what I'm doing. Now, would you please get in the van? We have a concert to attend, and I know Nevaeh would like you all to be there." She looked pointedly at Amber. "Especially you."

The family stood in silence, with the exception of a dog barking from inside a trailer.

The older man stepped forward. "Is that Wilson Range in your van?"

"It is."

He looked at his wife. She glanced at Amber. Harlow waited for someone to mention the guy in the Sasquatch suit.

"Then I want to change my shirt." The man shuffled back toward the trailer. "I'll be right out."

The Danes family scattered into various abodes to re-robe themselves. Amber remained in the yard, tears of anger and frustration welling up in her eyes.

Harlow crossed to her, feeling the uneven dirt beneath the soles of her Italian leather boots.

Amber crossed her arms more tightly around her middle.

"This is going to be good," Harlow said.

Amber twisted to look behind her, then over Harlow's shoulder at the van.

"I don't want people to laugh at her." Amber's voice was barely a whisper as she said, "I don't want people to pity her."

Harlow couldn't begin to imagine the hell school must have been for Amber. Forced to show up, then chastised for not magically picking up the skills she needed. Amber was protecting her darling, talented niece from a place where her own dreams and ambitions had been crushed.

"It's changed, Amber. It really has. Vander and the other teachers respect and care for Nevaeh and all their students."

Amber gazed at Nevaeh where she stood, resolute, next to the van. "She's a pretty good singer, I guess?"

"Yeah. She's our star."

"She's our star too," Amber reminded her.

Harlow gestured to the sky, stars hanging low enough they felt easily within reach. "Stars have plenty of light for all of us."

Amber held Harlow's eye for a moment, then nodded. "I'm gonna go put on my good jeans."

"Great." Harlow was filled with gratitude and joy. But also some impatience. "Please hurry."

In minutes, about half the Danes family had made it into the van. The others loaded up in a truck.

Nevaeh was quivering with energy as she buckled in next to Sasquatch. He patted her arm.

She looked up in surprise, as though she'd been so distracted with her family drama she just now realized he was there. Then she smiled at him.

"I like your hat. It looks good with your fur."

IT WAS SIX FIFTEEN, and the ballroom had been packed since five thirty. Harlow wasn't there. Nevaeh wasn't there. But Loretta Lazarus sure was, and if they stalled any longer, she would get up on the dais and start singing or selling real estate, possibly both.

Vander's stomach sank as he scanned the ballroom. Every last seat on the floor and in the balcony was taken, with the exception of the front row. Taylor was aggressively protecting those chairs for Harlow's guests, save two prime seats she'd offered to the elderly Mrs. Moran and her best friend, Flora Weston. Otherwise, she had eighteen chairs reserved for a group of six people who were clearly not coming.

It didn't take a lot of guesses to figure out whose fault that was.

Vander was startled by a gentle arm around his shoulder. Willa and the rest of his coworkers had gathered around him.

Great. A pep talk.

"You've done a wonderful job with this, Vander."

He tilted his head, debating her point with as much energy as he had at the moment. He'd done a great job of hurting an incredible woman and ruining any slim chance he'd ever had with her.

"Honestly, dude, look around you." Mateo gestured to the crowd.

Vander dutifully scanned the ballroom. The usual suspects were upright in their chairs. Pete, Mac, Today's Moment, folks from the Open Hearts Community, all the international students who weren't in the pageant. Even Aida's German shepherd, Greg, sat politely, staring at him in expectation. Mike, the actual foreman at Jameson Ranch, was there with his wife, who seemed to be recovering well. Angie was there, arms crossed, leaning back in her chair wearing a—

Vander pulled his head back in confusion.

"What's wrong?" Tate asked.

"Is Angie...? Is she wearing a scarf?"

The teachers turned their heads in unison, like a mob of meerkats.

"She's wearing a scarf and *a dress*!" Luci exclaimed, a little too loudly, then finished with a whisper, "Nobody look," just to make sure everyone stared harder.

Vander forced his eyes off the unlikely sight and scanned the rest of the crowd.

The type of details Harlow would have already noticed and categorized floated out to him. Pete wore an old leather blazer that looked like it had been the height of style in 1978. Raquel sported a black turtleneck, enlivened by an assortment of her own jewelry. With a few silver threads running through her hair and dramatic turquoise, she looked elegant, even beautiful.

Everyone did. The Pronghornians had gotten all dressed up.

The pageant had revived the old ballroom, a symbol of the glamor and elegance that had once been a part of this town. Everyone had dressed for the occasion.

These are your good old days, as a distressed piece of plywood might suggest.

"You did this, Vander," Tate said. "I know you

didn't want to, but Loretta never would have gotten the idea if it hadn't been for your playing. I know you prefer your privacy, but these kids and these families are never going to forget this."

"It's been fun," he admitted. In fact, it had been so fun, he wasn't opposed to doing it again someday.

A flash of yellow caught his eye as someone moved toward the dais, her loud voice calling out, "If Santa Claus is coming to town, he needs to step on a reindeer."

Who knew what would happen if Loretta made it to the stage?

Vander was the only one who could shut it down.

He grabbed his guitar and cut her off, striding onto the dais. Colter dimmed the wall sconces, so the room was lit by the sparking holiday lights and tumbleweed chandeliers. They'd planned for Harlow to do the introduction, but he was gonna have to do.

He gave the crowd a brief wave.

They roared back in approval, hooting and hollering, stamping their feet and clapping.

He paused, as he did with his students, waiting for them to quiet.

They didn't.

All of Pronghorn just kept cheering like he'd won *The Great British Bake Off* and the World Cup simultaneously.

"Quiet down!" Tate's loud voice cut through the crowd. "We can't start the show with everybody yelling."

The roar of the audience quieted but was quickly

replaced with the shutter click of phones taking pictures.

Vander looked out on an endless plain of little rectangles flashing at him, like a firefly's dating app. "Please, put your phones away. No pictures, or it will disturb the performers."

The crowd started to talk back, because of course it did.

He held out both hands, flailing for a plan. "Luci—I mean, Ms. Walker—has agreed to take pictures and share them." He glanced at Luci, hoping this was true.

She rolled her eyes and pulled out her phone.

He glanced at Mateo who was already pulling out his own device. "And Mateo is going to record the performance."

The crowd begrudgingly silenced their phones and put them away.

"And now, I present, the Pronghorn Pronghorns' Holiday Pageant." Vander gestured to the students, then retreated to his stool near the back of the stage where he would accompany the singers.

He lifted his hand to strum the first few bars of "Welcome Christmas," but a slice of light from the back of the ballroom interrupted him. The door opened, a triangle of yellow light obscuring the late-comers.

The entire community turned in their seats to stare.

Vander closed his eyes briefly, prepared himself, then looked up.

She was so beautiful and powerful, it felt like this could be the pageant right here, watching this woman claim her seat.

In the doorway, Harlow brushed her hair back. Head held high, as though there was nothing interesting or unusual about her actions, she led a group of Nashville elite, the entire Danes family, two men in stylized camo shirts with name tags and someone in a Sasquatch suit to the front row.

The only sound was Loretta whispering, "Like butter wouldn't melt in her shoe."

As they neared the dais, Harlow grinned at Nevaeh. The girl scampered over to where Taylor and Morgan excitedly greeted her. Harlow saw that her guests were settled, then took a prime seat, right in the center of the front row.

Finally, she turned her eyes on Vander.

He met her gaze, hoping she could read his feelings.

I'm sorry.

I'm falling in love with you, and that wild uncontrollable feeling scares me.

I missed you.

A relationship with you is going to take compromise, and I can't wait to start negotiations.

"Excuse me?" Raquel's voice cut through the moment. Vander blinked, then saw her tapping Sasquatch on the shoulder. "Excuse me, but I can't see a thing except *your fur*. Your torso is too long."

Squatch mimed a dramatic apology and did an

overstated Sasquatch creep to the end of the row, where he sat down next to Flora Weston.

She patted his knee, then signaled it was time for the show to start.

Vander took one last look at Harlow, trying to communicate everything he needed to.

She gave him a wry smile as she read his thoughts as clearly as if someone had pressed Play on the closed captions of his mind. She glanced down, then pressed her lips together in a smile.

Hope, and an unexpected desire to perform, shot through him.

THE PAGEANT WAS BRILLIANT.

Even by Harlow's standards, they had knocked it out of the park, past the parking garages and over the last guy hocking unauthorized merch.

The carefully orchestrated combination of personal student monologues, fun duets, moving solos and group numbers had all the feels. And even the little glitches and imperfections made it better.

Oliver's adorable story about Pete hiding a candy cane in his jacket pocket on Christmas morning had the crowd laughing, and nearly brought them to tears when Oliver pulled a candy cane out of his own jacket pocket and walked it over to his grandpa in the audience.

Mav and Antithesis described the Feast of the Sunrise, and Harlow was pretty sure there wasn't a person in the house who didn't want to try one of those lime cakes.

A rowdy rendition of "The Twelve Days of Christmas" had the audience in stitches. The group pretended to forget certain lines, throwing in items more common to Pronghorn in the place of the original gifts. Morgan hammed up "five golden rings" in a different voice every time. And all the while, Mav improvised a running commentary, confused about why his true love thought he needed so many birds and what he was going to do with one lord a'leaping, much less ten.

The show rolled on, wrapping every audience member in its magic. This was truly what live performance was meant to do, forge a connection between the audience and performers, creating an experience none of them were ever going to forget.

Then the stage cleared, leaving only Nevaeh and Vander.

Vander sat on his stool, arm draped over his guitar, and smiled encouragingly at Nevaeh. She drew in a deep breath, then stepped up to the microphone.

"Christmas is my favorite time of year at our place. Some people celebrate twelve days of Christmas, but we celebrate, like, a whole month."

The crowd chuckled, leaning forward to hear more about the Danes family. Amber sat stiffly next to Harlow, alert and on watch.

"My grandma makes the best cinnamon-and-sugar donuts. She only makes them at Christmastime, but she'll make them like, seven different times throughout the season. We never know when she's going to start, but then one morning in December, I'll wake up and smell the cinnamon, all the way from her house." Nevaeh's eyes brightened. "And that's the scent of Christmas coming."

Nevaeh spun the audience into her story, connecting them with their own memories of the scents of the holiday season. Nevaeh's grandma straightened and smiled as her husband patted her hand.

"But my favorite holiday tradition is the bonfire. On Christmas Eve, we always build a big bonfire, right in the center of our property. We burn things we no longer use or things that are broken. We do it because the fire is bright and pretty, and it's fun, but also it's like saying goodbye to the old year. Letting go of things that aren't working and making a fresh start for the next year. We sit around the fire and tell stories and sing songs. My grandpa tells the funniest stories, and even the ones I've heard before still make me laugh. And we sing. We sing every Christmas song we know." Nevaeh swallowed hard, then drew in a deep breath. "My favorite song is one my auntie Amber taught me." Nevaeh glanced at her aunt. "She has the best voice in our family, and that's saying a lot because we all love to sing."

Amber, who had been struggling to hold back tears, gave Nevaeh a warning look.

Nevaeh just grinned at her. "It's a song about how even in the coldest and darkest times, there is hope."

Nevaeh glanced at Vander. He nodded, strumming the first few bars of "In the Bleak Midwinter."

Nevaeh's voice filled the hall. The haunting, powerful song acknowledging despair and hope swept through their hearts. There was not a dry eye in the house, and next to Harlow, Amber watched in wonder as her talented niece brought the entire room to a bonfire at the center of the Daneses' property.

The last notes faded, and the audience was silent, as though if they were quiet enough the song might continue.

Then Wilson jumped to his feet, large hands applauding. The floor groaned as the rest of the room followed suit, the sound giving way to a torrent of applause.

Nevaeh gave the crowd a quick smile, then slipped off the dais.

But the applause kept coming, so eventually Nevaeh hopped back onstage. She motioned for everyone to sit down. "It's not over!" she admonished them.

Taylor joined her onstage. "Sit down. You have to see what's next."

Nevaeh nodded vigorously, backing up her friend, then they both looked meaningfully at Vander.

Vander looked like he was about to bolt.

But he stood, picked up his stool and moved it to the center of the stage.

"Well, that's a hard act to follow," he said, keeping his eyes on his guitar as he adjusted the strings. "And I'm not much of a performer."

"Bull brains!" Loretta yelled from the audience.

Vander flexed his brow in response, appreciative of the audience's chuckle.

"I'm not. I'm not real good at performing. I'm not

great about talking sometimes. I'm real bad at sharing my feelings, and sometimes even worse about figuring out what those feelings are. But I figured out one thing. I owe someone here tonight an apology."

Vander gazed at Harlow.

"You are amazing, Harlow Jameson. And sometimes that scares me. If you left, still mad at me, and I didn't take this chance, I'd never forgive myself. I'd never get over it because you are one in a million. Or technically, one in a little over eight billion, given the world's current population."

He plucked a few notes on his guitar, glancing at his fingers before refocusing on her.

"I don't know where to live or how to do this. But I know you're the person I want to figure it out with. We're gonna have some decisions to make down the road, but yours is the hand I want to be holding as we cross those bridges."

Harlow could feel all eyes of Pronghorn on her and Vander. And for once, she didn't mind a bit.

"To show you how truly sorry I am, Harlow, I'm gonna play you a song." His fingers plucked a few strings.

Harlow gave him a warming look as she recognized Justin Bieber's "Under the Mistletoe."

"Actually, I'm gonna play you a bunch of songs. For you, I have composed a medley of the worst Christmas love songs."

Harlow burst out laughing.

324   MISTLETOE AT JAMESON RANCH

Vander's face flushed. "And believe it or not, every word is true."

Vander's eyes sparkled as he played a few notes of "Merry Christmas, Baby." Harlow shook her head, but his grin grew wider.

It was the most absurd, beautiful performance. Vander played snippets of all the terrible classics, somehow making the cheesy songs feel straight from the heart. He reworded "Last Christmas" to paint himself as the one who'd messed up and added a verse to "Winter Wonderland" that included dragging a massive Christmas tree across a field. Then he switched up the tune again and gazed at her, launching into "Under the Mistletoe."

By this point, the crowd, which hadn't enjoyed a concert in Pronghorn in decades, if ever, could not be contained. The kids were bouncing off the walls cheering, the audience was on their feet dancing, everyone filled with joy and love.

Harlow sat in the front row, holding eye contact with Vander as he sang to her.

The last notes of "Under the Mistletoe" were absorbed by the crowd.

Harlow rose, drawn to Vander. As she approached the dais, he glanced up meaningfully to where a twig of mistletoe hung above him.

Not that she needed an excuse.

Vander set his guitar aside and stood, offering her a hand. If there was anyone in the room reacting as she fell into his arms, she didn't notice. This kiss was worth a little undue attention.

"Hey! The show is not over."

Harlow was brought sharply back to earth. Taylor was addressing the audience, iPad in hand, pointing at the program for the evening. "Sit back down." She turned to Harlow and Vander with just the right amount of impatience. "Final song?"

Vander cleared his throat, releasing Harlow's waist as he returned to the stool and grabbed his guitar. All the kids assembled back on the dais.

Taylor addressed the audience, "This is a sing-along." She pointed to the balcony, to the seats in the back, settled her finger on Wilson and the other Nashville visitors, then Sasquatch and finally Amber. "So sing along. Words are on the back of the program if you don't already know this song."

Harlow glanced at Vander. "This is teacher pride that I'm feeling right now, isn't it?"

"Taylor couldn't have asked for a better boss role model."

Taylor looked pointedly at Vander. "Are we gonna have some music?"

He hid a smile, then strummed his guitar, playing the opening sequence of "Put a Little Holiday in Your Heart."

And Pronghorn, never short on community participation, wasn't about to let the kids have all the fun. The audience sang along with the cheerful classic, on tune, off tune and with whatever words they had to express the joy of coming together and singing on a cold winter's night.

CHAPTER SEVENTEEN

As VANDER LIFTED his fingers from the strings, the audience let out a final rousing cheer and round of applause. Kids scattered into the crowd to find their families and friends. Nevaeh fell into a hug from her aunt, along with a reprimand for calling out Amber as the best singer in the family.

Vander set his guitar aside and secured his arms around Harlow. Her sweater was soft and sparkly, like her eyes.

"I'm feeling so charitable toward George Michael and Justin Bieber right now," she said.

"You like that?"

"Love." She placed her hand on the side of his face. "I loved it. I love you."

"It came from the heart." Vander took her hand and wrapped it in both of his, placing it against his chest so she could feel the powerful beat. He gazed at her, hoping she could read his thoughts but also realizing he needed to speak his mind too. "I adore you, Harlow. You are all I want. At Christmas, Easter, President's Day—"

"Valentine's Day?"

"Especially Valentine's Day. There's no one else I would accept a candy conversation heart from."

Harlow threw her head back and laughed.

Vander basked in the sound, aware they were surrounded by a crowd of people but in their own private chamber of conversation. He readjusted his grip around her hand, pressing it more firmly against his chest. He needed to speak, to let her know how serious he was.

"I saw you on the street, the first day. I can't even explain what happened. I knew it was you. I couldn't see how we would work out. But all I wanted to do was try."

Her breath caught.

Vander tilted his forehead to connect with hers, whispering, "I knew it was you. Harlow, please tell me you'll let it be me."

She nodded, keeping her forehead against his. "It's you."

He gave in and brushed his lips against her cheek. It was a real challenge to remember they were in a seriously crowded room right now.

"I want to be with you too." A sly grin spread across her face. "For this Christmas, last Christmas, under the mistletoe, walking in a winter wonderland."

Vander laughed.

Her gaze connected with his more seriously. "I want you for any kind of life we can work out together. We *are* different, but together we fit."

He moved closer to her. "A little like espresso and ice cream."

"We can do this," she whispered. "It's going to be a fun challenge."

Vander bent his head to hers and kissed her again, lost in the soft sweetness of her lips.

"Hello! Public venue?" Luci snapped.

How long had they been kissing?

"A long time," Luci answered his question.

"That was fantastic!" Wilson's booming voice drew their attention. He jogged over from where he was talking with Nevaeh and her family. Trey and the others joined him as he congratulated Harlow and Vander.

Wilson laid a large hand on Vander's shoulder. "Did Harlow talk to you? I hope you're interested in coming to Nashville for a visit."

Vander nodded, prepared to answer this time. "I'd love that." He looked past Wilson to Trey, "You want to do another jam session?"

"Yeah," Trey said, surprised but on board. "We got some good work done the other night."

"It was fun."

"It *was* fun, and I think we could have a Christmas hit on our hands with what we got started there."

Vander reached out to shake Trey's hand. "Sweet. Just let me know when. I'd love to sit in." He wrapped an arm around Harlow. "Obviously I'm gonna want to get over to Nashville as often as I can. A side hustle of helping out the songwriting team could go a long way toward airfare."

"Cool." Trey nodded enthusiastically. "We're all happy to come here too. If Harlow will let us crash her place."

She wound her arm around Vander's waist and gazed at him as she said, "I'd love that. I'll be spending a lot of time back here too."

Wilson looked confused for half a second, then shook his head at his daughter and her partner. "You two in on this plan to steal Vander for your song-writing team?"

"We'll do whatever it takes," Carol admitted.

"That's fair." Wilson leaned toward Vander, pointing over his shoulder toward Nevaeh. "You'll keep an eye on that one, won't you? Make sure she graduates? Because I would love to connect her with a few folks in the business when she's ready."

"We're all looking out for her," Vander assured him.

Wilson and his crew shifted away as the ballroom began to empty. Raquel greeted Wilson, then led the group into the hotel dining room for cookies, leaving the teachers and Harlow alone.

"You guys, that was awesome!" Tate said, holding up both hands for high fives.

Luci slid in next to Harlow. She pulled off her glasses and gazed up at her. "It was wonderful. Thank you for including all the kids from Open Hearts. I know it meant so much for them to be seen as a part of the community."

Vander warmed as Harlow wrapped Luci in a hug. "It was my pleasure."

"That was amazing," Colter said. "I just feel so full of... I don't know. I feel full of hope and holiday cheer."

"That was the goal," Vander said.

Loretta was suddenly at the center of the group, the way a mushroom can pop up out of nowhere.

"You know, I never really thought about how big this hotel is."

Everyone stared for a moment, confused by the segue.

"It's a hotel," Mateo noted.

"Well, I know that." Loretta rolled her eyes. "It just seemed to me there are a lot of rooms."

The teachers all looked at each other, their gazes connecting like a light-speed game of cat's cradle.

Willa tilted her head slightly, pinning Loretta with her teacher's gaze. "Where are you going with this, Loretta?"

"We have all this space. It seems like we should be using it."

"For *what*?" Luci asked.

Loretta shrugged. "Well, I'm sure I don't know. Housing?"

"Wouldn't rental space in Pronghorn cut into your real estate earnings?" Harlow asked.

Luci gave Harlow a nod of respect at that one.

But Loretta just smiled coyly. "Not if the residents are too young to buy a house."

The words hung in the air, as though they were italicized writing on a distressed piece of plywood.

"Oh, no," Mateo said.

It took Vander a moment to figure out what had Mateo so upset, then it hit him. Loretta was hatching a plan for a boarding school.

"What kind of an attitude is that?" Loretta snapped. "It's never 'oh, no.' It's 'oh, *maybe*!'" Loretta winked at Mateo, like she'd won a great battle of wits.

"I think 'no' is appropriate in this situation,"

Mateo said, with as much force as Vander had ever heard from him.

Loretta widened her eyes at the group, batted her spidery eyelashes and sashayed away to go chat up Sasquatch.

"She may be considering housing some students here," Willa said. "But I'm not gonna worry about it. There are legal reasons why it's highly unlikely she'll make it happen."

Harlow cleared her throat, reminding them that Loretta was never one to follow the letter of the law. Or even the spirit of it.

"You know what? I'm not gonna worry about it either," Luci said. She picked a Who-size piece of lint from her tartan plaid holiday top. "Christmas is only four days away. Are we still celebrating at the hotel? Or should we crash Harlow's place?"

"Let's make plans over cookies," Mateo suggested.

"Good call," Colter said. "I'm full of cheer but have plenty of room for cookies."

The group headed toward the exit.

Vander stayed right where he was and reached for Harlow's hand.

Her fingers slipped into his, a flush rose to her cheeks, and he knew she was thinking the same thing he was. They could sneak in one kiss.

She took his other hand and tugged him closer.

Vander closed his eyes, breathing in her spicy perfume, letting her block out the noise and excitement of the room. Her lips met his, and there was nothing in the world but Harlow.

EPILOGUE

"WHAT'S ALL THIS?" Vander asked, following Harlow into the living room. Sheets of paper with grids and numbers and notations, all in different colored ink were spread out on the ottoman.

"This is our calendar." She tucked a lock of hair behind her ear.

Vander kissed her in the same spot, and she laughed as he helped to tuck her hair back in place. She'd only been back from Nashville for two days on this trip, and he was going to kiss her every chance he got. No question.

"It looks like plans for a lunar space launch."

Harlow turned a dry look on him. "If we didn't have to plan our calendars with a songwriting team in mind, it would be a lot easier."

"Sorry," he said, grinning at her. "You're the one who wanted me to share my gifts." He shrugged. "There's nothing I can do about it now. They need me."

Vander had been surprised by how much he enjoyed working with Trey, Maria and Carol. Songwriting and playing with others hadn't been something he'd considered in the past. But that was life as Harlow's boyfriend: new ideas and avenues for adventure were constantly unfolding in her presence.

Harlow knelt on the carpet next to the ottoman

and shifted two pieces of the calendar. "Is it me, or is this actually going really well?"

It was going brilliantly. The last two months had been the happiest of his life.

"I feel like this is going well," she continued. "I'm managing the stress of work better now that I have more consistent blocks of time on the ranch." She focused on the calendar as a flush ran up her neck. "And time with you."

"It's been good for me too," he said. It had been great, fabulous, miraculous. As Vander opened up to Harlow, he was less inclined to mull over problems in his own head. Her perspective helped him reframe difficulties and release feelings he might have once kept bottled up. In turn, he helped her relax and let go of the intense stress of her job, allowing her to fight even harder for her artists.

She picked up a particularly colorful sheet of paper. "I've got some questions about next month. You know Abigail's case is coming up in April?"

Vander nodded. "I don't envy the opposing counsel."

"We're hoping to settle out of court, but there's a chance we may go to trial. It's possible I won't be able to work from the ranch at all that month."

"Then I'll come to you. Let's plan on it. We've got spring break in there anyway."

"You're willing to spend your whole spring break in Nashville with a woman who may be working fourteen-hour days?"

"I'll be in charge of coffee and foot rubs."

She rolled her eyes as she made a note on her calendar, but the little smile appearing on her lips suggested she liked that idea just fine.

Vander gazed at her, struck again by how he loved every single thing about her, soft and tough, silly and serious. He'd been planning on saving the big moment for sunset. But here, in her living room, in front of papers detailing every precious minute he got to spend with her, Vander couldn't seem to hold his tongue.

"I have a question to ask you. Hypothetically."

"Hypothetically you're going to ask me a question? Or you're going to ask me a hypothetical question?"

"I want to present a scenario for your consideration."

She sat back on her heels. "I'm listening."

"Let's say there were two people who were crazy about each other, really in love." Vander took her hands; he kissed the back of one. "Being together presents complications, one might even suggest impracticalities, but they're not insurmountable."

"Clarifying question, are they—?" Harlow fanned her free hand between the two of them, indicating the spark they'd both felt from the first moment they'd met.

"Yes. Despite obvious differences between the two, there is ample evidence to suggest those differences balance the couple in surprising ways. And they both want the same things in life." Vander's voice shook as he said, "Love, commitment, a life of service to others, children." Her fingers tightened around his. "Based on this evidence, does it make sense for these two to start their life together?"

Harlow's gaze connected with his, and tears appeared in her eyes. "I like everything about this hypothetical situation—" a gorgeous smile spread across her face "—except for the hypothetical part."

Vander reached inside his jacket and pulled out a small package wrapped in craft paper. His fingers shook as he unwrapped it, less nervous and more excited. The paper fell away, revealing a platinum setting with a fan of white diamonds surrounding an exquisite turquoise stone that half the town of Pronghorn had helped him pick out from Raquel's supply.

"Harlow Jameson, will you marry me?"

Harlow's gaze flickered to the stone, then back to his eyes.

"Yes," she breathed. "I cannot wait to marry you."

Vander wrapped both his arms around her waist, pulling her close, losing himself in the scent of her hair. They couldn't know what path life might take or where it would take them. But wherever he and Harlow were together, that was his home.

* * * * *

Don't miss the next book in Anna Grace's
The Teacher Project miniseries,
coming April 2025 from
Harlequin Heartwarming